LIMINAL*SUMMER

AN*ALICE*BURTON*BOOK

JAMIE*BETH*COHEN

D1521090

Black Rose Writing | Texas

The author grants the final approval for this literary material.

First printing

This is a work of fiction. Names, characters, businesses, places, events, and incidents are either the products of the author's imagination or used in a fictitious manner. Any resemblance to actual persons, living or dead, or actual events is purely coincidental.

ISBN: 978-1-68433-816-0
PUBLISHED BY BLACK ROSE WRITING
www.blackrosewriting.com

Printed in the United States of America
Suggested Retail Price (SRP) $19.95

Liminal Summer is printed in Palatino Linotype

*As a planet-friendly publisher, Black Rose Writing does its best to eliminate unnecessary waste to reduce paper usage and energy costs, while never compromising the reading experience. As a result, the final word count vs. page count may not meet common expectations.

READ JAMIE BETH COHEN'S WASTED PRETTY

During junior year of high school, star student and stellar lacrosse player Alice Burton grew four inches, and, thanks to her mom's experimental health food products, shed twenty pounds. Alice has mixed feelings about her surprising transformation.

On the plus side: Chris Thompson, the hot college guy she has a crush on, talks to her.

On the minus side: Her dad's creepy friend, professional athlete Karl Bell, lets his eyes, and his hugs, linger too long.

After a disturbing encounter in a dark hallway, Alice realizes the response some men have to her new body isn't just disgusting, it's dangerous. Her life is further complicated by her parents' crumbling finances and the family's entanglement with Karl.

Set in Pittsburgh in 1992, *WASTED PRETTY* is about a girl determined to protect her body, her future, and her heart.

* * * * *

Jamie Beth Cohen drew me in completely with this heartfelt and deeply honest coming-of-age story steeped in the world of rock 'n' roll and radio and shot through with the ache of first love.
—Kit Frick, author of *I Killed Zoe Spanos*

This book is dedicated to everyone
who read, loved, and supported
WASTED PRETTY.
This book is for you.

* * * * *

Lyrics used courtesy of Kate Beck.

TO —
MADELINE
BRIAN
HUGO
JUNIPER

LIVE INTO THE
LIMINAL SPACES!
(I think you might be doing that!)

LIMINAL★SUMMER

SAFE TRAVELS

♡ Jamie

Belfast, ME
5/2024

CHAPTER 1

I'm behind the counter with my head down, a ruler in one hand and a bright pink highlighter in the other, when I hear Cassie's *I'm-getting-pissy-and-I'm-going-to-lose-it* tone coming from the folk-punk section of the store. I try to ignore her. I think I've finally figured out a way to get corporate off our backs, and if I can just get these dots to connect—

"I'm not doing it!" she growls at Zach. "Make Alice do it! You always make me alphabetize. It's because you hate me!"

I can't help it. I look up.

I make eye contact with a customer in a black leather vest that's embellished with safety pins on the shoulders and short, fat, metal spikes down the front. It's 1997, not 1987, but whatever, dude, Rod's Records caters to music lovers of all genres. That's another thing corporate doesn't quite get. I shrug at him and smile.

"I don't hate you, Cassie. I can't ask Alice to do it right now, because she's not actually working today."

"Then why are we listening to The Indigo Girls?!" Cassie yells.

Zach puts his hands up to his temples, massages them, and then walks Cassie over to the counter.

"It's fine," I say. "Let Cassie put on whatever she wants."

"I'm not allowed to put on whatever I want," she complains. "Zach makes the rest of us follow the rules. You're the only one who gets to play albums from ten years ago. Because you know Tess Wilson from Liminal Space, and your dad's famous, and Zach wants to sleep with you! Blah. Blah. Blah!"

Zach has his back to me, but I can tell he blanches at his sister's jab. For her part, she sticks her tongue out at me. Because she's sixteen. And pissed her dad died. And her brother sold the family business–a beloved used tape and CD store–to a corporate entity that has enacted all sorts of stupid policies that might make sense in a strip mall in Vegas, but not in a college town like State College, PA.

"My dad's not famous," I say, even though he sort of is. "Just put on your Veruca Salt and go alphabetize the folk singers."

"Folk-punk," she corrects.

I stick my tongue out at her. She gives me the finger, changes the CD, and stomps off.

"Sorry about that," Zach says, coming behind the counter.

"Not your fault. After four years here, I'm immune to her outbursts. And I like Veruca Salt, anyway, so it's no big deal."

Cassie has always been prone to dramatics, but things got worse after Rod died two years ago.

"She's not twelve anymore," Zach says.

"Well, at least she's alphabetizing now."

He nods to my charts and printouts. "What are you doing with all that stuff, anyway?"

"Well, I know corporate has been giving you a hard time about year-over-years, so I thought I'd do some analysis. It looks like they don't take into account the academic calendar or, more importantly, the football schedule."

"What do you mean?" Zach takes a swig of coffee from his Grateful Dead mug. It was Rod's mug before it was his, and I'm still not used to seeing Zach drink out of it.

"When they send sales summaries," I tell him, "they control for weather, like they'll tell you what your sales were compared to last year and what the weather was compared to last year, but they won't tell you if the football team was in town. They don't know how to control for the way things work here."

Zach looks at me half-impressed, half-perplexed. "Do you really have to move?"

"Well, I did graduate last week, so…" I scrunch my face up and laugh. "I should probably, you know, start my life or something…"

I started working at Rod's Records my freshman year, right after I quit lacrosse fall-ball, because everyone was mean. I had had my share of mean girls in high school. Rod didn't hire many Penn State students, preferring to hire adults, or high school kids whose parents he knew. He said college kids were flaky and prone to hangovers, but my dad vouched for me and because my dad was a big deal "talk jock" at a radio station in Pittsburgh, I got the job. Still, that's not why Zach lets me flout corporate's "play only albums released in the last six months" rule.

"So … you graduated…" he teases me. "You haven't left yet. And now you can work full-time! I'll make you the assistant manager. You're better at reports than I am, anyway. It'll be fun."

"I don't think my life's work is to be the Assistant Manager of Rod's Records in State College," I tell him, and immediately regret saying it.

But he doesn't flinch. Instead, he drinks his coffee and, with a wry smile says, "Are you sure?"

I know the coffee must be cold by now, but he doesn't bother to reheat it.

Being the manager at Rod's Records wasn't supposed to be Zach's "life's work" either. When I started he was a junior, just two years ahead of me, and I had no idea he was Rod's kid until Cassie burst in one day, threw a bottle of water at him and walked out, because apparently that's one of the ways she shows her love. In explaining her outburst to me, he outed himself as the boss' son and we bonded over having dads with big personalities.

Zach got a degree in philosophy and was supposed to go on to grad school on the West Coast, but Rod died just after Zach graduated, so he didn't feel like he could leave. Zach's mom sold the store and made a deal with the head office that if Zach stayed on as manager, she and Cassie could still have health insurance.

"Come on, you don't have anything better to do," Zach cajoles. "You don't have to be the assistant manager forever. Just give it a try."

"You don't know that I don't have anything better to do," I say.

"That's because you won't tell anyone your big secret plan."

"Listen, about that... Burton'll be here soon, and he still thinks I'm moving back to Pittsburgh to work at the radio station, so let's not talk about my 'big secret plan' around him."

"Would be hard to talk about it, given you haven't told me what it is."

"Exactly."

"So, today's Picture Day?" he asks.

I nod to my cap and gown hanging from a shelf by the back door. "Yup."

I refused to go to my graduation ceremony last week because if I did my parents would have insisted on going, too. The thought of being anywhere with my mom and dad breathing the same air fills me with dread, so I skipped it. My dad's coming up to take me to lunch and snap a picture of me in my cap and gown in front of the Nittany Lion statue. He comes up for lunch at least one Friday a month anyway, so that part isn't unusual, but the whole *pretend today is graduation day so I can have a picture to hang in my office* is really very special and so him.

"I'll put these away." Zach moves the boxes of my mom's Butterfly Bars and packets of powdered Butterfly Shake Mix off the counter and onto a hidden shelf beneath the register. We sell my mom's concoctions, along with bottles of water and soda, to students who need something quick after class. My mom convinced Zach to stock her stuff on one of her infrequent visits. She made sure he knew she was doing him a favor—letting him be the "exclusive State College carrier" of her now-famous products even though he was sort of doing her a favor and he took shit from corporate about the whole thing. This is a special gift my mom has, convincing you she's doing you a favor when really it's for her own gain.

The guy in the leather vest with spikes and safety pins comes to the register and Zach rings him up: A used NIN disc, a used Billie Holiday disc, and a new copy of Green Day's *Insomniac*. People are endlessly fascinating. I ignore their small talk and continue to draw lines between points on the graph I'm making to get the home office to chill out.

"Where are you going for lunch?" Cassie's done alphabetizing and is leaning up against the counter, twisting her curls around her finger.

"I don't know, The Nittany Lion Inn's right next to the statue."

"Fancy," she says with a head wag.

"I guess."

"But you don't eat lunch, right? You just eat your mom's Butterfly Food."

"I eat lunch when my dad comes. It's easier than arguing with him about it."

"I wish my dad were here to argue with."

"I know, Cassie. I'm sorry."

"I'm sorry for being a snot before," she says, her eyes trained on the ground.

"It's fine." I give Cassie a wide berth. I can't imagine losing my dad when I was her age, even though I almost did.

"But I do think Zach wants to bang you." She raises her dark eyebrows several times in quick succession. It's over-dramatic to the point of comic. "Hubba! Hubba!"

"Shut it, Cassie," I say, purposely trying to keep my response measured, casual.

She doesn't know Zach and I have already had sex. Many times. No one in town does. The first time happened the second night of Rod's shiva, which also happened to be Memorial Day my sophomore year. I was hanging out at the house with the family, and the next thing I knew it was three in the morning. I walked Zach back to his apartment above the store, and we got stoned and hooked up. I thought it was a one-time thing and felt a little guilty that I might have taken advantage of him, given everything that was going on, but six months later it happened a second time, on New Year's Eve. Zach had a party for people from the store, and when everyone else went home, I didn't. This past New Year's we did it again, and we haven't stopped. We're together at least once a week. We've never talked about it as a relationship or anything, and I know he has a thing about not dating employees—especially now that corporate has all these stupid policies—but I just keep showing up, and he's never turned me away. We don't need to talk about it. I like it like this.

"Did you see we added an in-store tomorrow?" Cassie asks me.

"No. When?"

"Corporate called yesterday and put ACE on the schedule for tomorrow."

"It's Memorial Day Weekend! It's dead around here." I shout at her like she's the one who made the decision. "Gawd, I hate corporate! What are they thinking?"

"I don't know. ACE is playing The Hook tonight and their label called to request an acoustic spot here tomorrow."

"Weird. I've never even heard of them."

"Are you serious? They have, like, songs running in three commercials right now."

"No TV," I shrug.

At the start of my senior year, I moved into my brother Nate's house. He doesn't have a TV, which meant I had to give up my nightly *Jeopardy!* routine, but it was less expensive than all my other options, and he needed a housemate. It was a bit of culture shock to move from a house with six girls right in the heart of all the fraternity mansions junior year out to the quiet edge of town, but I got used to it. I got so used to it, I'm dreading leaving.

I've been studying Nate to learn how to be a grown up. My mom helped with the down payment, but Nate pays the mortgage and all the bills with money from his two jobs: an assistant coach on the Penn State soccer team and managing one of the weight rooms on campus. Another assistant coach will be moving in when fall pre-season starts, but until then, I have a room with a bed, a desk, and a dresser. Most of my stuff is in boxes in the basement. I've always known it was temporary, like a space between college and life.

"Oh, look, it's your famous dad!" Cassie says, as a bunch of skateboarders her age enter the store. My dad's bald head sticks up behind them.

Burton won't come to the house because my mother's money paid for some of it, which is why I'm at the store on my day off playing with charts and graphs, waiting for him to pick me up.

"He's not famous." I roll my eyes at her. *He's sort of famous.* His drive-time talk show is syndicated now, so people all over the

Northeast know who he is, but only like angry forty-year-old men, so it doesn't really count.

Burton and Zach greet each other, and Cassie wanders back to the folk-punk section. Before her dad died, she liked sparring with Burton, but now she prefers to avoid him.

"What are you doing there?" my dad asks. He gives me his left cheek to kiss. The right side of his face is permanently drooped from the fight that could have killed him five years ago. He claims to remember none of it. As far as I can tell, he knows he left the radio station event with Major League asshole Karl Bell and woke up in the hospital several days later. I've never believed his convenient memory loss, but it works in my favor, so I don't push it. Along with those lost hours and the droopy side of his face, he has occasional memory slips that I seem to notice, but no one else does. Other than that, he's made a full recovery, though sometimes his speech is slurred when he's tired. That could have meant an end to his on-air career, but Burton just acts like he's not slurring and because he's convincing—and a little bit scary—everyone pretends not to notice, too. "That looks like homework. Are you going to tell me you didn't actually graduate and that's why I couldn't go to commencement last week?"

"It's just some stuff for the store," I tell him. "I need to take it upstairs, and then I'll be ready to go."

As I'm gathering the papers, I hop off the stool and accidentally knock an envelope off the counter. Pictures of me in my cap and gown in front of the Nittany Lion statue fall onto the floor like a wreath at my dad's feet. While he leans down to pick them up, I freeze and lock eyes with Zach.

"What are these?" my dad asks.

I'm silent. Zach's silent. My dad is seething.

"You already took photos at the statue? Did your mom take these?"

"Yes," I say, eyes on the floor, like I'm sixteen-year-old Cassie.

"Well, what am I even doing here, then?"

I don't say anything.

"Look at me," he commands. "Why am I even here?"

"It's fine," I finally say. "You and I can take photos, too. I have my cap and gown. See?" I point to the shiny blue, paper-thin monstrosity hanging from the shelf. "I'm just going to take some stuff up to the office. And we can get lunch. You're here so we can get lunch."

I don't wait for a response. I just turn and head for the back door that leads to the stairs. Zach calls to Cassie to take the register, and I hear his footsteps behind me.

"You okay?" he asks on the small landing of the stairs between the office, his apartment, and the staff bathroom.

"Yeah, I'll be fine."

I throw open the office door and slam the papers down on the desk.

"You're not okay," he says.

"I'll be fine. I'm fine. I just … this is why I'm not moving back to work at the station. It's bad enough the two of them have to be in the same city. I don't need to be there with them. They can't even stand the idea of each other, and they'd just make my life hell."

"You should probably tell him you're not moving home."

I turn to face Zach. "It's not home anymore. And, to be fair, I never said I would go back, he just assumed I needed the experience before applying to journalism school. So, like, I never said, 'No, that's not what I'm going to do,' but I also never said, 'Sure, sounds like a great idea.'"

"So, what *are* you going to do?"

"Zach, I'm working on it. When there's something to tell you, I'll tell you."

"Understood. You sure you're going to be okay?"

"Yeah. I just need to get back downstairs." I turn back to the desk and try to straighten it up a little, so I can put my papers somewhere I can find them again when I come back. "The longer he stews the worse it'll be. And I'm sure he left his car running by the fire hydrant. Not that he'd ever pay a ticket if he got one…"

"Okay, just real quick—"

"What?" I ask over my shoulder.

"Are you going to The Hook tonight?"

"Probably. Cassie said I should hear the band that's playing."

"ACE? Yeah, they should be good."

"Great. I'll be there."

"Do you want to get dinner before?"

"I don't know. Where are people going?"

"Oh, I don't know. I mean with me. Do you want to grab a bite with me before the show?"

I stop rummaging and turn to face him.

"Yeah." I nod, and I feel my eyelashes batting, as if on their own accord. "That'd be great." I resist the urge to ask him if by "grab a bite" he means "go on a date," but I don't need to. His deep-set brown eyes are sparkling, and he has a little half-smile that's hard to ignore.

"Cool." He says, with a nod. "Get out of here. I'll clean up this mess. Call me after lunch, and we'll figure out the details?"

"Yeah. Cool," I say.

CHAPTER 2*

As expected, my dad's maroon Caprice Classic is on College Ave. idling in front of the fire hydrant. The Caprice replaced the Wally Wagon I had to drive in high school before I learned to drive stick, and then again when my RX-7 disappeared along with those hours my dad says he can't remember. This car looks deceptively like an undercover cop car, which I think he likes. The idea that he could arrest you at any moment gives him the same kind of authority in the real world that he's used to at the station—which he runs like a fiefdom—but I miss the Wally Wagon. Nothing was wrong with it. One Friday he came up for lunch in it and the next visit he had the Caprice. When I asked him what happened to the other car he blew me off, and I assumed it had something to do with a gambling debt, which is just another thing no one in my family talks about.

It's a short drive from the store to the parking lot by the Inn and the statue. I take a moment to lay my gown across the back seat and by the time I take shotgun, he's already on the car phone that sits between the two front seats. He holds up a finger that basically says, "Gimme a minute," which is fine by me, because that's better than arguing with him about whether or not I should have let my mom take fake graduation pictures of me two weeks before he gets to take fake graduation pictures of me. I consider how messed up it's going to be when I'm old and relying on photos for my memories. Today is sunny, but it rained on graduation weekend. Will I confuse the realities?

Forget that I didn't actually wear my cap and gown for graduation and just sat in the stands to watch my friends move their tassels?

I'm lost in the thought of divergent realities when I realize my dad is handing me the phone.

"It's Johnny."

Shit.

"Hey," I say into the phone.

"Hey?" he mocks me. "That's all you've got for me? I've been leaving messages for you at Nate's for a week. I talked to him last night. He said he told you. I even tried to reach you at the store. And you say, 'Hey?'"

"Hey," I repeat. Johnny works for my dad, but sometimes it feels like he's more my big brother than Nate is.

"Listen, I know you're avoiding me because you think your dad wants me on your case about when you're coming home, but that's not the only reason I've been calling you."

"Okay."

"Do you want to know why I've been calling?"

"Okay."

He lowers his voice. "Can he hear me?"

I look over at my dad who seems oblivious to my conversation. He probably feels safe in his assumption that Johnny is doing his bidding and getting some sort of commitment and timeline out of me. I love Johnny like a brother, but I feel bad he's hitting his late twenties still under my dad's thumb. That will not be me.

"I don't think so," I say, pressing the phone more tightly against my ear.

Johnny lowers his voice to a whisper.

"I was calling to talk to you about Chris Thompson."

Instinctively, I look over at my dad who, thankfully, remains oblivious. I know it's not an act, because there's no way he would be able to fake disinterest in this conversation.

"What's up?" I ask, choosing my words carefully, knowing that even if my dad seems disinterested, he can clearly hear my side of the conversation.

"You don't know?"

For a moment, I feel sick to my stomach, like something has happened to Chris Thompson. Even though he walked out on whatever it was we had five years ago with no warning, I always thought we'd at least talk again.

"Know what?"

"He's coming to town," Johnny reports.

"To town? To Pittsburgh?" I feel less sick but more confused.

"To State College. Tonight," Johnny says. "He's playing The Hook and doing an in-store at *your* store tomorrow. I tried to get in touch with you, but I thought by now you'd know."

"I don't. I didn't." I look over at my dad who has pulled into a parking space and is still either ignoring me or pretending to.

"His band is playing *your* store tomorrow."

"I heard you." Forcing myself to speak vaguely and calmly, so as not to draw Burton's attention, is not easy. "I just hadn't realized."

"You know they changed the band name from A Combustible Event to ACE like three years ago, right?"

"I didn't. I don't. How would I?"

"You do work in a music store, right? And their songs are in a bunch of commercials right now."

"My bad, I guess." Who knew I was missing more than *Jeopardy!* without a TV?

When Chris Thompson left Pittsburgh we weren't exactly dating, but we were … something. He left me, and the city, and his band Wasted Pretty, to move to Australia with A Combustible Event. Now, Tess Wilson—Wasted Pretty's lead singer, Chris Thompson's cousin, and Johnny's ex-girlfriend—is like a huge star in England. I still get postcards from her, but she never mentions Chris. Johnny doesn't either. He's never once brought him up since that night when my dad lost those hours and my car, and I lost Chris. I guess I just assumed they had grown apart. I guess I was wrong.

My dad gets out of the car to mess with his camera in the parking lot.

"I just want to make sure you're okay," Johnny says.

"Does he know?"

"Does who know what?"

"Does he know I'm here?"

"Yes." Johnny says cautiously.

"Chris Thompson knows I'm here? Does he know I work at Rod's?"

"Yes. Jeezus, Alice, can Burton hear you?"

"No, he got out of the car. Is there anything else you want to tell me that you should have told me, like, a week ago?"

"Don't get pissy at me, Wonderland. You could have called me back, you know? It's not like I could leave a message like this on Nate's machine."

He's right. I'm not angry at anyone except myself right now. And I'm not even actually angry. I don't know what I am.

"I'm sorry, Johnny. I should go. My dad's waiting."

"Are you going to be okay?" he asks.

"I'll be … something. Thanks for letting me know. I appreciate it. I'll talk to you soon."

I hang up before he can say anything else and then lean over to shut off the car. I take longer than I need to put on my cap and gown while I try to regain some semblance of the calm I felt just an hour ago, when I was drawing points on a graph, and Zach didn't want to take me out to dinner, and my dad wasn't mad at me for seeing my mom, and Chris Thompson wasn't on his way to my town. Or maybe he's already here. Which would mean it would be better if my dad left, ASAP. The last thing I need is to see Chris for the first time in five years with my dad in tow, given that one of the reasons we had to sneak around in the first place was how much my dad hated him. Though, at this point, I'm not sure my dad would even remember him. His foggy memory lapses seem to be worse around anything contentious related to his parenting. As if, maybe he's sorry for being such a jerk, but instead of apologizing, he just conveniently forgets trying to control every aspect of my life.

All of a sudden, the town feels too small. State College has always been my happy place. It's everyone's happy place. People actually call it Happy Valley. And for the last four years, it's where I've felt the most at home and in control and safe, hidden in the valley, surrounded by mountains with only one way in and one way out. I especially like the times classes aren't in session, and the population shrinks, and it feels like the small town it actually is. But now it feels too small, like Pittsburgh, but worse. What if we walk into The Nittany Lion Inn and Chris is there with his band? This summer was supposed to get me one last shot at things being happy, being slow, being quiet and uncomplicated. It was supposed to be my moment in between.

"What was that all about?" my dad asks. I didn't even realize he was standing right next to me.

"Just Johnny being Johnny. Wants to know when I'll be back." I don't want to bring it up, but Johnny deserves Burton brownie points, if nothing else.

"What did you tell him?" my dad asks.

"I told him I don't know yet."

CHAPTER 3

Photos in front of the statue go smoothly. It isn't mobbed, the way it was graduation weekend. I feel sort of dumb as people walk by and point and whisper about the girl in the graduation robe a week after commencement, but I remind myself that enduring some random people snickering is preferable to standing in line with a million other grads or being anywhere with both of my parents at the same time.

I rush through my lunch (grilled chicken on a bed of undressed greens), but my dad takes his time with his meal (burger, fries, side salad, and soup).

"Are you seeing Nate today?" I ask.

"No. He said he was too busy."

"Are you two fighting?"

"Your brother and I don't fight, Alice. He just prefers your mother's version of everything. Including reality."

"Sorry I asked. Everything okay at the station?"

"Alice, I've been patient. You graduated last week. Why can't you tell me when you're moving home? You and Nate must have discussed when his new roommate is moving in. What's the big secret?"

"His new housemate moves in in August. It's not a big deal. No secret."

"So, you're moving home in August? The beginning or the end?"

"I'm—" I'm about to lie through my teeth, or at least be incredibly opaque when I'm interrupted.

"Dennis Burton!"

Nate's boss, the head coach of the men's soccer team, comes up behind me and reaches across the table to shake my dad's hand. Coach Baker is not my favorite person, but right now, I'm thrilled to see him and his whiskey on the rocks.

*   *   *   *   *

"Where do you want me to drop you?" my dad asks after he pays for lunch.

I check my watch. I've known that Chris Thompson is in town—is in ACE *and* will be on stage at The Hook tonight *and* at my job tomorrow—for exactly one hour and thirteen minutes.

I need to talk to Meredith. And I need my dad to get out of town. In all the ways I imagined I might run into Chris Thompson again—and I certainly have thought about it—none of them involved my dad or State College. In fact, I always assumed I would see him in New York City on one of my many weekends to visit Meredith at NYU. Or maybe it would be sometime in the future, with me in journalism school at Columbia, walking down the street with my awesome future boyfriend who would shake Chris' hand firmly and then wrap his arm tightly around my shoulder, proud to be with me and feeling sorry for this guy who let me go.

It was plausible in my mind. There are lots of musicians in New York, and Meredith and I are always running into people we know at clubs and bars and on street corners. It's weird how small and huge New York City can feel at the same time, and how many Pittsburghers end up there. Occasionally, after a night out drinking with Meredith, I would think I actually did see him from behind—the feathery blond hair, a tall guy with broad shoulders—and I would drag Meredith half a block, only to accost some tourist looking for Times Square.

"I'm fine here," I tell my dad. "I need a walk."

"Having lunch with me is that stressful?"

"It's not that." I hug him. "I just have a lot on my mind."

"Starting to realize that being a graduate is harder than being a student?"

"I've always known that. Why do you think I'm staying here for the summer?"

"You're hiding."

"I'm not hiding. I'm just taking some time for myself."

This is sort of true and sort of not. I'm not hiding, I'm waiting. I'm waiting to hear from the Klein Fellowship which would allow me to move to New York City in August, work in a variety of newsrooms, provide me room and board and a small stipend for two whole years, and almost guarantee entry to Columbia's journalism school when it's done. But he doesn't know this, no one does, except Meredith and the two professors who wrote my recommendations.

"You'll make more at the station than you do at the record store, and you don't have to pay me rent. Just come home now, let's go get your things."

"What part of 'time for myself' do you not understand, Dad?"

"You mean time away from me? You just had four years! And you'll have the rest of your life to be wherever you want. I don't expect you to stay at the station forever. I know you're going away for journalism school. I just don't understand why you're dragging your feet here."

I make fists out of my hands but keep them at my side and take a long, deep breath.

"I'm gonna take a walk, Dad."

I turn to head back towards Nate's.

"What about your cap and gown?"

"I don't need them anymore. You can take them. You can throw them out," I call over my shoulder.

"Alice," he says sternly.

I turn to face him.

"What are you keeping from me?" He sounds angry, but not nearly as angry as I would expect him to be given I'm not doing exactly what he wants exactly when he wants it done.

I retrace my steps back to him and give him another hug. "Nothing. Everything's fine. I'll talk to you soon."

I turn my back on him while he's still leaning on the Caprice Classic. I know he's watching me. And I know he's sad or mad, or both. But I also know he pushes us all away every day with his *my way or the highway* B.S. and his gambling, which he swears he has in check, but I think he just has more money to blow now. A bigger cushion doesn't mean the problem is gone.

CHAPTER 4

Campus is pretty quiet, as is the neighborhood behind College Ave. Being in town while classes aren't in session is magical. I feel bad for my friends who've never spent a summer here. They think they know the town—they even think they love the town—but only seeing State College during the school year and thinking you know what it's all about is like only seeing me at The Hook and thinking I'm just a drunk party girl who flirts a lot. You'd never know there's this other super-over-achieving side of me after the hangover wears off. I know I can't stay here forever, I don't even want to, but I can already feel, in every inch of my body and every fiber of my being, how much I'm going to miss it.

At Nate's place, a pale-yellow sticky note hangs at eye level between the screen door and the heavy wooden door. My brother's rushed scrawl reads, *Listen to the messages and deal with your mail.*

Nate never resorts to sticky notes unless he's really pissed, but I have more important things to do. I grab the cordless, page Meredith, and turn on every fan in the house while I wait for her to call back. Thankfully, she's quick about it.

"What's up, Chicken?" she asks.

"Hey, do you have a few minutes?"

"For you? Always!" she slurs.

"You're drunk. It's like, two o'clock?"

"It's also the Friday before Memorial Day, and I'm in the Hamptons, so yeah."

"Right, I forgot."

"Forgot? I left you a message yesterday right before I left."

"Oh, sorry. I haven't checked messages."

"We need to get you a cell phone. Want me to get you a cell phone?"

Meredith believes money can fix everything, and while she's always generous, she's more so when she's drunk.

"Thanks. No, I don't need a cell phone. And, as much as I'd love to wait to talk to you when you're in a more sober place, I need to talk to you now. Can you focus, please?"

"This sounds serious. Let me go inside." I imagine her, barefoot with a bathing suit and a sarong, padding from a picture-perfect deck overlooking the ocean to a picture-perfect living room overlooking the deck, while I just head up to my room with its twin bed and desk fan. "Okay. What's up?"

"Well, it's about Chris Thompson."

She lets out an exaggerated sigh. "No!!!! It's been 362 days since the last mention of Chris Thompson. Why? Why? Why?"

"Shut up. And please tell me you don't actually keep track."

"Ehhh, I don't, but I'm thinking it's been about a year, and I was sort of hoping if we made it a full 365 days, he'd be out of your system for good."

"Hilarious," I say.

"I know you really wanted some sort of closure," she says, "and to rub it in his face that you survived his unannounced departure and thrived. But, please, can we agree no talk of Chris Thompson anymore? We've graduated. We're supposed to be adults or something."

"He's here," I say.

"He's where?" she asks.

"He's in State College. He's playing The Hook tonight. He's doing an in-store at Rod's tomorrow. He's here."

"Oh. This is serious." It's like I can hear her sobering up through the phone. "Are you sure? Have you seen him?"

"Yes, I'm sure. And no, I haven't seen him. Johnny called to tell me. And Cassie said something about the in-store this morning. I just didn't realize Chris was in the band she was talking about. They changed their name. They have songs in a bunch of commercials right now."

"Oh, do they do the song in the Sprite commercial? And the Saturn one? They are sooo good. I knew they were by the same people."

"I don't know which commercials. So not the point, Meredith."

"Sorry. Right. Okay. But this is what you've always wanted, right?"

"What is?"

"Closure."

Sometimes I don't know what I want until Meredith tells me what it is, but once she says it, I know she's right. "Right. Yeah. Closure."

"Ohhhhh nooooo…"

"What?!"

"Oh gawd, you don't want closure. You want him."

"I don't know. Is that what this feeling is?"

"Describe it."

I can't describe it. I can only remember what it was like to be alone with him, and I can't talk to Meredith about that because she never liked him.

"Alice?"

"Yeah. Sorry. I … I don't know. I just know I like how I feel when he looks at me."

"No, you *liked* how it *felt* when he *looked* at you *five* years ago. And then he left town and didn't even say goodbye, so, functionally, he's an ass, and you can't trust him. But, I'm all for closure, so, *if* he's still hot, and *only if* he's still hot, just fuck him and be done with it. Please. And then we really never have to speak his name again."

"Do you think it's that easy?"

"What? Fucking? I do think it's that easy. He's a musician on tour. Isn't fucking why they go on tour?"

"No, I mean, you think closure's that easy? Like, we fuck and that's it?"

"I certainly hope so. Because if you fall for him, I predict disaster." She's so right.

"What if he's married?" I ask her. "He could be married, right? He's what, twenty-five now? Do twenty-five-year-olds get married?"

"Why did I think he was so much older than us?" she asks.

"Back then, I think he seemed older because he had his own place."

"That place was a shit hole."

"Again, not the point, Meredith! Not everyone can live in a place up to your standards."

"Not this again."

"Not what again?"

"Nothing," she says.

"Can you please help me?"

When I thought about seeing Chris Thompson again, I always imagined it would be a chance run-in. I never thought I'd have time to think about it, time to prepare.

"Sorry, yeah," she says. "I guess my best advice is to look hot and don't go to the show alone."

"Shit."

"Shit, what?"

"Zach."

"What about Zach?"

"I forgot. He asked me out. He wants to get dinner before the show tonight."

"What?! Oh my gawd, Chicken. He finally asked you out?! And you didn't lead with that?!"

"Yeah. Sorry. The whole Chris Thompson thing scrambled my brain."

"Oh. Okay. Well that's actually perfect. Go to dinner with Zach. Show up to the show together. Make Chris jealous. Then if something happens with him, great. If nothing happens, you still have Zach. It's a no-lose."

"Not for Zach it isn't. Shit. Should I ask Zach if we can go out tomorrow?"

"I mean, you could. But he'll be at the show anyway, right? Wouldn't that be weird?"

"I guess."

"I think you give Zach a chance."

"Oh, I see. You think if I commit to Zach in the next few hours, I won't hook up with Chris Thompson. Is that it?"

"No, I know you're a total slut. Lord knows that wouldn't stop you."

"Ha ha. You know, it would be easier to take your advice if you didn't hate Chris so much on my behalf."

"Well, someone has to. Remember, it's me who gets to stick around and pick up your sorry, crying ass when he bolts, so I think I have a say here."

"Whatever. I can't believe Zach picked today to ask me out. After four years of me making myself incredibly available to him. And he talked again about me staying here and making me assistant manager."

"Oy! Not that again."

"Listen, just because you live in New York City, doesn't mean you get to 'Oy!' Oy is my thing, Daughter of the American Revolution!"

"Blah. Blah. Blah. I thought we were supposed to be planning your night."

"Yes, please, let's. My heart is racing. Am I too young to have a heart attack?"

"You know, you could have avoided all of this if you came with me this weekend. I told you, you should have come to the Hamptons."

"Let it go, Meredith. We can't always do what you want to do." The thing about having a best friend who pays for everything is that most of the time she gets to make all the decisions.

"Alright. Let Zach take you to dinner. Look hot. Play it by ear. Don't fall in love. That's all the advice I got. And I want to head out to the beach anyway." She's not happy with me, but she won't say it.

"But what do I wear?"

"Where's Zach taking you?"

"I don't know."

"And the show's at The Hook?"

"Yeah."

"That's tough. Because you want to look hot, but not too dressy. You absolutely can't look like you're trying too hard. For either of them."

"I know."

"Are you tan?"

"Yeah, a bit."

"Okay. What about that deep mauve t-shirt dress you got at The Gap?"

"Okay. Yeah."

"With my Steve Madden slides. I left them in your closet the last time I was there."

"Okay. Thanks."

"But you really need to do your nails, and your toes."

"Isn't that trying too hard?"

"Maybe. Just do your toes then."

"Okay, I can do that," I say. "Thanks, Meredith. Have a good weekend."

"You can thank me by giving me all the details. Tomorrow. If not sooner."

"Of course. I'll call you."

"Later, Chicken. Oh! And one more thing."

"What?

"Do not forget a condom!"

I hang up the phone and bring it back to the cradle in the living room. I stand over the table that collects the mail and throw away a series of GRE prep advertisements—I'm happy with my scores and have no intention of taking them again—and put aside my *New Yorkers*. Nate must have already snagged the copies of *Rolling Stone* and *Spin*. Jerk. Those subscriptions were a gift to both of us from our mom. But, the pile is also devoid of bills, and even though Nate can be a jerk, I have to accept I'd be lost without him taking care of all the grown-up stuff.

I lie down on the couch and reach behind my head to press the button on the answering machine.

"You have six new messages ... Message One, received Monday, 6:11p.m. ...

"Hey Burtons, It's Johnny. Call me back." Click.

"Message Two, received Tuesday, 8:04 p.m. ...

"Hi kids, it's mom. I'm in Pittsburgh for a few nights. Just got back from an event in New York City. Very exciting! Had dinner with Meredith. Would love to talk to you soon. Hope you're well!" Click.

"Message Three, received Wednesday, 11:32 a.m. …

"Hey, Wonder Twins – It's Johnny, call me back. I'm available at the station until Burton goes on air at 4:00 p.m.. Why am I even saying this? You know when he goes on. Why won't you call me back?" Click.

We're not twins, but ever since I followed Nate to Penn State, Johnny has insisted on referring to us as such.

"Message Four, received Wednesday, 7:06 p.m. …

"Wonder Twins! Burton just got off the air. Why haven't you called me back?" Click.

"Message Five, received Thursday, 4:18 p.m. …

"Hey Chicken! Leaving for the Hamptons in a few. Really bummed you couldn't come. I'll do some day drinking for you. Kisses … And. Hey! What's up, Nate?"

"Message Six, received Thursday, 9:26 p.m. …

"Hey, Wonder Twins … take the form of a reasonable human being and call me back. I can't even believe we live in a world where the Burton kids won't return my calls. Nate, I used to buy you beer before you could buy it yourself. Alice, I need to talk to you. Call me back. Now. Or before tomorrow night." Click.

So now I'm caught up on my life. All except for what comes next.

I call the record store, and Zach picks up. He does have a nice voice.

"Hey, it's Alice," I say, feeling a jitteriness in my abdomen that must be the internal equivalent to blushing.

"Hey, how was lunch?"

"I survived," I tell him.

"I know you typically don't like to eat two meals in one day," he says.

State College is so small that most people know about my mom's health food business and how I was her first success story. Her whole burgeoning empire is built on the fact that I lost 20 pounds my junior year of high school while sticking to her plan of shakes and bars and celery for most of the day and a sensible dinner at night. But this is also an out for me. I could tell Zach that because I had lunch with my dad, we should do dinner tomorrow night. However, Zach also knows I drink copious amounts of alcohol when I go to The Hook which is (a) not part of my mom's sensible eating plan, and (b) requires me to eat real food for dinner on nights before shows. He would absolutely know I was blowing him off if I tried to back out now, and that doesn't feel right.

"No, it's fine," I finally say. "I'm definitely up for dinner."

"You pick the place. Anywhere, on me."

I don't really blush, my skin is too olivey for that, but if I did blush, I'd be blushing.

"Is it too hot to sit outside at The Café?" I ask.

"Not if we start with some Long Island Iced Teas."

"Great. I'll see you there. Seven?"

"I can come get you... if you want."

Nate's place is just under a mile from the store and the store is only a few blocks from The Café.

"Nah, you don't have to walk all the way up here. I'm fine to meet you down there."

"I really don't mind. I'd like to."

"Okay. I'll be ready any time after six-thirty."

"Great," he says. "And also, your friend Johnny called here looking for you yesterday. Cassie just remembered to write it down. Sorry."

"No worries. I talked to him today. Thanks."

"Good. Okay. I'll see you later. Great."

"Yeah. Great."

And it is great. I've been wanting Zach to ask me out for years. But it's also weird. And maybe it doesn't mean anything at all. Like, how much would actually change in the next few months? We already have sex. And spend tons of time together at the store. If he wants to take me out to dinner, that's cool. It's not like we're going to decide to be exclusive right before I leave town. It's just dinner. And Chris Thompson just happens to be in town the same night. I'm sure it will all be fine.

I'm sure it will all be fine. I just keep repeating that to myself as I head down to the basement where Nate makes me keep the few boxes of stuff I have. I know exactly where to find the envelope Chris left for me when he took off for Australia. It's in the sturdy green and white liquor store box. I flip through the envelopes of photos inside and locate the one labeled "Summer 1992." It has a ton of shots from poorly lit bars where Wasted Pretty played and photos of parties at Chris' place after the shows, the ones everyone would eventually leave so it would just be me and Chris and Johnny and Tess Wilson playing cards. The photo I'm looking for is in its own envelope inside the 1992 envelope. I take it out and study it. It's the only picture I have of Chris and me, and it's not even really of us. It's actually a photo of Johnny and Tess one night after a show. But Chris and I are in the bottom corner, way in the back of the frame. We're out of focus, but we're there.

I flip the photo over to see where he has written "Us" on it. I don't read the letter in the envelope with it, the one telling me he was leaving, that he was already gone. I don't read it, because I don't need to. Just seeing it reminds me what it felt like that day—my dad in the hospital, my car stolen by Karl Bell who put him there, and Chris on his way to Australia with his new band.

Meredith's right: I cannot trust him. He left Pittsburgh without telling me. He left the continent without telling me. Even though he told me virtually everything else. Even though I was the first one he told he was dropping out of college, and I was the one who knew he dreamed of being a roadie because he never wanted the attention of being an actual rock star. I'm supposed to be furious, and part of me is, but part of me could never muster the strength to be mad at him at all. I have to admit, fleeing Pittsburgh makes even more sense to me now than it did then. It's a great place to be from, but its thick tentacles of connection act like a straitjacket.

CHAPTER 5

The doorbell rings at 6:30 p.m. exactly. No one rings our doorbell. Most of Nate's friends just let themselves in the back door, and I don't have many people over. Nate prefers it that way. But it makes sense Zach would ring the bell. He doesn't come by here very often.

On the way down the stairs to let him in, I let myself wonder if he might be holding flowers on the other side of the door, but then I realize I'm not sure I want him to be. The thoughts flick in and out of my brain so quickly: Yes, I want this to be a date, but also, I don't want him to go overboard. I want tonight to be casual, friendly. Maybe so I won't feel bad if I ditch him later for Chris Thompson. But also, I know so few people who actually go on dates, I'm not sure what to expect. And Zach and I have seen each other naked, so that probably changes things from whatever normal is supposed to be. Maybe this is why no one I know dates. It's very confusing.

To my relief—*is that what I'm feeling?*—Zach is not holding flowers when I open the door. But he does look… nice. I mean, he always looks nice—deep set eyes, shaggy brown hair, really deep dimples when he smiles—but he also always looks rumpled. Not tonight. He's wearing skinny, but not too tight, black jeans and a black and white bowling shirt. Instead of sneakers he's wearing red and black bowling shoes. Meredith would probably say it's a little too matchy-matchy, but he's definitely trying. I'm glad I took her advice and put on a dress and did my nails. I decided to do my toes and fingers, even if maybe that was too much.

"You look nice," he says.

"Thanks, so do you," I say, but I also laugh a little, even though I don't mean to, and Zach tips his head to the side and makes a pained face.

I step past him to get out of the house, but he moves the wrong way and we bump into each other. More forced laughing and grimacing ensue.

"This feels a little awkward, right?" he asks.

"Yeah, I don't know why. I don't want it to be awkward."

"Okay, so it won't be. Cool?"

"Yeah, cool," I say with a smile and he takes my hand, and it's not awkward. Then he sort of nuzzles me—his nose and lips against the skin behind my ear—and it's really not awkward. It's hot. I feel … smitten… a word I'm sure I've never uttered or thought before.

At Café 210 West we take an empty two-top on the front patio by the sidewalk railing. It's not crowded because of the holiday weekend, but it's not empty either. I know several people on the patio, and I feel them taking note of us, me and Zach together, out for dinner, alone. Or maybe I'm imagining that. But we did walk in holding hands and there are some nosy, astute people in this town.

"Hey guys," Dara says as she comes up to the table. She's my favorite server— a local with straight, jet black hair, unbelievably short bangs, and big hoop earrings, who doesn't put up with any B.S. "Alice, you missed happy hour, by like, a mile."

"I know," I tell her, with a laugh.

"I thought maybe you took off."

"What do you mean?"

"Like, left town without saying goodbye."

"I'd never, Dara. I'm here for the summer. Promise."

"Good. And Zach," she turns to him. "It's been a while."

"Hey Dara," he says.

"So, what are you drinking?" she asks us.

"Long Island Iced Tea," I tell her.

"Same," Zach says.

"Separate tabs?" she asks.

"Just one," Zach says. "I'll take the tab."

"I see," she says. Dara raises her eyebrows a bit and then smiles at me as she turns to put our order in.

"Thanks for asking me out," I say, a grin spreading uncontrollably across my face.

"Thanks for saying yes." Zach puts his hand on the table, and I take it. I'm surprised by the jolt of giddiness I feel.

We talk about the store while we wait for our drinks. He asks me for details on the project I'm working on to which will hopefully explain to corporate that they can't treat us like every other store, And he reminds me they can treat us any way they want.

"Are you sure you don't want to stick around for a year or two?" he asks. "I don't have the energy to fight with corporate the way you do."

"No, but thanks for the offer."

"Why won't you tell me what you're up to?"

"Okay, I'll tell you. But really, no one knows what I have planned, so it needs to stay between us. Well, Meredith knows, but no one else."

"Of course, Meredith knows," Zach says with a smile.

"Yes, of course."

"How is she?"

"Drunk on the Hamptons," I say.

"I think they say 'in' the Hamptons," he corrects me.

"Well, whatever they call it, she was already tipsy when I talked to her this afternoon, so I'm sure she's drunk by now."

"She's a trip," he says.

"She is," I agree. "But she's always liked you."

"You know she hit on me your freshman year?"

"Of course she did. Of course, I do."

"Does she know about us?"

"What about us? Tonight?"

"Well, yeah, but also…"

"You mean that we sleep together on national holidays?"

"When you put it like that…"

"Yeah. She knows."

"You really do tell each other everything, huh?"

"You don't have a friend like that?"

"Not really. Most of my high school friends left for college and didn't come back. And most of my college friends graduated and left. I guess my dad was really my closest friend."

"Sorry," I say. "I miss him, too."

I wonder if it's the wrong thing to say. I do miss Rod—he was like a normal parental figure for me while my parents were getting increasingly selfish and childish—but I obviously don't miss him as much as Zach does. I'm about to apologize when Zach opens his mouth to speak.

"You know, talk about someone who really liked someone. Rod loved you."

"That's nice of you to say. He was always great to me. I mean, I always figured it was because I'm Burton's kid, but that's okay."

"No," Zach says. "It wasn't that way at all."

"What do you mean?"

"I'm sure you got hired because of Burton, but my dad always thought he was a bit of a buffoon and that you were twice as impressive as your dad."

"He said that?"

"Yeah."

"Why didn't you ever tell me?"

"I don't like talking about the things he said because he's not here to explain himself. Like, if I misquote him, or there's some nuance I miss. It's just the things I remember him saying are so final, and I don't like passing them on. But you should know he liked you for you, not because of who your dad is."

"Thanks, Zach. I really appreciate you telling me."

"Sure."

It's weird how different but comfortable it feels to be with Zach on a date. Like, we talk in the store all the time. And at The Hook. And at parties at his place. But this is different. And even though we've seen each other naked and I know exactly how soft the skin between his shoulder blades is, and how the birthmark on his chest looks like a heart, we never really talk in those moments, not even last week, when he must have been at least considering asking me out. It's almost like we're different people in his bed—not Alice and her manager, Zach—but just two people who can't figure out how to be with anyone else.

We're just sitting, holding hands, and silently looking at each other, when Dara puts our drinks down a little too hard and some of the liquid sloshes onto the metal grating of the table.

"Sorry that took forever!" she says. "Summer help is the worst."

"No worries," I tell her. "No rush."

I kinda just want to sit quietly with Zach for a while.

"Are you two love birds eating or just drinking tonight?"

"Nice, Dara," I say. "I'll have a burger and sweet potato fries."

"No bun, right?"

"No, I'll have a bun."

"Oh, so you're drinking tonight, huh?"

I consider what it says about me that my favorite server at my favorite day-drinking spot knows I only have buns when I'm planning to get trashed, but I chalk it up to her good service and not my own questionable choices.

"Yes, Dara, I'm drinking tonight."

I pick up my pint glass and clink it to Zach's while he orders a burger, too.

"You two headed over to The Hook later?" Dara asks while she's still writing down his order, a true professional.

"Yup," I say.

"That band that's playing tonight," she says. "ACE? They were in for happy hour. Seem cool. They have all those songs playing in commercials right now. Good tippers."

My breath catches, and I cough a bit, and then I sort of burp/choke. *Great.*

"You okay, Alice?" Zach asks.

"Yeah. Fine," I say. "Sorry. Swallowed wrong." *Ugh.* "You coming to the show, Dara?"

"No, I'm here 'til late. Maybe I'll catch up with you all after hours."

"Cool," I tell her as she glides away, quickly, as if on roller skates.

"So, your plan?" Zach asks. And for a moment I wonder if he's talking about my plan for tonight, for Chris Thompson, or for him, but then I remember I was about to tell him about the fall.

"Okay, so, I applied for this fellowship in New York City, and if I get it, I'm going. It's a really big deal and most people who do it go on to journalism school at Columbia or Northwestern, like no problem. And, if I don't get it, I think I'm still going to go. But, it'll be hard, because the fellowship would make it financially doable and get me the experience I need. But without it, I'll probably be waiting tables or something, so then my dad'll pressure me to come back and work at the station, and honestly, that would probably make the most sense. So, I can't stay here, because like, I mean, it would be fun, but you know…"

"That makes sense, I guess. I mean, I don't love it, you being hours away in either direction, but it does makes sense."

My gawd, he really likes me.

"Zach, why did you wait until now to ask me out? Is it just because we work together? That you're technically my boss?"

"No. It's because if you said no, you could tell me it was because you were leaving or whatever, and I wouldn't have to feel bad about it."

"But if I said yes…"

"I know. I should have asked you out a long time ago. I'm sorry."

"No, don't say sorry! That wasn't a nice question."

"No, but I am. Really."

"Well, it's no problem on my end."

"So, when do you hear from the fellowship?"

"I thought I would have heard by now, so I guess any day. It's stressful, but I have a good feeling about it."

"And Burton doesn't know?"

"No. I wanted to get it on my own. I wanted to know I could."

"Yeah, that makes sense. It's sort of hard knowing everything you have is because of your dad."

"I didn't mean it like that, Zach. You do a great job running the store."

"I do a better job with you around."

"That's sweet," I say.

"And it's more fun, too." He holds my hand up to his mouth and kisses my knuckles.

CHAPTER 6

When we get to The Hook, two guys who are regulars at the store are onstage playing guitar and singing covers of songs by The Police. Everyone from the store is here tonight, like most nights, because The Hook is essentially an extension of Rod's. It's owned by Rod's brother, Stu, which explains Cassie's presence even though she can't pass for 21 or get into any other bar in town.

"Alice!" she yells at me as a greeting. "You look so pretty! Like you actually tried tonight!"

"Thanks, Cass."

Because The Hook is always dark, it takes her a minute to notice that Zach and I are holding hands.

"Wait!" she says, her own hands up to her face and her eyes wide like the kid in Home Alone. "Are you two here together?"

"We grabbed a bite," Zach says, and his tone communicates to Cassie that she needs to leave it at that.

I wonder if it's just something he doesn't want to talk about with Cassie, or something he's not sure he wants to talk about with anyone, when I see Chris Thompson over Cassie's shoulder. There's a mix of relief and disbelief in the pit of my stomach. It's not until I see him that I realize I didn't actually think he was going to be here. It's not that I thought Johnny was messing with me, that's not like him, it's more like he's overcautious and over-protective so he might have assumed Chris was going to be here when really he left the band two years ago, moved to Japan, and some other dude is playing guitar for ACE now.

But Chris Thompson is here, down the hallway that leads out the back door. I watch as he crosses from the bathrooms into the little area they have set up behind the stage that functions as a green room. I see him for a split second; it's just his profile. His hair is different, shorter, but it's Chris Thompson—I can tell by the way he runs his hand through the hair on the top of his head.

Johnny was not being over cautious. Chris Thompson is backstage at The Hook. And I'm at The Hook. I simultaneously feel the urge to go backstage—no one would stop me here, they'd assume I was on official business for the record store—and flee the building.

The two locals on stage finish their set and the room applauds. Zach puts his arm around my waist making it even more clear to everyone we're together, even if he doesn't want to talk about it. Of course, it feels more complicated than it did twenty minutes ago—slightly claustrophobic and presumptuous even—though I do like the way his chin length, light brown curly hair—like Michael Hutchence pre-haircut—brushes my face.

My head is on his shoulder when I see Chris Thompson again. I know the set-up of the room means I can see the people on the stage, and they can't see me, but the impulse to flee comes back. Like I'm not ready for five years of pining to be over, especially because I don't know how they're going to end. And of course, there's Zach.

"Do you have weed on you?" I ask him.

"Uh, yeah, but I thought—"

"That I only smoke in your bedroom?"

"Something like that, yeah."

"Well, things are different tonight," I tell him. I know he thinks I mean something different than I do, but maybe I don't even know what I mean.

We step outside and duck between the buildings. He hands me his one-hitter and a lighter. I take a drag off it, close my eyes, and lean up against the wall. The hot, wet summer air feels like a steam room, but that's not why my muscles are relaxing. Zach refills his pipe and takes a hit himself. He leans next to me. We're both staring at the wall of the building next to The Hook. It's grey and cinder block, and I wonder when it was repainted last, not that it matters to anyone or anything.

"Do you want to take off? Go back to my place?" he asks.

It doesn't sound like a bad idea. The warm fuzzy feeling I have when I'm stoned is so closely tied to the impulse to push my body up against Zach's that I take his hand in mine. We could go back to his place now and pretend it's just a regular night, like I haven't graduated, like he didn't ask me out, like Chris Thompson isn't on the other side of the cinder block we're leaning up against—

"We should go inside!" I blurt out and let go of Zach's hand. "We should … check out the show, right? Everyone's so excited about this show."

"I guess," Zach says. "Not sure how The Hook got added to ACE's schedule last minute. They're about to really blow up. It's pretty cool and all, but we can catch them at the store tomorrow."

It's tempting, but even in my relaxed haze, I know I'll regret skipping the show and the opportunity to parade Zach in front of Chris. But I'm not so stoned that I don't know that's not fair to Zach. I guess in my fantasies of being a successful grown up at an Ivy League school with a hot, fake boyfriend in NYC, it didn't occur to me that I might still be attracted to Chris Thompson.

"Let's just go in."

I don't wait for Zach to respond. I lead him by the hand.

Inside, we find Cassie near the bar. I take her Coke out of her hand without asking and take a swig.

"Cass, there's rum in here."

"Shhhh…" she says in an exaggerated stage whisper.

I don't give it back to her. Instead, I suck it down myself.

Normally, I'd give her shit and get her in trouble with Zach over this, but I can't get worked up about it now. This is why I should only smoke when I'm alone with Zach in his apartment. It's just so hard to care about anything else when my edges are fuzzy. But then ACE takes the stage, and nothing seems fuzzy at all.

CHAPTER 7

Watching Chris Thompson play guitar probably doesn't look like much to most people. He's tall and blond with bright blue eyes, but on stage he keeps his head down—hair in his face, eyes focused on his own fingers, or maybe they're closed—and tries to blend in. I've never seen anyone on stage actively try to disappear the way he does. But still, I stare. To me, watching Chris Thompson play guitar is everything; it brings me right back to being sixteen. When he was on stage under the lights, he couldn't see me. It meant I could stare openly and unabashedly. Before we even kissed, I would sit in the clubs where Wasted Pretty played and take note of each of his small, controlled movements. Even after we kissed, after I spent nights in his bed—silently begging him to screw me and wondering why he wouldn't—I still couldn't look him directly in the eye, but when he was on stage I could take him all in.

Tonight though, his movements are slightly more animated, even though he still looks down, his eyes shielded by his bangs. It makes me realize just how much time has passed since we knew each other. A feeling I'm not prepared for works its way into my soggy brain. It's a hope that his more relaxed movements mean he's happy. I'm not prepared to want him to be happy. But I know he wasn't happy in Pittsburgh. The moodiness comes back as a flash—the way Johnny and the guys in Wasted Pretty complained to me. The way I could sometimes cheer him up, but not towards the end.

In the middle of the set, Zach brings me a lemon drop, even though I haven't asked for a drink. Then he brings me another. He's never bought me drinks before, not unless he was buying a round for everyone. But I look around and we're the only ones holding oversized shots. We clink our plastic cups together and throw our heads back. The cold, acidic liquid chills my whole body.

Before I've even felt the liquor hit my knees, Cassie grabs my hand and pulls me onto the dance floor. We bounce up and down and accidentally-on-purpose knock into one another, laughing and sticking our tongues out at each other the whole time. I'm much more fucked up than I mean to be, which, if I'm honest, is sort of a pattern for me.

"ACE is really good," I say to her.

"No shit! Where have you been?"

"No TV," I remind her. "Do they even have an album out?"

"Not recently," she says. "I think they're in the States to record a new one!"

"How do you know this?" I ask her.

"How do you not?" she asks me.

"I guess I was busy, I don't know, trying to graduate!"

"The guitarist is super-hot," she tells me.

"You're sixteen," I say. Exactly how old I was when I met the hot guitarist. But he was five years younger then, too.

"I'm sure that wouldn't stop him," she says with her damn bouncing eyebrows again.

I take her by the wrists and make her stop dancing. "What makes you say that?"

"Rock star. Loose morals," she says with a knowing laugh that makes her seem older than sixteen, and also possibly drunk, even though I haven't seen her try to sneak anything since I took her rum and Coke.

I know Cassie's just saying dumb shit, but I don't like her talking about Chris Thompson this way, like a conquest. It's probably not smart to feel possessive about someone I haven't talked to in five years—someone who dropped me like a sack of potatoes, or a dumb kid—especially while I'm on a date with Zach, but it's hard not to.

I'm about to put Cassie in her place, when ACE starts playing a familiar song.

"Oh my gawd!" Cassie screams and then starts singing along … *In this morning's rain, And this one single day, What does it matter to this morning's rain? And I still feel like I'm yours, And I still feel like I'm yours…*

It's a Liminal Space song. An old one from their first record with Tess.

"I love this song!" I scream-whisper at Cassie.

"Right? Gut wrenching," she tells me, hand over her heart. "I want someone to write a song like this about me."

"Doesn't everyone?" I ask. "Tess is totally the best songwriter ever."

* * * * *

When ACE's set is over, Cassie, Zach, and I hang out by the bar with the rest of the Rod's crew. Zach stands next to me but is engaged in some conversation about the Grateful Dead—a conversation I have no interest in—with two of the guys.

"Anything happening back at your place?" Cassie asks Zach.

I know she's trying to scheme a way to get Chris Thompson alone. Which is actually something I should be doing. I need to talk to him without freaking Zach out. I need to talk to him without freaking myself out. I need to not freak out. The whole set was such an overwhelming sense memory experience that I'm not even sure if I'm mad at him or over him or what.

"We should probably see if the band wants to come hang out," Zach says.

"Are you going to ask them, or do you want me to?" Cassie asks, bouncing on her toes.

"You know what?" I say. "It's tight quarters back there. I'll go talk to them."

I hear the slur in my words, but I don't even wait for Zach or Cassie to respond. I'm not sure if I'm trying to save Cassie from embarrassing herself, or if I'm worried about how Chris might respond if she came on to him. I just know I want to be the one in control when we make contact.

The narrow hallway is crowded with people trying to get to the bathrooms or to the loading dock or the band. I can see the back of Chris' head and neck and the slope of his shoulders above the crowd. Just the sight of them, the particular angles at which his body fits together, brings back what it was like to touch his skin, to rest my fingers on his palm, to wake up in his bed, and drape my arm across his bare chest, still wondering why things had only gone so far the night before.

He's talking to one of the guys who opened for them. There are a few people between us. I wait for the flow of the crowd to push me closer to him, enjoying the idea that an invisible force is responsible for our coming together, like whatever happens next is up to the crowd, not me. When I'm standing close enough to reach him, I stretch out my arm to tap his shoulder, but I freeze, my arm in midair. I'm distracted by my own hand and the thought that maybe we use a base-ten counting system because we have ten fingers. Apparently I'm still a little stoned.

It's loud, and I can't make out what anyone is saying. Their voices are just a woosh of sounds. I'm convinced my hesitation means I should bail. I look to the backdoor and then back to the main room. The hallway is clogged with people either way, the invisible force won't let me flee. More out of embarrassment that I've been standing with my arm outstretched than anything else, I let my hand drop to Chris' shoulder and feel the soft cotton of his tee shirt between my fingertips and his broad muscle.

"Yeah?" he says, as he turns around. But then he sees me and says, "Oh, wow."

"Yeah," I say. "Wow."

I look at him expectantly.

He looks at me expectantly.

And after an initial moment of relief, based on the sheer fact that I can tell he knows who I am, I realize I was worried he wouldn't remember me, but I hadn't even given that thought space in my mind until I was sure it wasn't true. I panic, desperate to run away. But then he pulls me into him, one arm wrapped tightly around my waist and the other around my shoulders.

My whole body softens into his. The sensation is comfortable yet exciting. Electric. His body feels like home—not a physical home or a home I've ever experienced, but the way I want a home to feel. Alive, energized, and safe. I take a deep breath in and fill myself with him.

Shit.

Meredith would not like the feelings I'm feeling or the thoughts I'm thinking. Neither would Zach, who very well may be watching us right now. I should not have gotten drunk, or stoned, or come here at all. Disaster is imminent.

I exhale when he releases me.

"It's sooo good to see you," he says.

"Yeah. Wow," I say again, though I'm not sure why.

"I thought that was you on the dance floor, but I wasn't sure. I didn't want to be wrong."

"You could see me dancing?"

"Yeah. I thought it was you, but then I thought … your hair, it grew out."

"It's been five years." I tug on my long, brown waves. "But, you always told me you couldn't see the crowd from the stage."

"Did you always believe everything I told you back then?"

"Well, yeah." I knew Chris when a lot of people in my life were lying to me about a lot of things. "Didn't you tell me you'd never lie to me?" Even as I say it, I want to take it back. I'm not supposed to care whether he ever lied to me or whether he ever will. I'm just supposed to get him in bed and out of my system. My very drunk system.

"Would you believe me if I told you that was the only thing I lied about?"

"I don't know," I say, hoping my mock outrage hides my actual outrage.

"Mostly I can't see the crowd, but at certain bars, let's just say, I could see you staring."

I put my hand to my forehead and cover my eyes.

"Don't be embarrassed," he says. "I always loved it."

He reaches out to caress the length of my hair.

"How are you?" he asks.

"Drunk," I say.

"Really?"

"Yes, very. And a little stoned. How are you?"

"I'm not drunk, but I am happy to see you."

"Oh my gawd. I forgot. You don't drink, do you?"

"It's not a big deal." He looks like it might be a big deal.

"Sorry, I shouldn't have…" I trail off, because I'm not really sorry and even if I am, I'm not supposed to be. I may have come to his show, but he came to my town, my bar, with no warning. This is what I do. I drink, I hang out with my friends. This bar and the store have been the only consistent places in my life since my parents divorced. And I'm not sorry. I like to drink.

"It's fine, really. Everyone around me drinks all the time. And you don't owe me anything."

"No, I don't, do I?"

I think we're both surprised I say it out loud.

"No. You don't."

We look at each other silently.

I'm not mad at him. I don't want to be mad at him. I am mad at him. I'm not mad at him. I want to be mad at him. Should I be mad at him? I'm woozy. Abort. Abort.

I have to get out of this hallway, but there are too many people crowded around us for me to make a quick getaway and a slow getaway seems more awkward than staring silently into his dumb blue eyes that take me right back to his bed in that dingy apartment just off of Pitt's campus.

"We should probably talk," he finally says, but I'm already trying to change the subject.

"The set was amazing. The music seems… different."

I have an ACE album, or rather an A Combustible Event album, that I picked up used at Rod's my freshman year. Either they sound way different live or their music is changing. Or I'm that drunk.

"You want to talk about music?" Chris asks me.

There are people all around us trying to get his attention, and even though this whole thing is incredibly awkward, he seems somehow at ease… with himself, with me, with what appears to be a little bit of fame.

"What do you want to talk about?" I mean it to sound like a challenge, like I'm coming from a place of strength, but it ends up sounding bratty, like the kid I feared he took me for back then.

"Let's go somewhere quiet," he says.

"Oh, yeah, I'm supposed to be asking you all to come back to Zach's place."

"Zach's Place?"

"Yeah, Zach's apartment. Zach runs Rod's Records. You're playing an in-store there tomorrow? He lives upstairs, and if you want, you can all come back and hang out. We'll get some pizzas or subs, and some beer … or water, sorry, or whatever. Sorry. It's what we usually do after the shows here."

"Is Zach your boyfriend?"

"Zach's great. He runs the record store. I work there."

Chris doesn't say anything, but it looks like he's about to. Rather than let him speak, I blurt out, "I don't have a boyfriend."

Which is true. I think. *This is going well.*

Chris smiles, one of his many, varied smiles. This one is kind, knowing, like maybe he's as nervous and confused as I am but he's just better at hiding it. I don't ask him if he has a girlfriend, and part of me knows it's because I don't want to know. Get in, get out, get closure. I'm on a mission.

"Let me talk to the guys," he finally says, pointing to the green room. "And we have to get the gear into the van. Do you want to come in and meet them?"

"It's okay," I say, realizing some space might be a good idea. "I'll be by the bar. Take your time."

I turn to go back into the main room when his fingers catch mine. I feel the charge of his touch all the way up my arm. I spin around to meet his gaze.

"It's good to see you," he says. "I'm so glad you came."

And even though I don't know what to say, I'm glad he's glad.

CHAPTER 8*

Back by the bar, the room has mostly cleared out. Zach and Cassie are hanging out with a couple of other people from the store and even more people who want to be invited back to Zach's, but only if the band is coming.

"So?" Zach asks.

"He's talking to them," I say, hoping to sound casual.

"Who's talking to who?" Zach asks.

"Oh, sorry, uh, Chris, the guitarist, is asking the other guys what they want to do."

Cassie takes a swig of her drink and then says, "Why are you being weird, Alice?"

Great. The kid can read me like a book. Or she's just mad I talked to the "hot guitarist." If she only knew.

I take her drink out of her hand and smell it. "Zach, there's rum in Cassie's Coke."

"Bitch!" Cassie spits.

"Cassie!" Zach growls.

Their argument takes the heat off me for a minute, so I lean over the bar and pour myself a seltzer from the soda gun. When I hop back down, Chris and the other guys from the band are walking towards us. I get Zach's attention and Cassie flips me the bird. *Fair.*

"Zach, this is Chris Thompson. Chris, this is Zach Berman. His place is just a few blocks down."

They shake hands, and it hits me: the complications of tonight crystalize in front of my eyes like steps in an M.C. Escher drawing.

"Nice to meet you," Chris says.

"Yeah, you too. No accent?" Zach says. "I thought you guys were from Australia."

"Derek and Tau are." The guys nod a hello. "I'm from Pittsburgh." Everyone in the group looks at me.

"Chris and I know each other from his last band." I wave my hand nervously as if I'm gesturing to history. "Wasted Pretty."

"You were in Wasted Pretty?!" Cassie gushes. "With Tess Wilson?! Oh my gawd! So cool! Is that why you did Liminal Space's song?"

"That's our song," Tau said. "It may be their hit, but Chris wrote it."

I still feel like I'm yours. I still feel like I'm yours. I still feel like I'm yours.

Chris does his best to deflect attention as everyone looks his way. Thankfully, no one is watching when I stagger backwards and have to hold onto a chair for stability. That song is old. Four years old. It came out the summer I graduated from high school. It was Liminal Space's breakout hit. It's an angry, romantic ode to passion and loss. And Chris wrote it.

"That song is the best!" Cassie squeals.

Luckily, there's a swirl of activity as people introduce themselves, so no one pays attention to me trying to regain my composure. I'm watching the guys I know from the store do stereotypical guy things—I don't have to hear what they're saying to know they're asking Derek about his drum kit and Tau about his bass—while the girls are all trying to get Chris' attention. I feel their desire charging the air. I know what it's like to encounter him for the first time. How it feels when he's looking at you, and it's like you're the only person for miles. I'm thinking about the first time Chris and I spoke, before I knew he was in a band, before I knew what we'd become, before I knew he'd leave—but part of me always knew he'd leave—and that's when I realize Zach is watching me.

I feel busted, even though Zach and I are not … anything. And even if we are something, whatever it is, it's certainly not exclusive, but I am sort of on a date with him, and I have no desire to hurt him.

I've hooked up with a few of the musicians who've come through town in the past, maybe more than a few, but I'm always discreet about it. My refusal to overtly flirt with anyone in Zach's presence has unintentionally given me an air of disinterest that turns out to be irresistible to aspiring rock stars. Occasionally, I will walk one of them back to their hotel, if they have one, or tour bus, if they have one of those, but it turns out sex is always better with Zach, in that warm, fuzzy, comfortable, stoney kind of way, so I typically don't let things go too far. But tonight ... tonight's going to be a hard one to manage.

I try to smile at Zach, but I'm sure I look guilty.

He motions for me to come over to him.

"You ready to get out of here?" he asks.

I nod.

"You want to grab a case out of the cooler? I already called in the subs. Meet you back there?"

"I think we might need two cases tonight," I say, looking over the sizable crowd that has formed around us.

"That's fine. Tell Uncle Stu I said it was fine."

"Got it."

"See you back there." He gives me a quick, friendly hug and a kiss on the cheek before he taps two guys to go with him to the Sub Shop.

This leaves me to round up the crew and move them a few blocks down College Ave. to Zach's place. I ask Cassie to help me with the people and she walks right through the crowd to Chris, takes his hand, and leads him towards the door as if it's the most natural thing to do. And everyone follows them, because why wouldn't they? It's kinda cute—watching Cassie make her play—but also a little cringeworthy, because I can't help but see myself in Cassie. But I was never that forward with Chris Thompson, at least not in public. No one could ever know we were together back then, but she's acting out a scene I had always imagined for myself in my head—being "with him" for real, and not hiding it. For his part, Chris looks over his shoulder at me, and I give him a nod, as if to say, *Don't worry, I'm right here.* I get two of the guys from the store to carry the beer and we walk down College Ave. following Cassie and Chris like they're pied pipers.

Our crew beats Zach and the food to his place, so I use my key to let everyone in through the back door. Zach's apartment is a big room with lots of mismatched couches in it and all the kitchen appliances on one wall. It's a really big room. It functions as an extension of the store, and it's where we do projects like inventory and have staff meetings. It's still strange to me when Zach runs them. I can still see Rod sitting on the mid-century modern, avocado green couch—he called it the Power Couch because it sits on a small platform up against the large windows giving you the best view of the whole room—and it's weird when it's Zach up there instead.

I walk around the room lighting a few candles and some incense sticks, and make sure the door to Zach's bedroom is shut, the way he likes it when people are over. The guys with the beer pass out cans and then put the rest in the fridge

"Do you live here?" Chris asks me while I straighten some magazines on the table Zach uses for everything—eating, folding laundry, unpacking boxes of CDs.

"No, I just have keys because of the store." I don't mention that they're also useful for the nights when I take Cassie back to her mom's house and then walk a big loop around town, so no one knows I'm coming back here to get high and screw Zach.

"You seem really comfortable here," Chris observes.

"Here in State College, or here in the apartment?"

He says both, but I think it's a cover. I think he's wary of how easily I move around Zach's place. Which is fine, let him be wary. He may have written the most amazing song of longing ever, and it may be about me, but he's the one who's been M.I.A., and I don't like the implication of his question: that I should have been waiting around for him to reappear.

"Well, State College is home, and I'm in the apartment a lot because of the store."

"Home, like forever?"

"For now. And for the past four years. Pittsburgh's too complicated since my parents split."

"But Johnny told me you're moving back to work at the station."

"That's interesting," I say.

"What's interesting?"

"You've been talking to Johnny?"

"Yeah."

"See, I was under the impression that when you moved to Australia you didn't have access to a phone. Or like, paper and stamps." I force a laugh so maybe he'll think I'm joking. Maybe I am. "But somehow you managed to talk to Johnny. About me? And my plans?"

"Alright, Alice. That's fair." Chris smiles, like I couldn't possibly really be mad at him, and I hate that he might be right. "Listen, I know it's quieter here than it was at the bar, but not by much. Is there somewhere we can talk? Please?"

I'm considering my options: Do I want to leave with him right now? Where would we go? Nate gets pissy whenever I have people over to his place, and Chris Thompson is the last person I'd want to test him with. Do I want to talk? Or do I want to let the past go and just hook up with Chris? Because he's still so damn hot and every part of my body is drawn to him. It's actually hard to keep a respectable distance, though I notice he's actually giving me a wide berth. I'm just about to suggest a walk, when Zach and the guys come in with food.

Zach. *Shit.* I can't just go for a walk with Chris. Even if it is just to talk. I mean, I could, but I'd have to explain it somehow.

I see Chris eyeing the food that Zach is spreading out on the table.

"Go ahead, grab some food." I tell him. "We'll find some time."

"You're not going to eat?"

"Not that."

"Are you still eating the … mosquito snacks?"

"Nice try," I say with a laugh. "You mean The Butterfly Food? Yeah."

I almost forgot how well we once knew each other.

"That go well with beer?"

"I thought you didn't care if people drank."

"I don't. But I do care if you eat."

"I eat. I just don't eat crap."

"Add it to the list of things we should talk about." He flashes me a smile and puts half a sub on a plate.

I'm headed to the kitchen-wall to grab what I need to make one of my mom's shakes when Zach asks me to go down to the store. He won't leave a crowd of this size in his place without either me or him in charge, so he taps me to choose the music. He has a boom box that's fine for most of the gatherings here, but the apartment is also wired to the store's sound system. I guess he wants to impress ACE.

"Sure," I tell him while Cassie makes a fuss about why I shouldn't be allowed to choose the music.

"That's where we're playing tomorrow?" Chris asks. "Can I go down and check it out?"

"Sure," Zach says, but he looks at me a little too long, like he's trying to figure out what isn't being said.

*　*　*　*　*

I love being in the store after-hours. The only light I turn on is the desk lamp on the counter. It looks like an entirely different place than it does during the day, when the fluorescent lights hum and the wall of windows lets in the natural light that bounces off the lawn in front of Old Main—green and lush in the spring and covered in icy white snow in the winter. Tonight, it's just the warm glow of the yellow bulb under the brown shade by the stereo system.

I have my back to Chris as I flip on all the necessary switches to fire up Rod's old system, but I can tell he's standing impossibly close to me. There's no more wide berth now that we're alone, and while I'm not exactly sure how I want this night to go, I know I like the feeling of heat radiating off his body. He reaches over me to take down one of the CDs we keep for in-store play. I turn towards him and our chests are nearly touching.

"Is this the Ben Lee set from the Livid Festival in Brisbane?" he asks.

"Probably. One of our regulars brought it back for Zach from his year abroad."

He looks more carefully at the handwriting on the case. "This is last October. I was at that show."

"Whoa. You're a Ben Lee fan now? How very Australian of you." I can't believe we're talking about music right now. I'm staring at the place his shoulder becomes his neck, right above the collar of his t-shirt, and I can remember, *I can almost feel,* what it's like to press my lips into his skin right there.

He hands me the disc. "Can you put that in?"

"Sure. But be prepared for Cassie to flip out."

"She seems … spunky."

"That's one word for her," I say.

I turn my back to him to put in the disc and make sure it's feeding to the speakers upstairs. I keep my back to him, pretending to mess with levers, but even though it's fairly dark, I'm sure he can tell I'm just stalling. Finally, I take half a step back so that the length of my body is pressed up against the length of his. He folds his head into my hair and reaches around me to put his arm around my waist. I don't know if it's him or me shuddering, but I can feel my heart banging on my chest and his heart banging on my back. I can feel his breath on my ear and then his lips on my neck. I can't feel my knees and I'm sure if he weren't holding me close, I'd fall or just float away. But the spell of impending ecstasy is broken when I hear the sound of Cassie on the steps. I've extricated myself from his embrace by the time she throws open the door and flicks on the overheads. Tau is right behind her.

"Are you seriously playing this shit in my earshot?!" she yells.

"Jeezus, Cass. Put on whatever you want. Just turn out the lights and lock up when you're done."

"Mate, where'd you go?" I hear Tau ask Chris, which is sort of a dumb question, because he's obviously right here.

I bolt out of the store and up the stairs not sure how my legs are even working given how weak my knees are.

CHAPTER 9

When the party thins a little, Zach and I sit on the Power Couch discussing the logistics for ACE's in-store tomorrow with Derek. When Chris and Cassie and Tau came upstairs from the store, Chris gave me a conspiratorial smile from across the room, but he's kept his distance since then. He's with Tau and Cassie by the fridge and they both seem stuck to him like groupies.

"I can bring the kit in if there's room," Derek tells us. "But I'm just as happy to sit out the show. Sometimes they do in-stores without me."

"Do you want to see downstairs?" I ask.

"I'll take him," Zach says, before Derek even answers. "I want to change the music anyway."

This means I have to stay upstairs, because Zach doesn't like to leave people in his place if one of us isn't up here. He's never actually said that, I just know it's true. Because after all these years in the store, I've made a hobby out of reading Zach. I'm starting to think he can actually read me, too, which makes tonight very strange.

"Make sure you take Cassie with you," I remind Zach. "Unless you want her screaming about your shitty taste in music when you come back up here."

Zach and Derek go over to the kitchen. I'm willing Chris not to go with them, but he follows when they head for the door. At the last minute, however, Chris turns around and heads towards me. It doesn't seem like the rest of the reconnaissance party even notices him peeling off from the group. There's a rush of heat between my legs as I try to figure out how close to me he's going to sit—how close I want him to sit—when he stops short, right in front of me.

"You're not headed downstairs?" he asks.

"No, I'm in charge up here if Zach is down there. Gotta make sure no one steals a pasta pot, or something."

"I thought you said you didn't have a boyfriend."

"I don't. I told you, we're not together."

He climbs up on the platform and it looks like he's going to straddle me—which is when I realize I want him to straddle me—but instead he stands in front of me looking out the window behind me. I'm eye level with his groin. I put my fist up to my mouth and push my lips into my own knuckles to keep myself from burying my face in his crotch. I'm not drunk anymore. Just reckless. Because Chris Thompson makes me reckless. I've always known that. It doesn't matter how mad I am at him, how mad I should be. It doesn't matter he broke my heart. I wish it did, but I have to admit to myself it doesn't. I just want to see him naked again. I hope his hotel is close by. We have to get out of here.

When he finally sits down, he sits close, but not as close as I'd like.

"What were you looking at?" I ask him.

"The street. Parking. Wondering if we should move the van now or leave it behind the club."

"You can pull into the loading dock out back, if you're worried about your stuff. But it is State College, so I wouldn't worry too much."

"No, not worried. But it's not just our stuff. We're sleeping in the van."

"You're what?" I am disappointed on several levels.

"Don't freak out, it's by choice."

"I thought you guys were doing well," I say before thinking better of it.

"We are, Princess."

There it is. I haven't been called that in five years, because only Chris Thompson has ever called me that.

"I'm not saying doing well is all about money," I clarify, "but sleeping in a van?"

"It's a nice van. And it's by choice. Mostly."

"What does that mean?"

"We worked it out with the label. We're going old-school and low budget on the east coast, so we can max out the budget in LA. We're recording out there and we just wanted to be able to, you know, enjoy it. And have some space from each other when we're not in the studio."

"I mean, there's low budget and there's no budget."

"Plus," he continues, "they weren't too excited about this tour to begin with. We haven't put out a new album in a while, but we wanted to capitalize on the songs running in those commercials, so we made some concessions. I borrowed the van from some guys I know in Philly."

"Concessions are one thing, but you don't have to stay in a van."

"No?"

"Zach will put you up here. That's what all these couches are for. Bands stay here all the time."

"And where do you stay?"

I don't know how to answer him, because I don't know what he's asking. Where do I stay when bands stay here? Where will I stay tonight? But we're locked in deep eye contact, and I have a desperate desire not to say the wrong thing. I think this is what's called a pregnant pause.

"What do you mean?" I finally ask.

"Are you sure there's nothing going on with you and Zach? You seem really comfortable with each other."

I feel the need to press him to be explicit.

"Chris Thompson," I narrow my eyes and pout my lips, hoping humor will save me from embarrassment if I'm off-base … but how could I be off-base? This is finally happening, isn't it? Gawd, I hope it is. "Why in the world does it matter so much to you if I'm with Zach? Are you having impure thoughts about me?" More pouty lips that I hope come across as half-seductive, half-teasing.

"Come with me." He takes my hand and leads me towards the door.

"Chris, I can't leave."

"We won't go far," he says.

In the small space outside the apartment there are two other doors, one to the office and one to the small staff bathroom. I know the office is locked, and I'm not carrying my keys, so I open the door to the bathroom, and we slip in before anyone sees us.

I'm not claustrophobic, but this bathroom isn't big enough for me by myself. When I'm working, I always use Zach's bathroom in the apartment. But the two of us—me, almost six-foot and Chris, over six foot—really don't fit. But it doesn't matter. We're all but fused together. He has me backed up against the wall while he kisses me, his thigh between my legs. I lean into him putting the best kind of pressure on my crotch. I feel like I can't breathe, like I don't even want to breathe, like breathing is inconsequential when I'm alone with Chris Thompson. There is sweat pooling everywhere. Maybe I do need to breathe.

"Can we go to your place?" he pants in my ear, his hand up my shirt.

"No."

"No?"

"No. I live with Nate." I take a big gulp of air. "You may remember, he's very particular. I'm allowed to live there, but he frowns on visitors. Also, he doesn't like you."

"It's been five years since I've seen him. Longer since we played against each other and all that shit."

"I'm sorry, we're not going back there. Can you get a hotel room? Just for tonight?"

"That wouldn't be a good idea. The guys. You know?"

He kisses my face, lifts my ass onto the corner sink, which is essentially the size of a mixing bowl and very likely cannot hold my weight, and then drops to his knees, head under my dress. I grip the sink under me and do all I can to stay quiet, knowing the group from downstairs will be coming up at any moment. A silent scream rattles in my chest as I tip my head back as far as it will go.

"You can't tell me you've never snuck anyone into Nate's," he whispers when he comes up for air.

"I have not, and you're not going to be the first. You know he wouldn't hesitate to kick me out on a whim. And I need a place to live."

"But Johnny said you were moving back to work at the station."

"I'm sure he did."

He's kissing my neck, but he stops. "Aren't you?"

"He and my dad think I am. But in truth, I haven't said yes, and I haven't said no. Frankly, it's my back-up plan, but they don't know it."

"What's your actual plan?"

Rather than answer him, I press my hand against his zipper and then undo it. He digs his fingers into my shoulders, his face pressed hard against mine. He stops asking questions.

CHAPTER 10

When the music pouring from the speakers changes from Garbage to U2, I know that everyone from downstairs will be heading upstairs soon.

Without explaining myself, I kiss Chris just below his ear and silently slip out of the bathroom and into the apartment. There are even fewer people hanging out than there were when we left, which makes me feel more conspicuous. I walk casually through the room trying not to arouse any attention or suspicion. I imagine I look like hell. I feel ravished, but also invincible. I let myself into Zach's empty bedroom to get to his bathroom and clean myself up. I stare at my reflection in the mirror. Is it possible he's come all this way, I've waited all this time, and we still might not get to fuck? Is it possible I actually want more than that? Is it possible he does?

When I make it back to the main room, Zach and Derek are talking by the table and Tau has Chris essentially pinned to the refrigerator.

"What's going on?" I ask Cassie.

"Zach and Derek are trying to figure out tomorrow. And if they're going to stay here tonight. And if they should move the van now or later. Boring." She rolls her eyes and tips a red Solo cup back. I take it out of her hands. "Chill, Alice," she says. "It's just water."

I smell it and give it back to her. "What about Chris and Tau? What's going on over there?"

"Tau's pissed about something. I can't tell what. Something about Chris staying up here while they were checking out the space downstairs. Also, boring."

I laugh at Cassie's assessment of the situation, but I'm not sure I agree.

"It's one a.m." I tell her. "I should probably walk you home."

"You really don't have to do that."

"I'd feel better if I did." It's the same conversation we've had a million times.

"I think I'd like Chris Thompson to walk me home," she says, batting her eyelashes, looking like a caricature of a sultry woman.

"I'm sure you would."

"Didn't you used to date someone in Wasted Pretty?" she asks.

I'm caught off guard by the question.

"No," I say quickly and plainly.

I can imagine it being something I said once, a long time ago, an exaggeration in an effort to impress people when I first got to Penn State. It was never exactly true, but it was not exactly untrue either. I certainly never expected my half-lie to show up here with his new band.

"Um, I think you said that back when Liminal Space was getting big. You said you knew Tess Wilson and you dated someone in her old band. Was it Chris Thompson?"

"I hung out with all of them."

"Alice, your face is all red."

"No, it isn't. You know I don't blush." I straighten my back, highlighting the several inches I have over Cassie, and look down my nose at her. "I need to get you home, Chicken."

I walk over to the guys. "I'm going to head out. I'll walk Cassie home on my way."

"Can you take me to the van?" Derek asks. "I'm going to move it down here for the night. Is that on your way? I'm a little turned around."

"Sure," I say. "No problem."

"You okay?" Zach asks me.

"Totally. I'll be back to set up in the morning. Do you need me before 10am?"

Zach looks confused, then hurt, then he looks at Cassie and back at me.

"No, that should be plenty of time."

He leans in to hug me, friendly, like we always are in public. I make it quick, worried he'll be able to smell Chris on me and worried Chris, who's watching this whole exchange up close, will read too much into it. Zach notices my discomfort, but doesn't say anything, because he's Zach, too gentle, too kind. I say a few more goodbyes, including a perfunctory one to Chris that everyone seems to be watching, before Cassie, Derek, and I head out into the night.

As soon as we're on the street, Derek lights up a cigarette. "Zach says we can expect a small crowd tomorrow." He offers me a drag. I shake my head, but Cassie takes it from him before he even offers it to her.

"Yeah, classes are out and it's a holiday weekend in the States. Pretty sleepy here."

"No offense, you all seem like lovely people, but I don't know why Chris insisted we add this date at the last minute. I thought maybe there would be more of a crowd."

So, it was Chris' idea to be here. I feel this new information in my chest. It swells as I take a deep breath.

"Well," I say. "We're happy you're here."

"Yeah, yeah, you guys are great. Seriously."

"Cassie said Tau and Chris were arguing. Is that… common?" I try to sound like I'm just making conversation, not fishing for information.

"Only on tour."

"Yeah? Why?"

"You know Chris from Pittsburgh, right?" Derek asks, and I realize I may need to back off the questioning, especially in front of Cassie.

"Yeah. We knew each other when I was in high school. Why?"

"Ah, no reason. Yeah, they only fight on tour because Chris lives with Tau's sister, so Tau gets all protective if he flirts with anyone when we're on the road."

This new info hits me in the gut.

"Oh. Was he flirting with someone?" I ask cautiously, forming the words in my mouth rather than my throat in hopes they will come out casually.

"No. He never does. He and Talia have a really good thing going. He wouldn't mess with it. But everyone always flirts with Chris, and Tau doesn't think he does enough to put them off. But the label tells us that girls should see him as available. He's our pretty face."

"You're cute, too, Derek," Cassie says. "Mean it." She hands him his cigarette and wanders ahead of us.

I say the bare minimum the rest of the walk to the van.

*   *   *   *   *

As soon as I get inside Nate's, I page Meredith. I spend an excruciating 12 minutes getting ready for bed, and when she still hasn't called back—do they go to sleep earlier in the Hamptons?—I call her apartment in the city so that I can at least leave her a message and hope she calls in to check it remotely.

"Hey, it's me. We need to talk. But don't call me back on the off chance you get this tonight, because I'm going to bed, and you know how Nate is with phone calls this late. So, we can talk tomorrow, but to recap: Number One: He's still hot. He cut his hair and still looks great. Number Two: We hooked up in the staff bathroom at the store. Not sex, but that might have been a space issue, though we managed to do, you know, other things. Number Three: He seemed to sense something was going on with me and Zach and he wanted details, but I mostly ignored his questions. But it sort of had me thinking that maybe he wanted, you know, more than a casual fuck. AND then, number... is this number five? I don't know, whatever. Number Whatever: I find out he's with the lead singer's sister. Like, with her, with her. Like, lives with her. Happy. Devoted. I'm sure you would say it doesn't matter. Just fuck him, and close the book, right? But, I can't figure out why he was so interested in my situation with Zach when he has something going on with someone else. What's that about? And lastly, Number ... Fifty-Two? ... I think Chris added this date to their tour. Like, it was his idea to come to State College, so, what's *that* all about? Okay, call me when you get this, but only if it's tomorrow, not tonight. Talk to you."

I put the phone back in the cradle and before I go back upstairs, I go into the kitchen to get a glass of water. That's when I see the note from Nate.

"In Philly with Angela until Monday. No parties. Don't break anything."

I have the house to myself for the weekend. Interesting.

CHAPTER 11

The in-store is lightly attended, as predicted, but I think there are actually more people than Zach expected. The guys in ACE hang out after for a bit going through our stock of used CDs and they each pick up a bunch. All of this is good stuff to report back to corporate, but an hour after the show, the store is, not surprisingly, dead. It's a beautiful day. Hot for May—but not too hot—and it's not muggy at all. Outside the large plate glass windows, the sky is a rich, cobalt blue with big, fluffy white clouds that move slowly, but noticeably, through the air.

Zach is ringing up Chris' haul of CDs when he tells me I should clock out.

I can't read his tone. Is it, "I can't look at you after I took you out to dinner and you bailed on me, so get out of here?" or is it, "The store is dead, get out of here?" or is it, "You're dead to me, so get out of here?"

I look at Chris. I know he's with someone and he kept it from me. But he doesn't know I know.

"No, it's fine," I say to Zach, making sure Chris hears me. "I like that it's quiet. I can get some more work done on the report. Cut Cassie or Brian."

"It's okay, Alice. There's no rush on the report. Like, literally no one even knows you're working on it. You gave yourself homework."

"Are you sure?" I still can't read him, and it's bugging me.

"Yeah, take the guys out to lunch somewhere. Show them around town or something."

"Not me," Tau says. "I'm going back to bed."

"I could go for a kip," Derek says.

"He means a nap," Chris tells us.

"Yeah, I got that," Zach says with a slight edge. It's very slight, but I notice it.

"Well, I'm good to go." Chris is either ignoring or missing Zach's subtle attitude. "Alice, let's get lunch and catch up. You do eat lunch, don't you?"

"Very funny," I say.

"She actually doesn't," Zach says, which is not cool on his part, but I suppose he suspected he was sending me to hang out with the whole band and not to have an intimate one-on-one with Chris Thompson.

"I do sometimes," I say, too defensively. "I did yesterday."

There are a bunch of complicated looks being passed between the guys in ACE. I choose not to watch whatever silent conversation they're having.

"Maybe I am actually hungry," Tau finally says.

"I'll bring you something back," Chris tells him in a tone that communicates the discussion is over.

Tau heads upstairs in a huff.

Even though I came in early to help set up, Chris and I haven't spoken about anything other than sound levels and recording equipment all morning. I did watch him watch me eat a Butterfly Bar even though I brought bagels and donuts for everyone else. I feel like everyone in State College is used to my eating habits, so it's weird to feel weird about them. I eat one of my mom's bars or shakes for two of my three meals a day, and I eat a regular meal for the other one. It's actually far more balanced and healthier than what most of my friends eat. But lunch is making me nervous for another reason. I haven't spoken to Meredith yet, even though I paged her as soon as I woke up. I'd feel better if I could talk to her first. I feel like there's something about this situation that I'm not quite getting my mind around—like why I care he's living with someone even though I don't want to care—and I bet Meredith would have no problem putting her finger on it. I'm trying to think like her, but it's futile, because Chris Thompson has always scrambled my brain and my judgement.

"I'm going to run these discs out to the van," Chris says. "I'll be right back."

I nod as he goes through the backdoor.

"How long are they staying with you?" I ask Zach.

"Just 'til tomorrow. Then they go to Pittsburgh."

Interesting.

"What's your history with him?" Zach asks.

This is not the question I want to hear.

"Complicated," I say. "Or not. You know, just the typical hot guy in the local band. But I guess we were friends. Listen, Zach, about last night—"

"What about last night, Alice? It was just dinner."

And with that, he retreats back into his Zach shell. Quiet, reserved, kind. He lets me off the hook. He doesn't fight for me, and he won't hold it against me. And while that makes today much easier on me, it also makes me sad. Like I'm not worth fighting for. And what if I'm supposed to be with Zach, I mean, not forever, but Chris will be gone in a day. And while I eventually want to be gone, too, I didn't mean to screw things up so badly with Zach. And he doesn't deserve to be treated this way.

"Listen, Zach, it was a long time ago. It was complicated, and I was sixteen."

"Who's sixteen? Are you talking about me?" Cassie asks, appearing out of nowhere.

"No, we're not talking about you," I tell her.

"Are you talking about me?" Chris asks, returning through the backdoor.

"No one is talking about anyone," I say.

"Okay, well, I'm hungry. You ready?"

I look over to Zach. He's already involved in some paperwork, or he's pretending to be.

"Yeah, sure," I say to Chris. "Let's go."

I don't say goodbye to anyone in the store.

We step out onto College Avenue and the quiet is heavy.

Between the hum of the AC and the music that's always flowing through the PA, the store is never quiet. But a gorgeous Saturday on a holiday weekend in a small town is thick with a blanket of silence. I'm thinking of what I can say, how I could possibly open the valve of the pressure that seems to be growing in my head, when Chris Thompson wraps his pinkie around mine. It's such a small, unexpected gesture, I'm momentarily confused. When I look over at him, he's just looking straight ahead, like what he's done is the most natural thing in the world. Like he doesn't have a girlfriend in Australia. Like I'm his girlfriend. And though it's confusing, it has a calming effect on the buzzing inside my brain. But I still want to jump him. And also yell at him. But mostly, run away with him. It's the pinkie wrapped around my finger that makes me realize that. That all my grand plans for my future, a fellowship in New York and Columbia for graduate school, may mean nothing if he wants to be with me. And I hate myself for it, even though it's just a fantasy, because he lives with someone. In Australia.

"We can go here," I say, stopping outside The Corner Room. "Or The Diner is just up the street. They have these famous sticky buns that everyone talks about. Grilled Stickies."

"You eat something called Grilled Stickies?"

"Uh, like once a year. When I'm super drunk. But I thought you might want to try them while you're in town."

"Let's go here." He motions for me to go through the revolving door ahead of him.

As if by magic, or preordained destiny, we're seated in a booth in the back, far from any windows. When I slide in, he slides in next to me, which I'm not expecting, but I'm not upset about it. Typically, I hate it when two people eating alone together sit next to each other, rather than across from each other, but maybe I've just never been out with someone I want to be this close to.

"I'd stick with the burgers," I tell him, as he looks over the menu.

"Will do," he says. "So, you eat food these days?"

"I eat one meal a day and the rest are shakes and bars and celery. Same as always. Mostly. Why are you so interested in what I eat?"

"Because your body's different than I remember it. Your shoulders are broader." He leans over and kisses my shoulder through my t-shirt. "In a good way," he adds.

"I swim now, so I do consume more calories on the days I'm in the pool." I pause. "You really noticed the difference in my shoulders?"

"You don't think I have every part of you memorized?"

A rush of heat blooms in the lower part of my core and then I blurt out, "Chris, are you here because of me?"

He blinks a few times. "Here in the US? Or here in State College?"

I hadn't considered the first one and the thought of a whole tour being about me is disorienting.

"Either? Both? I don't know," I stammer.

"No, the tour, or really the mini-tour, is about the commercials. We were always planning to record in LA this summer, but we convinced the label to add a few dates on the East Coast after the commercials started running. But, if you're asking if I added the spot at The Hook and the one at the store today to make sure I saw you after Johnny told me you hadn't moved home yet? Yeah. I did that. And in case you were wondering, 'This Morning's Rain' is about you."

I am speechless and stunned. I spent hours in my bedroom listening to Liminal Space's version of that song on repeat. It said everything I was feeling about Chris Thompson, everything I was feeling about him being gone, and it turns out he wrote it for me. It's like a dream come true—every fantasy I've ever had, being the one who got away, being the subject of a rock anthem, being his.

"Alice?" he prods.

"But you didn't call. And 'I still feel like I'm yours?' I never felt like you were mine. You were always just out of reach."

"I've always been yours."

"I don't know what to say. You never called. Not then. Not now. You didn't even tell me you were coming. How is this all about me if I didn't even know?"

"I knew Johnny would tell you. Not as a favor to me, but to warn you, right?"

"Yeah."

"So, I didn't need to tell you. And, honestly, I didn't want to know if you were mad at me, I just needed to see you."

This should make me feel great, desired, wanted. The dream I had as a sixteen-year-old—of dating a rockstar, of dating Chris Thompson, and touring with him—is all wrapped up in what he's saying. He's come here for me. But it doesn't feel great. It feels … itchy, constricting, weird.

"But, you live with someone."

His shoulders slump and his lips twist up. He's about to speak when the waiter comes over.

We both order burgers; I ask for mine without a bun. Chris takes this interruption as a good moment to shift around to the other side of the booth, which makes sense, because we need to be looking at each other—not pressed up against each other—right now.

"Okay. You're right," he says. "I think we have a lot to talk about."

"Yeah, sure, we can talk, but this just seems like a long way to come for a casual fuck."

He stammers out a few muffled sounds and then takes a deep breath. "I deserve that. But can I tell you my side of the story?"

And for some reason, even though part of me wants to strangle him, the way he just accepts my low blows and doesn't return them is sort of endearing.

"Sure."

He reaches for my hand across the table. "I guess I just sort of hoped you'd be happy about it. I didn't think it'd go like this."

"Happy you're here? Or happy you're with someone? 'Cause, I'm not trying to be a bitch. I am really happy to see you, even if I really wish I could stay mad at you. But you do have a girlfriend, which is fine, whatever, but you seem really focused on whether I'm with Zach or not, so that just sort of feels like a double standard. And what about the bathroom last night? Does your girlfriend know about that?"

"Listen, are you with Zach?"

"See? What does it matter? I know about Talia."

"It matters because of what I'm about to tell you."

The look in his eye is both excited and pleading. It seems like we're in two different conversations, and I'm fairly certain I don't know what we're talking about, but it feels like honesty might be the best way to go.

"Zach and I have been friends for a while and …" I'm trying to figure out what and how much to say when two girls I vaguely know approach us. Chris and I pull our hands back to our own sides of the table. I'm not sure who lets go first.

"Hi Alice!" the blonde one says as she flips her hair from one side to the other.

"Hi…" I stammer, searching for her name, but she's not here for me. She's already turned her attention to Chris.

"You're the guitarist in ACE, right?" she says to him.

He flashes one of his smiles, one that seems charming, but I can tell is totally fake. "Yeah."

"You're really good. We saw you at The Hook last night. How long are you in town?"

"Just until tomorrow," he says.

I watch how he navigates this interaction. It's clear he wants to seem approachable but not too interested. There's a purposeful understatedness about him in this situation. Not dark and brooding, that would only garner more interest, but not too engaged, either.

"Well, we'll have a keg tonight, if you all want to come by. Alice knows where we live."

Chris looks at me, and I nod and smile, willing the girls, whose names might be Jen and Brooke, to move along.

"Okay, see ya!" the brunette says.

"Bye!" I say, with a big smile, wide eyes, and an exaggerated wave.

"Who are they?" Chris asks.

"I have no idea."

"Are you serious?"

"I am. Lots of people know who I am. That doesn't mean I know who they are."

"So, you're 'local famous?'" he teases.

"Something like that," I say with a smirk.

"You're not moving to Pittsburgh, are you?"

It's like he can see through all the shit and actually see me. It's exhilarating and terrifying. "What do you mean?"

"This is your home now, isn't it?"

"No, it's not like that."

"But you're not moving home?"

"Honestly, I know this is going to sound dramatic, but I don't really have a home. I mean, my dad's still in the place where I grew up, but it's not really 'home' anymore. Not since my parents split."

"I heard about that. I'm sorry."

"Thanks. I wish I could say it's not a big deal. People's parents get divorced all the time, you know, but they're just ... so... I don't know, childish about it. They make it a big deal. Like, why should it matter to me? It shouldn't, but they're always trying to use me to one-up each other. And like, I've always been closer to my dad and Nate's always been closer to my mom, but my dad pretty much leaves Nate alone and my mom still pretends like, I don't know, like, we're close, and I don't want to 'take my dad's side,' so I pretend, too. So now we're 'fake-close.' It's too much. I haven't been back since Thanksgiving my junior year. I stayed here straight through last summer."

"You haven't been in the 'Burgh since last year?"

"Well, almost two years."

"Oh."

"What?"

"I mean, that sounds serious. You're only three hours away. I haven't been back in five years, but I've been all the way across the world."

"I know, that's what I'm trying to tell you. I can't be there. Not working for my dad while my parents bitch about who I love more. I'm 21 years old. Enough with their bullshit."

"So, you're staying here?"

"No. Here is like a sleepy little dream that I get to play in, but I'm in Nate's extra bedroom and there's a time limit on that. And I can't do what I want here, anyway. So, there's no real home for me to stay in or move back to."

"What do you want to do that you can't do here?"

"Why are you so curious about my plans? Did Johnny put you up to this? You can't tell him I'm not moving back. Not yet."

"No, it's not Johnny. It's me, I want to know."

"Why? What does it matter to you where I'm going to be in three months?"

"That's what I need to tell you. I'm moving home. To Pittsburgh. Talia and I broke up before the tour. It was totally amicable, she's totally cool, but we're not right for each other long term, and I'm ready to be back in the States. We haven't told anyone yet—which is why Tau is monitoring me like a hawk. He thinks he's defending his sister's honor or whatever—but, it's over. Me and Talia. Me and Australia. Me and ACE. I'm moving home."

The waiter puts our food down, but I can't move. And I'm not hungry. This information is more than I can process on an empty stomach, but also too much to take in along with food. Chris doesn't seem to have the same problem. It's like he's been waiting to get this off his chest. He picks up his burger with both hands and digs in.

"You okay?" he asks when he notices I'm not eating.

"Um, well, this isn't about me, is it?"

"Me leaving the band? No. That's been coming for a long time."

"Okay. But…" The question is right there, but I can't bear to ask it, because I think I know the answer.

"Yes," he says, before I can formulate the right way to put it. "In thinking about being in Pittsburgh, about moving back now, I thought you would be there, too. That's what Johnny told me."

Chris just keeps eating while I can barely breathe. Does Chris being in Pittsburgh, and wanting me there, too, change anything?

He reads the panic on my face. "This isn't meant to pressure you. I honestly thought you'd be there anyway."

"Yeah, okay, about that." I look around the room to make sure no one I know is within earshot. "I'm planning to be in New York City."

"Oh." He mimics me looking around the room but does it in an exaggerated way, like a bad spy. "Is that a state secret?"

"Sort of," I say with a laugh. "I applied for a fellowship in New York. It would be a fast track to journalism school at Columbia. But I didn't tell my dad. I didn't tell anyone. Because if I get it, I want to get it on my own, not because I'm Dennis Burton's daughter. And he hates New York anyway because my mom is always there doing stuff for her company, so I didn't want to have that fight. I figure if I get in, he'll be so impressed, it won't be a fight, but there's no way he would have 'let' me apply if I told him about it ahead of time. So, I'm waiting to hear from them. But, that's my plan. New York. In August."

"And he thinks you're coming back to the station?"

"Yeah. But like, that's a last resort, if I don't get the fellowship, and I can't figure something else out there."

He reaches across the table for my hand again. "But I'll be in Pittsburgh."

I don't take his hand, opting instead to pick up my water glass with both hands.

"Yeah. That's wild. But it doesn't really change that I'm planning on being in New York."

He looks hurt. Like he really expected me to be there waiting for him. Which, I mean, it's flattering, but he could have called. Anytime in the last five years, he could have called. But I don't want to bring that up right now, because even if I don't plan on being with him in Pittsburgh, I do still want to fuck him today.

"So, you're really leaving the band?" I ask after taking a sip of water.

"Yeah."

"What are they going to think of that?"

"I assume it will be … awkward, but ultimately, okay. It's why I haven't told them yet. Or the label. I want these dates and the recording to go smoothly for everyone. But I'm sure it'll be okay eventually."

"How can you be so sure?"

"You know how this all happened in the first place, right? Like, how I joined the band?"

"You replaced their guitarist, right? Who met someone in The States?"

"Yeah, in California. He's ready to move home, to Australia, and I'm ready to move home, too. So, the band'll be fine. Oliver's a great guitarist. He's a better fit. They developed their sound with him. I've just sort of been holding his place for him."

"So, wow, it's really happening? Like it's a done deal, you'll be in Pittsburgh…"

"And you'll be in New York."

"I mean, I hope so."

"Well, I hope it works out for you."

He puts his hand out again, and this time I take it. "Do you?"

"Honestly? I'll be less disappointed if you end up back at the radio station than you will, but it's more important that you're happy."

"Thank you."

Chris Thompson and I are holding hands in public, and even though the booth makes it feel like we're sequestered, there's a small thrill in knowing that we really don't have to hide this from anyone. At least not here in this restaurant, at this moment.

"Well then," Chris says, a big, wide grin lighting up his face. "We have about twenty hours. What do you want to do?"

CHAPTER 12

The walk from The Corner Room to Nate's is fast and silent. By the time we get upstairs to my room, we're already practically naked. I have just enough time to snag a condom from the bottom drawer of my dresser before we both end up in the twin bed.

The sex is good but quick. Not bad quick. Not rushed quick. Just urgent. Like in finally doing what we've never done before, we can only focus on doing it and can't think too much about how it might feel or what it might mean. It's like once it was clear it was going to happen, we couldn't afford to let anything else bubble up. There's been too much build up, anyway.

I've been thinking about it for five years. It's not fair, and I wouldn't admit it to anyone—in fact, I've outright denied it when Meredith has accused me of it—but I've always compared every guy I've been with to what I thought it might be like to be with Chris Thompson. In and out of bed. And they've all fallen short, miserably. How could they not? I was comparing them to a fantasy of sex and a relationship that existed mostly in secret, in Chris' apartment where we didn't deal with the outside world, and we didn't bring the outside world in.

But sex with Chris is not a fantasy anymore. It's way more real than anything I could have imagined. Visceral in a way I could never have conjured. I knew we'd fit together—our bodies had always come together easily, even if he used to find ways to keep things from going too far—but I didn't know how vulnerable it would feel to be pressed up against someone so familiar, or how good it would feel to let myself be that exposed. Lying naked next to Chris, his bare arm thrown casually across my skin, is better than any sex I've ever had. I have failed Meredith's get-in-get-out-get-closure-at-all-costs mission. I'm here for the connection, the afterglow. My mind is not occupied with ways to get out of bed, out of the room, ways to escape without being rude, but willing to be rude, if it came to that. With Zach I always had the excuse of the secrecy, knowing that it would look bad if people at work knew we were sleeping together. He never pressured me to stay. But other guys on campus? I sort of developed a reputation for being hard to pin down, though most of them didn't actually care. They were happy to have me slink out in the middle of the night.

But now? I don't ever want to leave. I don't ever want him to leave. Even if the bed is a little cramped. The twin bed in the sparse room does not hold us well, even intertwined as we are. It's also weird having anyone in Nate's house, let alone Chris Thompson. I'm aware of the heat I would take if Nate came home unexpectedly, but I don't want to sneak around anymore. I know it was a factor in whatever Chris and I had back when I was in high school, but I don't want to be anyone's secret anymore. I roll over in the bed, pushing my back into his side and trying to make a little more space for my knees.

"You okay?" he asks.

"More than okay," I tell him. "You okay?"

"Yeah." He shifts his legs and ends up kicking me. "Sorry!"

"No, it's fine. I'm sorry about the bed."

"It's really small."

"Yeah. I've never brought anyone back here."

"So, Nate's still Nate?"

"Yeah, but it's still better than being at my dad's, so it's fine."

He rolls over to wrap himself around me from behind and kisses my shoulder. "Can I ask you something?"

"Yeah?" I turn towards him, putting a little space between our chests so I can actually see him, even though it means we're both likely to fall out of bed.

"I know what you're going to say, but I have to ask."

"Uh. Okay. But I try to avoid having difficult conversations naked."

He wraps his arms around me, and I bury my face in his neck.

"Will you please come to Pittsburgh tomorrow?"

"No," I say without even a second of hesitation.

"Hear me out," he says, and I roll away from him, turning my back to him again. "I'm not saying you have to move there. But I don't want to say goodbye yet. Just come for a few days."

"And what? Stay with you and Tau? In the van? How would that work, exactly?"

"Well, no. And we're actually staying with my parents. But that's the thing. Pittsburgh is as much your home as it is mine. You could just be home. It could have nothing to do with me."

"Oh … so … yeah, of course. I'll just stay with my dad. Or maybe my mom? I wonder which would piss the other one off more?"

"I know it's complicated. And it's a big ask. Just come for a few days?"

"I'm not a groupie, Chris."

"I didn't mean it like that."

"I'm not going back there unless I have to. I'm sorry. Not even for you."

"I'm not asking you to move back. I'm just asking for a few more days with you."

"No. I'd need like, a month to get mentally prepared for that."

"Alice? Is Pittsburgh your Plan B, or is there something else?"

I stare out the window at the bright blue sky and slow-moving clouds. I have a history of telling Chris Thompson things I don't tell anyone else, but mostly because in the past he seemed to exist outside of my real life. Lying naked in my bed makes him a lot more real. And yet, not. Because tomorrow he'll go his way and I'll go mine. And I'll know he's in Pittsburgh, not Australia, and I'll know he wants me there, too.

"I haven't figured anything out yet. Can we not talk about it?" I don't wait for his answer. "I have an idea. Do you like to swim?"

"You want to swim laps?"

"No. Not laps. I have something to show you. Get up. Get dressed."

I'm out of bed and into my bathing suit while he's still lying there looking stunned.

"Get up!" I tell him, a big smile on my face.

*   *   *   *   *

On the way to the quarry, Chris rests his hand on my thigh, like it's the most natural thing to do, but it's unbelievably distracting. I have to force myself to concentrate on driving. If I wreck Nate's car, I'll never hear the end of it. I'm lucky they took Angela's to Philly or we would have had no way to get out of town.

I've heard the quarry filled with water when a spring was unintentionally hit by some machinery. Some people say the abandoned equipment is still down there along with multiple cars that people have driven off the cliffs. Everyone on campus knows the story of the cook from one of the restaurants in town who jumped headfirst and came up bloodied and partially paralyzed, but that doesn't stop us from sneaking past the No Trespassing signs and throwing our own bodies into the void.

"You're kidding, right?" Chris says when I lead him to the edge.

"I'm not. It's amazing."

"*You* jump off *this* cliff?"

I nod with a smile, excited that I've surprised him. "You don't have to, if you're scared..."

"No, I'll do it. I just can't believe you do."

"Do you think of me as someone who is afraid of things?"

"I think of you as careful."

"You think of me as sixteen."

"Maybe. Not in a gross way. It's just interesting to see you … this way."

"Shall we?" I ask, taking his hand and kissing his cheek.

We jump together. It's more than exhilarating to hurl yourself off a four-story cliff holding the hand of a man you just fucked after a five-year wait. We hit the water with a smack. I surface first and wait for him to break through, his fine, blond hair plastered to his head.

"That was amazing!" he says, once he shakes the hair out of his eyes, like a cute, wet dog. He's typically so understated in all of his reactions that his excitement makes me proud, like I've shown him something he never expected.

He swims over to me and threads his arm under mine while we both dog paddle in the emerald green water.

"I don't think I could have ever imagined jumping off a cliff with you," he says with his face close to mine.

"See what you've been missing?" I say with a laugh.

I swim towards the edge of the water and hoist myself up onto the low rocks. It's shaded down here, and I'm eager to get back up to where we left our towels, on the outcroppings of limestone in the sun. I hold Chris' hand behind me as I lead him through the undergrowth to the trail that will take us back up top.

We're sunning ourselves on our respective towels when a car of guys pulls up to the ledge behind us. It's a big old beater, American made, and Lynyrd Skynyrd is pouring out of the sound system. In clown-car fashion it seems like seventeen guys get out of the one car, but maybe some of them have hiked up from the road, the way we did. They're young—underage teens, for sure—skinny and shirtless, with start-of-the-summer pale chests and long, scraggly hair. Two of them take a large blue cooler out of the trunk and start passing out cans of beer.

"What year is it here in Happy Valley?" Chris asks with a laugh.

"Here? At the quarry?" I say with a smile. "Time doesn't exist."

It's true. The quarry exists outside of time and space. Chris is right. I am careful. I don't typically ignore No Trespassing signs or jump off forty-foot cliffs, but at the quarry I can be someone else. More me. Or less me. I don't know. The past four years, I'd come here after sleeping with someone I probably shouldn't have to pretend it didn't happen. The quarry allows for a moment when school and my parents and my brother and even the record store don't exist. It allows for a break from reality, an escape from any decisions I have or haven't made, any deadlines or looming consequences. It's hard to think of anything else when you're running full speed off a forty-foot cliff.

One of the teens sees me watching him and brings over two cans of beer, in a gesture that's either neighborly or payment for not narcing on them. I take the cans without thinking, open one, and pass it to Chris, but he shakes his head.

"Right. Sorry," I say. But it's already open.

"I don't mind," he says, using his hand to shield his eyes from the sun making it hard for me to tell if he really does mind or not.

But it's hot and sunny and I'm happy, so I take a swig. And then another. I finish half the can before I lie back down and close my eyes with a pleasant buzz. My whole body is comfortably warm, either from the sun or the beer or just the fact that Chris Thompson is lying next to me. And then he wraps his pinkie around mine, just like he did on the street a few hours ago—how could that be only a few hours ago—and I feel something inside me come loose. There's a tension my body has been holding for years, and it just goes soft. It feels amazing, but also scary, like my protective reflexes won't be there if I need them. And for the first time, I think it might not be so terrible if I don't get the Klein fellowship. If I end up in Pittsburgh, at least he'll be there, too.

CHAPTER 13

I pull the car into the space behind the house and we go up the back stairs. Chris is standing close to me with his hand on my waist as I fumble with the keys. We're talking about what we should do tonight when I finally get the door open to reveal Nate and Angela sitting at the kitchen table. Chris must feel my body stiffen, but he doesn't take his hand away, in fact, he intensifies his grip just a bit. It reminds me of the night my dad sort of caught us in a sort of compromising position, and Chris wouldn't budge, as if he weren't afraid of my dad at all, even though, on some level, he was. That was the night he left, but those two things are unrelated.

I have the impulse to move away from Chris, to put some distance between the two of us so maybe Nate won't call us out, but I know it's too late, so instead I lean into Chris' hand. He responds by stepping even closer to me.

"What the fuck, Alice?" Nate is never subtle, but he is often vague.

Angela mouths *sorry* from her seat at the table.

"What's the problem?" I ask, not knowing exactly what part of this situation he finds most objectionable.

"You know you're supposed to leave a note if you take my car."

I relax just a little.

"Uh, I thought you weren't coming home until tomorrow. Who was I supposed to leave a note for? The coffee maker? The kitchen table? 'Dear Kitchen Table—I'm taking the car. Going to the quarry. Be back by dinner.'"

Nate ignores my jab. "I called the store and Zach said you disappeared with someone in a band before lunch—typical Alice, right?—but," he motions to Chris, "this is an interesting development."

Chris steps out from behind me, one hand still on my waist, one hand extended to shake Nate's. "Hey, Nate, long time."

Nate doesn't move. "What are you doing here?" he asks Chris. "What are you doing with him?" he asks me.

"Nate, Chris and his band are in town. They played a show last night and they leave tomorrow. I took him out to the quarry. I'm sorry I didn't leave a note." This is me trying to diffuse the situation.

"Remember when you tried to convince me nothing was going on with you two back in Pittsburgh?"

"Nothing was going on with us." This is not a lie. The night Nate thought he caught us together we hadn't even kissed yet.

"Then why the deep depression when he split?"

It's like all the air has left the room.

Chris, clear Nate is not going to take his hand, retreats behind me. Angela puts her elbows on the table and her head in her hands. Nate and I just stare at each other. Part of me is embarrassed. I don't want Chris to know what it was like after he left. There was a lot going on. He wasn't the only reason I was stressed out. But there's another part of me that can't believe Nate noticed, or remembered, or cared. He wasn't even really around then, but I have to assume even though no one dared to mention Chris' name to me, they must have been talking behind my back. I'm sure I have Johnny to thank for whatever Nate knows about my senior year of high school. But now it seems Nate's not mad at Chris for something that happened between them on the soccer field ages ago, at least not exclusively. Now, he's mad at Chris for hurting me.

No one says anything for too long. Like, really too long. Like, maybe only siblings can get away with staring at each other and not saying anything for this long. Except we are saying something, just not with words. He's asking me to double-down, to defend Chris, but it's not for Nate to decide how I move forward through this.

Chris takes a breath as if he's about to say something, but I put my hand up to stop him.

It's Angela who finally speaks, softly, to Nate. "We should really get going."

He goes into his room, directly off the kitchen, without saying a word.

"We just came by to dump some stuff off and pick some other stuff up," Angela tells me. "It turns out, I screwed up and thought Laurel was covering my classes this weekend, but she thought I was covering her classes. Huge screw up. Anyway, we're going to stay at my place tonight. And we'll be at Brooke and Jen's for a bit, if you want to hang out … or avoid us."

"Thanks, Ange." I'm giving her a hug when Nate blows back through the kitchen and out the front door.

"I'm sorry, Alice. I feel like this is my fault," she says.

Angela was my yoga teacher, and friend, before she was Nate's girlfriend. Never in a million years did I expect super-jock Nate to fall for a spiritual girl from Philly, who wears her hair in an amazing afro like her namesake, Angela Davis. As a couple, they stand out on campus and have had to figure out a way to bridge a couple of divides and respond to a lot of shit talk. I can't help but think if they've made it work—been able to really see each other in spite of all the ways other people see them, been able to see the good in each other, because there is good in Nate, I know there is—that there's hope for me and Chris.

"It's not your fault. You're perfect." I tell Angela and kiss her cheek.

"I'm Angela. Hi," she says reaching her hand out to Chris.

"Chris. Hi."

"Sorry I have to run. Be good to her," she says before she makes a rushed but graceful exit.

I turn back to Chris to apologize for all the drama, but before I can get the words out, he has me enveloped in a hug.

*   *   *   *   *

Upstairs, I take a shower, but Chris doesn't have anything to change into—he wore his shorts in the quarry—so he says he'll shower back at Zach's. He's sitting on my bed when I come in wrapped in a towel and close the door behind me.

"These from Tess?" he asks, pointing to the postcards I have tacked up to the back of my door.

"Yeah. Whenever she's on tour she sends me something from the road."

"I thought they looked familiar."

"Wow. All these years we've been getting the same postcards?"

"I guess."

"Weird."

He makes a pinched face and then holds something out to me, "And this?"

"That's the picture you left for me. With the note." I pick up the note from my desk.

"I didn't leave a picture."

And again, the air leaves the room, or maybe it's just my body.

"Yes, you did. Johnny gave me an envelope with this note and that photo."

"I left the note, but I can honestly say, if I had a photo of the two of us, I would have taken it with me." He turns it over. "It's messy, but I think this is Tess' writing."

"Really? I guess that makes sense." I try to sound casual, but I'm shaken. I can imagine Tess tucking the photo into the envelope, but all this time, I thought he left it for me. I thought it was him calling us an "us."

"Alice, I need to really apologize. And I need you to hear me, and I need you to forgive me. If you can."

"What are you talking about?"

"What Nate said. The way I left. All of it. I'm sorry."

"Chris, Nate doesn't speak for me. I know you needed to leave. I was collateral damage. I'm not mad. Not anymore. I don't know if I ever was. I was just … sad."

"It's really hard to apologize to someone when the person you're apologizing to won't admit you did anything wrong."

"I mean, you didn't. Not really. It was so long ago. Can we just forget it?"

"Princess, Nate said 'deep depression.'"

"Nate wasn't even around. He was already up here. If anything, he got that from Johnny, and you know how Johnny exaggerates. Plus. There was other stuff going on around the same time. My senior year was hard for a lot of reasons, but I'm fine."

"Can we talk about the other reasons?"

"Nope."

"Come here," he says.

I adjust my towel and sit next to him at the foot of the bed.

"I need you to know I'm sorry," he takes my hand between us. "I felt horrible about leaving, but I had to get out of that city."

"Oh, I get it," I tell him. "Which is why I think you, of all people, should understand why I'm trying to avoid going back."

"I do. But it doesn't mean I don't want you to. I know that's selfish. I just thought we could—"

"We can't."

"We can't what? You don't know what I was going to say."

"Sorry. What were you going to say?"

"We could give this a try for real."

"Yeah, that's what I thought you were going to say. You don't get it. I don't want to sneak around anymore and if I move back to Pittsburgh, it would be more of the same. You think Nate was hard to deal with? He learned it from my dad."

"I'm not afraid of your dad."

"I know you're not. It's not about you being afraid of him. But you'd be one more thing my parents would use against each other. I can totally see it, my mom inviting the two of us over for dinner, letting us use her condo when she's away on business, and my dad forbidding me to see you if I live in his house. So, then our relationship becomes their pawn. That's not giving it a real try, that's setting it up for failure. I'd rather stay here than go there."

"Is that what you're thinking? If you don't get the fellowship?"

"It's an option. I already have a job. Zach said he'd make me assistant manager. I could find a different place to live. Maybe write a few articles for the local paper that would help with my J-School applications. I mean, I know it's sort of pathetic to stay in the same small town you went to college in, but lots of people do it. People like it here. I like it here."

"I get that." He seems sadder than I've ever seen him. "And you and Zach?"

Zach. Shit.

"It's not about that. And it's not about you. Pittsburgh is complicated for me. You get that, right?"

"I do," he says, but I get the sense that he's deeply disappointed, not only in the situation, but also in me. I don't like the feeling, so I let my towel drop. That's all it takes for him to smile.

We take our time this time. I don't even care that Nate's in town and could come home at any moment, or that Zach and the band are probably wondering where we are. I can't think of anything beyond the space of the twin bed, Chris' muscular arms, and the sweat dripping from both of us. I feel things I've never felt before, things that make me wonder why this sex and the sex I've been having with other guys are both called "sex." Because they're just not the same thing. This is about being as close as I can be to someone. Entwined with one another, inside one another, not for the promise of something explosive, but for the sheer pleasure of not being able to tell where I end and he begins. This is what I've been missing and not even knowing I was missing it. Are other people having this kind of sex, and I just assumed they were having the other kind? The kind I have with Zach and frat house boys? Transactional. I do you and you do me. We're both satisfied but not satiated. I didn't know satiated was an option. I didn't know I could feel so full. I didn't know I could feel like this. Complete and whole. And of course, it will all be over soon.

He rolls over, his face next to mine, no space between our noses, our legs layered on top of each other. "You good?"

"I'm good." I curl into him, and he presses his lips to my forehead.

CHAPTER 14

The sun has started to set by the time we make it out of Nate's and down to Zach's. On the loading dock, I stop Chris before I put my hand on the back door.

"In there..." I gesture up to the second floor.

"I know," he says. "Come here."

He wraps me in a hug and plants a kiss square in the middle of my forehead. We haven't figured a damn thing out, but we both know we need to keep our distance. It's for the best. Because of Tau. Because of Zach. Because tomorrow they leave, and I don't know when I'm going to see him again.

"Where the hell have you been?" Tau asks when we enter the apartment. He, Derek, and Zach, along with Cassie and a few of her high school friends, are sitting around the big table eating pizza.

"Just catching up with Alice," Chris tells him.

I grab a slice and Cassie, always monitoring my food intake, raises her eyebrows. "Did you swim today?"

"Not laps, but I took Chris out to see the quarry and we jumped." Cassie has seen me eat pizza before, but probably only when I'm drunk.

"I would have gone to the quarry with you!" she whines.

"Weren't you working?"

"I would have blown it off!" she says. "It was dead."

"Slow day?" I ask Zach.

"Very," he says.

"Is there a plan for tonight?"

"Beyond this pizza? No."

"I heard Brooke and Jen are getting a keg," Cassie says.

"Why do you know that?" I ask her. She flips me off.

"You know I won't go to a college kegger," Zach says. Like most graduates who stay in town, Zach doesn't like to be seen hanging out with undergrads.

"Well, apparently Nate and Angela are going to be there, so I don't need to be there, either."

Angela gets a pass because most of the undergrads are her yoga students so it's not weird when she shows up at their parties and Nate doesn't care what he is or isn't "supposed" to do.

"So, The Hook?" Zach asks.

"Sure," I say.

*   *   *   *   *

No one's playing at The Hook tonight, so we turn our attention to the CD jukebox. I get the override key from Stu. No one has to pay, but I get to approve all music choices. If I don't like a choice, I require a drink in payment.

> Cassie: "Fighting Entropy" by Liminal Space.
> Me: Heck Yeah.
> Tau: "Big Bang Baby" by Stone Temple Pilots.
> Me: I'll allow it.
> Some guy I don't know: "Wannabe" by —
> Me: No. Drink.
> Cassie: "Napoleon" by Ani DiFranco.
> Me: Girl, you know I love you and you know I love her, but that's not the vibe we're going for tonight. Two Drinks.
> Tau: "Freak" by Silverchair.
> Me: Fine. But. Drink.
> Derek: "Hound Dog" by Elvis.
> Me: Perfect.
> Another guy I don't know: "Wrong Way" by Sublime.

Me: No. Two drinks.

He tries again: "Inbetween Days" by The Cure.

Me: Perfect, but you still owe me two drinks for the Sublime request.

It goes on like this for several hours. We've played this game before, but never with this many people or for this long. By the time I realize I'm drunk, I'm beyond trashed. The problem is, I don't specify what drink I want in payment and end up combining and mixing and sloshing around. At one point I slip off the high stool I'm perched on, and Zach rushes to keep me from hitting the ground. Chris sits at the end of the bar, sipping water and chatting with Cassie and Derek. He does not rush to save me.

* * * * *

I am throwing up in Zach's sink. Not his bathroom sink. Not even the staff bathroom sink. The kitchen sink. In full view of everyone in the apartment. But thankfully they all seem to be passed out. The clock on the microwave says 4:14. I wipe my mouth with a paper towel and slide down the wall next to the fridge.

* * * * *

It is somehow light out. Too light. There are no shades on Zach's windows, not in the living room. Just full walls of plate glass. That I wish had shades. I'm on the Power Couch, a light blanket over me, a backpack for a pillow. The microwave clock says 12:37. The apartment is empty.

CHAPTER 15 *

I spend Sunday in my bed. Alone. It still smells like sex and Chris Thompson, like sweat and Irish Spring. I miss him. I know I *can* see him again, now that he's back in the states, but I don't know *if* I'll see him again. Flashes of Saturday night come back to me, images of his face appear like a slideshow, one disappointed smirk after another.

Monday, Memorial Day, I spend at the store, my headache mostly gone. Zach is distant, and he doesn't ask too many questions. Thankfully, he keeps his voice and the music low. Cassie takes great pleasure in telling me, very loudly, just how stupid I got Saturday night. It rains, a light drizzle, and it's slow, so I leave early and get back into bed. Alone. The cordless phone next to me. When the rain lets up, I smell grilling meat and hear the voices of people in their backyards celebrating Memorial Day, but I just eat a Butterfly Bar I find in my backpack at the foot of my bed and go to sleep early.

Tuesday, Meredith and I finally connect. She only wants to talk about sex. I only want to talk about feelings.

"But was he big? I bet he's big," she says.

"Meredith. Stop. Please, I need your help. I fucked everything up!"

"I bet you did!" she jokes in a sing-songy tone.

"No, I'm serious. I think he hates me. He didn't even say goodbye. Or if he did, I missed it. But if he didn't hate me, he would have called by now, right? Like if he weren't pissed at me, he would have called."

"I don't understand. What does he have to be pissed about? Because you got shitfaced? Has he met you?"

"But he doesn't drink, Meredith. He's been sober since before I knew him. And he's never seen me drink."

"Well, he has now. And he's gone now, anyway. So, problem solved!"

"Gawd, you never liked him."

"No, I didn't. But that doesn't mean what I'm saying is wrong. He's the one who bolted without telling you. He's the one who didn't write or call."

"Meredith, I have to tell you something, and you're not going to believe me, but it's true."

"Oh, gawd, what?"

"'This Morning's Rain,' by Liminal Space. It's about me. Chris wrote it, and Tess recorded it. But it's about me."

"You're shitting me."

"I'm not."

"My gawd, it's like your dream came true four years ago, and you didn't even know it. You're a muse to a rock star. You can die happy now."

"Stop making fun of me."

"I'm not. This is what you always wanted, someone writing ballads about you. And you love that song."

"Right, but that means something, right? Like, he didn't want to leave me. He wanted to be with me; he just didn't want to be in Pittsburgh."

"Yeah, but he could have, like, I don't know, given you a fucking head's up?"

And I know she's right. I mean, no communication for five years, and then he just thinks I'd be exactly who he wanted me to be just because he magically reappears? But the thing is, even though Meredith is in my head, she's not in my heart. She doesn't understand there's a real connection, a way my body softens and my mind quiets when he has his hand on my lower back. How I feel like I have a purpose when he's around and he's my purpose. Not in an *I'll follow you anywhere* kind of way, but in an *I'm right where I'm meant to be* kind of way.

"I guess you're right," I finally say.

"Listen, I know it's flattering that he wrote an amazing song for you and came back looking for you. But I don't want you to feel bad about getting drunk. You're allowed to get drunk. You shouldn't feel bad about yourself just because Mr. Boring Straight Edge might be disappointed in you."

"You're right. I guess."

"Of course, I am! Anyway, have you heard from Klein yet?"

"Not yet."

"But you're moving here anyway, right?!"

"I mean, probably, but shit's complicated. I'd have to find something to do to put on grad school apps. And I can't sleep on your couch forever, and I don't know what kind of place I could afford."

"We'll figure it out. I'm sure I know someone who can hook you up with something."

This is always Meredith's answer to everything.

My phone beeps. "Hold on. Call waiting." I click over. "Hello?"

"Hey Princess, it's me."

"Hey!" My body goes warm and fuzzy. Chris Thompson doesn't hate me. "It's you!"

"You busy?"

"No. Let me just get Meredith off the other line." I click over. "Hey, let me call you back. It's Chris."

"Barf," she says.

"Classy," I say. "I'll call you back." I click over again. "Hey. I'm back."

"How are you?"

I consider my possible responses and go with the truth. "Mortified?"

"Mortified? Why?"

"Well, I know I got shitfaced Saturday night, and I'm pretty sure you weren't happy about it, and you probably heard or saw me puking, probably both, and now you're gone. So, yeah, not how I wanted the weekend to end."

"Me either. But I'm not mad at you. I think I just get it now. You know?"

"What? What do I know? I don't think I know anything. I'm just glad you're not mad at me."

"I mean, I just don't think we're in the same place right now."

"Well, obviously. You're in Pittsburgh, and I'm in State College, but like, is that what it comes down to?"

"I think so. Yeah." He sounds measured, like maybe he knows he needs to say this, but he doesn't actually believe it. "But it's not just that. I mean, like, different places in our lives, you know?"

"Oh." I feel a little lightheaded. "So, this *is* about me getting drunk?"

"Not necessarily. Part of it is the distance, which, if you move to New York, will be even bigger, but yeah, part of it is about me wanting to get off the *hanging-out-in-bars-every-night* thing. Like, it's one of the reasons I'm moving back here. I don't need to keep holding people's hair while they vomit."

"Oh my gawd, did you hold my hair?"

"Of course I did."

"Shit." Long pause. "Thank you?"

"It's fine. I didn't mind it. I'm not saying this because I don't want to hold *your* hair. I just … I think you're right, I think I thought it would go back to the way it was when we just hung out in my apartment and forgot about the rest of the world, but it was always more complicated than that. Even back then. And things are still complicated now, maybe even more complicated. And you've changed—"

"Of course I've changed. I'm not sixteen anymore."

"Right, I know. And I've changed, too. And I'm not mad at you. That's why I called."

"Then why did you wait until today?"

"Because Johnny was being weird about giving me your number. I think Nate might have gotten to him."

Of course. So, this is it. He doesn't want me the way I am. He wants me the way I was then. Or the way he thought I'd be, frozen in time, waiting patiently for his return. A legal, adult version of the girl who hung on his every word, movement, touch. I know now my heart has always been just that, unable to let anyone else in, but everything else about me has grown up.

"Okay," I say. "So, I guess, thanks for calling?"

"You get this isn't about you, right?"

"Yeah, sure. I mean, except that it is."

"Why do you say that?"

"Would we be having the same conversation if I didn't pass out Saturday night?"

He doesn't say anything.

"Right. So, it sort of is about me and the choices I make, and the way I live my life. So, it's sort of all about me."

"Alice, no. You absolutely should do whatever you want. I'm just realizing now that what you want probably doesn't include me. I'm trying to make things easier for you. Like, I'm about to be really boring, and I don't want to hold you back."

"Don't I get to make that decision?"

"Well, yeah, but haven't you already decided you're not moving here?"

He has a point.

"I've decided Pittsburgh isn't my first choice. Beyond that, I have no idea what comes next."

"Well, I do know what comes next for me. This tour. Recording in LA. And then being really boring in Pittsburgh. I realize it's not an attractive offer."

"Are you asking me to stop drinking?"

"No."

"But if I didn't drink, you'd want to be together?"

"Alice, I want to be with you, regardless, but I don't want to hold you back. I don't want to be the reason you come home if you don't want to come home. I want you to be happy, and I don't see a way for you to be happy with me."

"So, this is it?"

"I wish there were some other way. Maybe in another five years?"

After a long pause, in which everything inside me seems to come unattached from its moorings, I say, "I'm going to go." And I hang up.

I hold the cordless on my chest. Suddenly my little twin bed feels too big. What if I never find anyone? What if I spend my life chasing the high of being alone with Chris Thompson? What if Zach doesn't speak to me ever again? And shit, why would he? What if what I want in a partner is not viable in the real world? What if I'm not viable in the real world? What if without grades and class rank and fellowships, I can't motivate to do anything? What if I can't stop drinking?

The phone rings.

"Hello?"

"Meet me in New York," Chris says. "We're there this weekend. Meet me there."

I hate how much I need to hear him say this. To hear the desperation in his voice. To hear the longing for me, even though he just dumped me.

"It won't fix anything," I say, the cracks in my shaky voice are sharp.

"I know. But at least we'll have a few more days."

"I don't know."

"We get in Friday. We play Mercury Lounge on Saturday. Sunday we take the van back to Philly and fly out to LA. Just, meet me there. Please?"

I go to New York to visit Meredith so often the Peter Pan bus drivers know me by name.

"Okay, I can do that."

"One more thing," he says.

"For someone who called to break up with me twenty minutes ago, you certainly have a lot of demands," I say with a small laugh through my quivering voice.

"Just don't count Pittsburgh out, okay?"

Something fuses in my body, something I didn't even know was cleaved.

"Call me tonight," I tell him. "I'll have everything worked out for New York by then."

CHAPTER 16

The AC on the bus from State College to New York isn't really working, so when I step onto the subway car beneath Penn Station, I'm relieved to be blasted by the frigid air. A few stops later though, I'm chilled, my sweat crusted on my skin like a thin sheet of ice. Then, when I come above ground at West 4th Street, it's like stepping into a sauna, which is pleasant for the short walk to Meredith's place, But would be gross if I had to walk any farther. So many climates in just a few minutes and State College feels like a world away.

Meredith May's apartment isn't just a different world, it's a different universe from Nate's small, sparse house. When Mr. May bought the one bedroom for her sophomore year, Mrs. May came up to decorate it in her trademark French Country aesthetic, but six months later, Meredith's grandmother hired a decorator to redo it a la Monica's apartment in Friends, and that look stuck. Everything is overstuffed, tufted in purple velvet, gilded in gold with a black and white checkerboard motif anywhere it can be employed. The place is like a royal chess game on acid.

I've let myself in with the spare key I picked up from Lou, the doorman, and I'm stepping out of the shower when Meredith arrives home.

"Chicken, is that you? Are you alone?" she calls from the living room.

"Yes. In here!" I yell from the bathroom.

"Perfect. Do your face. We're meeting Philippe around the corner."

"We're doing what with who?" I come out to the living room wrapped in a plush towel, softer than any comforter I've ever owned. Meredith's wearing a short sleeve black dress with a black velvet choker and clunky black shoes.

"I told you about Philippe."

"I don't think you did."

"He's my new gay best friend. And he's French. Or, well, French Canadian, I think, but let's just say French. Anyway, it's his birthday and we're meeting for drinks at that place around the corner before his boyfriend takes him out for dinner."

"I should probably wait here for Chris." I say it cautiously, like I know she's going to give me so much shit.

"You… should probably just do your face. We'll leave word with Lou and Chris will find us."

I'd rather stay here. It would be easier to not drink here. But I don't want to upset her.

"Fine. What should I wear?"

"Anything from my closet. You're not in Cow Town anymore. And let me do your face."

There's no arguing with Meredith and she means well, so I let her dress me in a deep purple sundress and black slides. She piles my long, dark hair on top of my head and puts makeup on me with fancy brushes instead of the ones that come in the compacts from the drugstore. She tries to spray me with expensive perfume, but that's where I draw the line. "I don't want to smell like you, no offense."

"Dear gawd, he likes the way you smell, doesn't he?"

"He might." I can't help my lips from turning up at the corners.

"Gross."

The bar is dark, which is weird for four o'clock in the afternoon on a blazing hot Friday, but the temperature inside is pleasantly cool, like being in a cave of dark wood and twinkling lights. There's a courtyard out back, but Philippe's friends are all sitting in a semi-circle booth that takes up most of a small interior balcony. There's a dainty chain with a *Reserved* sign at the top of the stairs. Meredith unhooks the chain as if it doesn't apply to her, and we slide into the booth next to a few guys who seem to be wearing eye make-up, which is totally cool, but not something you see in State College, unless you're hanging out with the goth high school kids.

Meredith makes the introductions. There's Philippe, who's turning 24 today, and his boyfriend John, who could be anywhere between 19 and 29. I don't catch anyone else's name, which is fine, because Philippe shoos everyone away to the other end of the booth so he can have me to himself.

"We need to be best friends," he says in a strangely French but not French accent.

"Okay." I laugh. "How do we do that?"

"Well, you're Meredith's straight-girl best friend and I'm her gay-boy best friend, so either we have to hate each other or love each other."

"Oh, I didn't ask why. I asked how. I'm totally on board with being your best friend. But we have to bond over something more than Meredith to make it stick."

"What are you saying about me?" Meredith calls from the other side of John. Somehow it seems she's already drunk, or she's faking it.

"Nothing, silly! We're actually actively *not* talking about you!"

"That sounds boring!" she says with a hair flip.

"Cosmos!" Philippe says to me. "We bond over cosmos!" I don't even know what a cosmo is, but it's safe to assume it's a drink, and he's clearly had a few. I would prefer not to drink before Chris gets here. Or after Chris gets here. I'm not going to stop drinking completely, not for him, but I have thought about cutting back now that I'm not in college anymore.

"I'm good," I say.

"What do you mean?"

"I don't need a drink," I explain.

"Oh, but you do need a drink. It's my birthday and they make the best cosmos here!" He signals to the bartender below us. It's a subtle sign, but the man behind the bar starts moving quickly.

"How do you know Meredith?" I ask Philippe.

"She hasn't told you? I live in the building, and I was eyeing her bag in the elevator. 'You can touch it,' she said, and we both died laughing. BFFs ever since. But I'm no Alice Burton. I certainly can't compete with someone who's known her since birth and is dating a rock star. Dish!"

"Not birth, kindergarten," I say. "And I'm not dating anyone. We're just, you know, hanging out. And he's not a rock star. He's just in a band."

"He's in ACE, and they're about to break big. Thanks in no small part to smokin' hot Chris Thompson."

Hearing super-hip Philippe say Chris' name gives me a jolt of something I can't define. It's part embarrassment and part pride. "Did Meredith tell you to say that?"

"Stop talking about me if you're not talking about me!" she yells from the other end of the booth.

"No, Meredith didn't tell me to say that. It was in *Time Out*."

"What?"

Philippe fishes the magazine out of a bag beneath the table, opens it up for me, and points to a sidebar column with the heading, "You'd be an ACEhole to miss this" with a small picture of the band at the top.

ACE was last seen in America five years ago when they were known as A COMBUSTIBLE EVENT. The Australian band is back and better than ever, thanks in large part to their scorching hot guitarist, American Chris Thompson, whom they picked up at the end of their last stateside tour. Thompson saved the band from sure-death and disintegration when their former lead guitarist fell for an American girl and refused to return Down Under in 1992. Thompson had impressed A COMBUSTIBLE EVENT when his Pittsburgh-based band, WASTED PRETTY, opened for them in his hometown. (Tess Wilson, also a WASTED PRETTY alum, currently fronts UK-based mega-stars LIMINAL SPACE.) Thompson got his footing with A COMBUSTIBLE EVENT in their hometown of Cairns while they recorded *Everything and Everyone*. He had a hand in shepherding them from "A COMBUSTIBLE EVENT, Australia's Favorite Alternative-Pop-Rock-Band" into a more mature musical persona known simply as ACE. You've heard the new sound in all your favorite commercials this spring.

When asked to explain his vision for the band at a rehearsal in Philadelphia prior to the opening night of this mini tour, Chris Thompson demurred, saying, "It's all just music." ACE is stateside to record a new record and a set opening for NIGHTSWIMMING at Mercury Lounge this Saturday is your last chance to catch them before they go into the studio on the West Coast.

The bartender has made it up the stairs with a tray of rosy pink drinks in martini glasses and puts one down in front of each of us. There's a chorus of toasts in different languages and then Philippe starts singing Happy Birthday to himself in French while everyone else hums along. I just keep reading the little piece in *Time Out*. I can't believe I'm sleeping with, if not dating, Chris Thompson, and I can't believe he's about to give up on the band.

When the din of everyone dies down again, Philippe points to my untouched cosmo and says, "Do not rebuff my kindness."

"I'm sorry, I don't mean to rebuff anything. I'm just not sure I want to drink right now."

"Are you pregnant with the aforementioned scorching hot rock star's love child?" he asks. And the way he says it, it sounds exciting and dangerous, but I blanch at the thought.

"Alice is pregnant?" Meredith yells.

"Alice is not pregnant!" I yell back. We don't need to be yelling. We're the only people on the small balcony and there are only a few other people down at the bar. But Meredith gets louder when she's drunk. I've learned everyone does.

"Chris Thompson doesn't drink, so I try not to drink around him."

"Are you serious?" Philippe pretends to fan himself. "Hot, bad boy who's really straight edge?"

"He's not straight edge. I mean, not in an ideological way. He's just sober."

"Well, this just keeps getting better and better!"

"What does that mean?" I ask.

"America's next heartthrob is squeaky clean? Please tell me he has a dark and stormy past he's running from."

Chris was a cocky teenager who had a bad year when he was a freshman in college and possibly fathered a child in Indiana. I'm not sure that counts as a dark and stormy past, but even if it did, I wouldn't share it with my new best friend.

"You clearly know something," he prods. "I can see it as a cover story for sure."

"A cover story? I don't think they're there yet."

"They will be," Philippe insists.

CHAPTER 17*

An hour later, I'm on my third cosmo when Chris stands at the top step on the other side of the *Reserved* chain with his guitar case slung across his body and a duffle bag balanced awkwardly against his leg.

"Damn, if that's not a tall drink of water." Philippe fans himself and laughs at his own corniness. "Does he look better in person?"

I want to hop up and remove the chain for him, but my comfortably buzzed body feels heavy. Plus, I'm nuzzled into Philippe and trapped in the booth.

"He does look better in person," I say. "Photographs don't do justice to his eyes."

While I'm frozen by the dead weight of my buzzing body, Meredith gets up, removes the chain and does a deep, royal bow to usher Chris in.

"Your highness," she says.

"Hi Meredith."

"Glad you could join us. You could have left your stuff with Lou. I promise no one would have taken your duffle from my lobby."

"I don't mind," he says.

The balcony has gone quiet as everyone watches Chris enter into our midst. I see him as they see him: tall, broad, blond, black jeans that are almost too tight and a shirt made of thin heather grey cotton that just barely contains his shoulders, but somehow hangs perfectly. I try to wiggle out of the booth to greet him, but Philippe puts his hand on my arm and says, "Let him come to us."

I want to tell him that it's not like that with Chris. We don't play games like that, but I know I'm drunk, and I'm better off sitting anyway. Plus, I can tell Philippe likes it when I listen to him.

When Chris makes it to our end of the booth he stands over us, does a chin-tip and says, "Princess." Philippe does something between a squeal and a gasp which I think is the equivalent of an audible swoon. He puts his hand out to Chris and says, "I'm Philippe. I'm your new best friend."

At first I think Chris might be pissed, at the alcohol, at the clear display of wealth, at the gay guy hitting on him and the pretentiousness of the *Reserved* chain, but then he just laughs and everyone else laughs, too.

"Sit," Philippe says. It's half-invitation, half-command, but Chris complies with a wry smile on his face.

The booth is crowded, and it's killing me that Philippe is the one smashed up against Chris. I catch his eye while Philippe blathers on, asking him questions about the tour and saying things like, "Obviously this is off the record," which is just such a weird thing to say, and in his French Canadian accent it seems even more bizarre, like he's a spy in a movie.

My body is vibrating with alcohol and desire. Chris is so close, he's here—in The States, in New York, in this booth—but I can't touch him. I do the only thing I can think of and pour what's left of my cosmo on myself. "Oops!" I say in a dramatic and clearly fake way. "I think I need to go back to the apartment and change. Chris, walk with me?"

I basically shove Chris and Philippe out of the booth. I'm a little unsteady on my feet, but I manage to take Chris' hand and lead him towards the steps.

"Chicken, where're you going?" Meredith calls after us in her drunk voice.

"Spilled!" I say and awkwardly climb over the chain.

"I guess I'll just meet you back at my place?" she calls.

"Sure, yeah, whatever," I mumble. "No rush! Thanks Philippe! Bon Anniversaire!"

Outside it's bright and hot and humid. I stumble a bit on the pavement but stay close to Chris for support.

"So, those are your friends?" he asks.

"No, those are Meredith's friends."

"Interesting group."

"You don't mean interesting."

"No, I mean rich and pushy."

"I'm sorry."

"You don't have to apologize. You're not like that."

"No, I am neither rich, nor pushy. I am jobless and at your disposal." I laugh.

He doesn't. "How much have you had to drink?"

"I'm fine. But I am sorry. I wasn't going to drink this weekend, but Philippe is… well, rich and pushy. And he wanted me to drink with him. Did he mention it was his birthday?"

"He did," Chris says in a clipped way.

"What's wrong?" I ask.

"It's always something with you, isn't it?"

"What does that mean?"

"Nothing. Sorry."

"No, really, you're pissed."

"I'm not."

He is.

"You are."

"No, don't worry about it, you're perfect. You're you."

I'm so relieved, I giggle, but he looks… serious and smitten. He wants to be mad at me, but he can't be. I think my heart might explode.

Upstairs the AC is whirring, and Chris and I settle into the purple, velvet couch. I don't even bother changing out of Meredith's dress as the liquor has already dried or evaporated. I put my bare feet up on Chris' lap, and he rubs them.

He lifts up my leg and kisses my ankle. I've never been kissed there before, and it's magic. How does he know to do that? Has he kissed other women's ankles? Why has no one ever kissed my ankle? Does it always feel like this? If anyone else kissed me there, would I feel the warmth through my whole body the way I do now, or is it just him? Just Chris Thompson's kiss?

He slides his hand up my leg, and my body shakes with pleasure. I know I should be concerned about Meredith coming home and finding us in the living room, but it's worth risking her barging in on us to keep feeling this way.

Chris is on top of me. The pressure of his body pushes mine into the plush couch. I feel strong and alive, connected to something infinite and beyond me. It's like there's nothing standing in the way of anything I want, even though I'm still aware, through my vodka-soaked brain and shuddering body, that there are roadblocks everywhere, out there, but not here, not on this couch. I concentrate on his touch, his skin, the expanse of his shoulders above me, the rippling of his abs and strength of his thighs. I rub my face against his like a cat, maximizing our contact points, legs, hips, chest, face. I know my future is fucked because nothing will ever be as important as fusing myself to him.

*   *   *   *   *

I don't know what time it is when Meredith walks in, but it's still slightly light outside and she's complaining that she's hungry. I could have been asleep on the couch for ten minutes or two hours, it's hard to say, but I'm refreshed and, thankfully, not drunk at all. Chris is sitting in a gold brocade armchair across from me, hunched over his guitar, jeans on, shirt off.

"Good morning, Chicken! Time for dinner?" Meredith is still very drunk.

I look to Chris.

"Oh, it's up to him, is it?"

I shrug.

Meredith can be unbearable when she's drunk and in a mood. I'm sure she's pissed that her new best friend is out with his boyfriend and her old best friend just had sex on her couch.

"Pray tell, Rock Star, what do you want to do tonight?"

"Whatever Alice wants to do is fine."

"Nice abs," she says.

He takes this as a cue to put on his shirt.

"Chris said there's a band he knows at Mercury Lounge tonight, Small Hours, and the rest of ACE is going to be there. They want to check out the space before their show tomorrow…"

"Okay. Let's do that," she says, inviting herself. "You two shower. I'll snack." She shoos us through her room into the master bath.

"Sorry," I say to Chris.

"About what?"

"About her Meredith-ness." I sit on the edge of the tub watching as he pulls his shirt over his head.

"Don't worry about it. I'll suffer a night with Meredith if it means being with you."

"You have to stop this," I tell him.

"What do you mean?"

"Making it seem like … I don't know … like this is easy. Spending a night in New York City with Meredith just to be with me? She's going to make it hard."

"I didn't say it was going to be easy. But you're worth it."

"I am?"

"Princess…"

"Yes?"

"We don't have a lot of time. I'll spend it any way you want."

He knows this isn't going anywhere, and I know this isn't going anywhere. This is just now, nothing more.

I stand up and kiss him. "Thank you."

*   *   *   *   *

Chris stops at a hot dog cart as we walk across Washington Square Park. To my surprise, he buys three and tries to hand one to each of us. I take mine with a smile, but Meredith rolls her eyes in response. I silently beg her to keep her mouth shut. I don't need them fighting this early in the evening.

"You eat hot dogs now?" she asks. "From street vendors? What would Lois say?"

"I'm just hungry," I tell her, pissed that she invoked my mother. And I am hungry. Famished. It's been years since I've had a hot dog, and it tastes like the most perfect food in the world. I thank Chris as he eats his. We split the one he got for Meredith.

My New York City has always been Meredith's New York City. We do what she wants to do, when she wants to do it, and because she knows all the best places and all the best things, and because she always pays, I've never had reason to push back. But now I'm trying to juggle what she wants to do and what Chris wants to do, which is whatever I want to do. It makes me jittery.

I wish I could spend the weekend in bed with Chris, pretending time isn't moving forward. I wish Chris and I lived in New York City, together, like a real couple, being real adults. Why couldn't we? Why shouldn't we? Maybe we actually could. It's the first thing that's made sense to me in a while.

"Chicken!" Meredith yells as she grabs my arm. I hadn't realized I had zoned out thinking about a life with Chris in this city and almost walked into a busy street. "What's going on with you?"

"Nothing. Sorry. Country Chicken," I say, referring to her freshman year nickname for me. The city overwhelmed me then. It's been a while since I felt like that.

Chris wraps his arm around me as we wait for the light to change.

"I'll protect you," he says. It's a joke, but Meredith rolls her eyes in full view of both of us.

The bar at Mercury Lounge is already packed when we get there. Chris leads us through the crowd like he's used to people parting for him. And they do. I can't imagine he's recognizable as part of ACE—the picture in *Time Out* was so small, and I don't think they're getting bigger coverage in the States yet—so I think maybe it's just his regular Hottest Guy Ever appearance that makes people step back and gawk at him. I feel special as he leads me past the bar and then into the room with the stage. I like it when people look at us like this. I want to tell everyone he wrote "This Morning's Rain" and it's about me. I want people to know someone feels that way about me, that the Hottest Guy Ever feels that way about me.

We totally could move to New York City together. This could be real life. I don't know why it didn't occur to me until tonight.

We find Derek and Tau, but it's too loud to say anything so there are a lot of head nods and chin tips. I turn around to grab Meredith, to make sure she's included, but she's not behind me. Somehow, in snaking through the crowd I've lost her, and I'm sure I'll pay for it when she finds me. But I can't deal with that now because Tau is glaring at me. And I'm glaring back. But then Chris steps between us, turns to face the stage, kisses me on the temple, and slings his arm around my shoulders. I could definitely get used to this. I'm relaxing into his body, remembering how well we fit together, when Philippe appears shoving another pink drink in my face.

"How did you get here?" I practically yell.

"I took a cab. I know I look otherworldly, but I'm human, just like you!"

I laugh even though I'm still confused.

"I called him," Meredith yells in my ear. "He has a cell phone." She pantomimes a phone pressed to her ear. It's hard to detect with all the noise, but her tone is clipped, and I think she may have done a shot at the bar.

I mindlessly take a swig of the cosmo I've been handed and then remember it's Chris I'm leaning on. I look at him sheepishly and he gives a half nod which could mean either he's bothered or not. Being around him makes me hyper-aware of how often I seem to fall into a beverage.

"I mean *why* are you here?" I ask Philippe. "Isn't this your big night?"

"Right after dinner, John got a work call, so here I am. Aren't you lucky?!"

"So lucky!" I like that Meredith will have Philippe to hang out with. It takes the heat off of me.

"Anyway, this band is super-hot right now," he says.

"Let's dance," Meredith says as she grabs Philippe's hand and they disappear into the crowd. It's not really dancing music, but I'm happy if they're happy.

I finish my cosmo and lean into Chris. I can still feel Tau's eyes boring into my skull, and all of a sudden it's too much. I need to not be in a club. I need to not be next to Chris. I need Meredith and

Philippe not to be dancing and buying me drinks. I need Tau to not hate me. I need to figure out who I am away from all of them. I squeeze Chris' hand and smile when he looks at me.

"Be back," I mouth and then take off for the door.

The crowd doesn't part for me the way it did when I was with Chris. I end up bumping into people and getting elbowed. When I finally make it outside, I'm happy for the movement of the air, even if it isn't exactly cool. The traffic on Houston speeds by. Cab drivers are honking and women in stilettos and shiny tank tops play an ill-advised game of real-life Frogger. It's a chaotic display of life, but it serves to settle me. I like the way New York is what it is without regard for me or the cabbie or the woman about to fall out of her shoes. I should be here. Right here. In this city that doesn't care about me. That isn't watching me. That doesn't think I can save it and isn't trying to save me. It doesn't care if I like it and because of that, I love it.

CHAPTER 18

When I make it back inside, Small Hours has come off stage and the sound system is blaring Deee-Lite. The psychedelic, synthetic house music is totally out of place, but I get a kick out of it because Lady Miss Kier grew up in Pittsburgh, and I may not want to live there right now, but I can still claim her. Meredith dances up next to me. It occurs to me she probably paid someone to put this song on.

"Chicken, where'd you go?"

"Just needed some air."

"Your boyfriend went somewhere with the band."

"He's not my boyfriend."

"How long do you think we have to hang here? I'm still hungry. There's this great new place up the street I want to take you."

"I already ate," Philippe says.

"So, you'll eat again." Meredith shrugs. "I'll go to the gym with you tomorrow while this one spends quality time with the rock star."

She likes connecting with Philippe via digs at me. I wonder how they bonded before tonight.

"We don't have to hang here at all. Or you don't. I can catch up with you, or you can eat without us. I don't know how long he has to be here." When I turn back to the stage, Chris is up there with a guy from Small Hours pointing at speakers and checking amps. "I literally have no idea what's going on. Ever."

"Well, to be fair, you are the one who bolted," Meredith says with an air of superiority. "Your boyfriend was looking for you when the set was done. He looked all puppy-dog-eyed without you."

"Yeah. My bad."

"What's going on with you?" she asks me, exasperated. "You don't seem happy at all. Isn't this what you always wanted? The Hottest Guy Ever hanging on your every word? Your every sneeze? Why are you being so… I don't know… weird?"

"There's just a lot up in the air, and it's hard to know what matters."

"Yeah, that doesn't make sense at all," Meredith says with a head cock. "There's something you're not telling me and that's fine, but you're not fooling me."

"Meredith, you're being really hard on me—"

"Ladies! Stop!" Philippe insists. "I won't have my new best friend and my other new best friend fighting on a night like this. It's my birthday! Alice, go get your rock star, and let's get Meredith something to eat. No one likes a hungry Meredith."

Philippe cups Meredith's face in his hands and kisses her on the nose. It's sort of gross and sort of endearing, but when she laughs, I laugh, and when I shrug in her general direction she shrugs back, and I can tell we're fine. Just in time for Chris to step off the stage and join us on the dance floor.

"Are you staying for the next band?" I ask.

"I don't need to. I saw what I wanted to see. Where to?"

"Meredith wants to eat at some new place she's discovered."

"Let's do it."

We head out of Mercury Lounge and start walking up 1st Avenue as if we're the best of friends. It's not long before we're under the sparkly lights of the Indian restaurants at 6th Street.

"Please tell me we're eating here," Chris says with a wide smile, as we wait at a light to cross the street.

"I mean, we could, if you want to eat like everyone else," Meredith purrs. "But I know a better place around the corner. It's a raw vegan place where everything sounds horrible but tastes amazing."

The three of us react in horror.

"Raw, vegan?" Chris asks.

"It doesn't sound like there will be alcohol there," Philippe says.

"Meredith, did Lois put you up to this?" I ask her.

"She didn't put me up to anything. She was here last week and introduced me to the place, but I genuinely enjoyed it and you will, too."

"I won't, actually," I say.

"Trust me," she says. A different kind of friend might try to whine to get her way, but not Meredith. She's still in full-on demand mode.

"She said no," Chris says flatly.

Everything in my body tenses. It's not so much that I don't want him to come to my rescue—I can use all the help I can get with Meredith, sometimes—it's more that I know it won't work.

"Excuse me?" Meredith glares at him. "She doesn't need your help here."

"I just don't think that's where we should eat tonight," he responds.

I had forgotten Chris' talent of staying calm in situations like this, but I remember thinking it was mostly because he was misreading the potential for disaster.

"What if I don't give a shit what you think?" she yells.

I expect people on the street to stop to see what's going on, but mostly people only grimace and keep moving.

"How much have you had to drink, Meredith?" Philippe tries to intercede, but she swats him away.

"This isn't about me!" she yells. "It's about this fool." She points to Chris like he's a peasant and she's royalty. "You think she needs your protection from me? Where were you when she really needed your help? Where were you when I was dealing with Karl Bell?!"

It's like the whole city stops when she says his name. Maybe even the whole world.

I rock back on my heels. Chris' body is there to stop me from falling over. I want to yell, but I can't. I croak out one word, "Meredith," but she doesn't respond. It seems she's shocked herself silent.

We don't say his name. The name of the man who touched me, who made me touch him. We never said it again, not after the night she stepped between us and put an end to it. Not after that night which was the same night my dad left with him and ended up in a coma for six days. Not after that night, which was also the night Chris Thompson left for Australia.

Meredith's attorney father handled everything which meant no publicity and no trial. He went after Karl Bell for assaulting my dad which resulted in a large payout that allowed me to go to college and graduate with no debt. I'm not even sure what Mr. May did was legal, or how it's different from blackmail, but Meredith's dad and mine kept me out of it. I don't even think Mr. May knew about Karl assaulting me, and I don't know what my dad remembers. He claims to not know why he and Karl got into a fight, though I find that hard to believe.

I don't know how long the four of us are standing on the street corner before a homeless person comes up to Chris and asks him for money, and I'm pulled back into the reality that is my very present disaster.

"I think …" I stammer.

"No, I'm …" Meredith stammers.

"Don't." I say.

Chris steps towards me, and Philippe steps towards Meredith, but we don't let them near us, and they respond by giving us plenty of space, wandering out of earshot.

"I need—" Meredith says.

"You need?!" I screech. "How is this about what you need?"

"No, wait," she says, less a demand than I would expect. "I need *to apologize.*"

"Like I said, don't. I get it, you hate Chris. You hate him so much you went somewhere you've never gone before. Don't apologize. You wouldn't mean it."

"I do mean it. I'm sorry I said what I said. But, you're right. I never liked him. You should have been once and done. Fucked him in State College and let him go. He's literally on tour and you're all gaga over him like he's your real boyfriend. I don't know what you're thinking. He left you once. He'll do it again. And I'm the one who'll be left putting you back together, just like I did back then."

She glares over my shoulder where Philippe and Chris are talking by the door to a bodega.

"He's not leaving."

"What do you mean?"

"He's staying. In the States. In Pittsburgh. He wants me to move there, too."

"What?! How is that going to work? What about the band? What about your plans?"

"He's leaving the band. But you can't tell anyone."

"He's leaving ACE? Now? When they're about to blow up? For you?"

"First of all, you don't have to sound so surprised. And secondly, no, he's not leaving the band for me. He's leaving the band. And he wants me to come with him."

"What about the fellowship? You're moving here!"

"That's still my first choice. And he knows that. But I haven't heard from them and nothing's decided."

"So, your Plan B is to move to Pittsburgh with Chris Thompson?"

"Not necessarily."

"But you're considering it?"

"It's flattering."

"Uh! You're not that girl! Don't be that girl! You'd really give everything up for someone who bailed on you?"

"What would I be giving up? Sleeping on your couch?"

She takes a long, deep breath. "Is he really that good in bed?"

"Meredith!"

"I mean, come on, he's hot, but take away the rock star street cred and what are you left with? A college dropout who once played in a band?"

"Stop it. Just stop it. This isn't a contest between you and him. This is my life."

Meredith looks stunned. And defeated. As if the last chip she had to play fell onto the street and bounced down a sewer grate.

"So, are you going to do it?"

"I don't know. I don't know what I'm going to do. But my point is, he's not trying to bail on me, and you don't need to hate him on my behalf."

"But seriously. What are you going to do? What about grad school?"

"I'm not talking to you about any of this until you promise to be nice to him."

"Fine." She doesn't even hesitate, and I can't tell if that means she's lying or she's over it, all of it: any grudge she might be holding from five years ago or five minutes ago. She walks right past me and extends her hand to Chris. "Truce. We both want what's best for her. Right?"

To his credit, he doesn't look to me for approval—Meredith would tear him up for that—he just takes her hand and shakes it.

"Now, for raw vegan fare! Follow me!"

She hooks her arms in mine and Chris'. Philippe takes my other side. It's like she's Dorothy, and we're the Tin Man and the Lion and the Scarecrow being led down the yellow brick road. Or maybe I'm Dorothy. Hard to say.

CHAPTER 19*

The restaurant is a total hippie nightmare: tapestries on the wall and mis-matched cushions thrown everywhere. We're just supposed to grab one to sit on at the long, low tables. The fresh-pressed juice is good though. I'm glad to have something non-alcoholic to drink, but then Philippe pulls out a silver flask and spikes his drink and Meredith's. He passes the monogrammed flask across the table to me, but I put the cap on and hand it back to him. He makes what I think is supposed to be a "prissy" face at me.

"I think we should take this quiet moment to really figure things out." Meredith announces, after she orders for all of us. There is new age-y music playing in the background, but thanks to the mostly empty restaurant, it's fairly quiet.

"What are we figuring out?" I ask.

Chris is sitting close to me, his hand on my bare knee under the plank of the table. It's hard to concentrate on anything else.

"Your life?" she says, raising her voice as if it's a question, when it's clearly a statement.

"There's nothing to figure out," I tell her. "We're in a wait-and-see-mode."

"Who's we?" she asks, eyeing Chris Thompson.

"Anyone interested in figuring out my life."

"Well, what are some of your options?"

I look around, but no one is jumping in to help me.

"Um, you know I'm waiting to hear from The Klein Fellowship…"

"And…"

"And I hope I get it."

"Because you'd move here if you did?" She bats her eyelashes dramatically at Chris.

"That's Plan A."

"And Plan B?"

I laugh nervously. "I don't exactly have one."

"What does that mean?"

"Well, I have a couple options, but I don't know which is actually, like, the next best one."

"But if you had to decide today?"

"Meredith, can we talk about something else?"

"We don't have anything else in common except you, Chicken. Come on, you love being the center of attention."

"Well, if I don't get the fellowship, I could still come here and try to get a job, or I could go to Pittsburgh and work at the station for a few years and then apply to J-School."

"Well, that's convenient." Meredith raises her eyebrows in a challenge but keeps her voice breezy. "Then your dad gets what he wants, and Chris gets what he wants."

Chris takes his hand off my knee. "You told her?"

"Sorry. I tell Meredith everything."

"Told her what?" Philippe pipes up. "Tell me everything like you tell Meredith everything!"

I look to Chris for permission. He looks frustrated but nods at me. "Chris is leaving the band … and moving home … to Pittsburgh."

Philippe's mouth hangs open, and it's hard to tell if he's really shocked or just pretending to be.

"I'm not going to lie," Chris says to Meredith. "Of course, I want Alice to be in Pittsburgh. But not if she doesn't want to be there."

"She doesn't want to be there."

"I can speak for myself, Meredith. He knows my concerns."

"What's wrong with Pittsburgh?" Philippe asks. "Aside from it being Pittsburgh?"

"Have you ever been to Pittsburgh?" I'm still defensive, protective of it, even when I have no desire to be there. Except, maybe I do. Maybe the best part of tonight is Chris' hand on my knee, and maybe that's all I need.

"No, I'm Canadian," Philippe says, as if that's an answer.

"It's her parents," Meredith explains. "Bad divorce. Lots of bad blood." Meredith gets it. "You should have heard Lois complaining about Burton last week," she continues. "Right at that table over there."

"Listen, I really don't want to think about it until after I hear from Klein, okay?"

"That's so unlike you," Meredith chides. "You usually have a Plan A, B, and C, all the way down to Z."

"I'm sort of counting on Plan A here, Meredith." It feels like even giving too much thought to alternative options could somehow mess with my chances. Like, if I don't want the Klein program more than anything else in the world, I won't get it. Even though I'm not normally superstitious like that.

"I'm sure it'll work out," Chris says, leaning over to nuzzle me.

"Barf," Meredith says quietly. This is her being nice. "Come on, Chicken, you must have other options..."

"I don't know. Zach's offered me an assistant manager position. I could stay in State College for a little while and write stories for the local paper."

"Zach! I forgot about Zach. Sad, sexy, dreamy Zach." Meredith turns towards Chris. "Chris, have you met Zach?"

"Good guy," Chris says, choosing not to engage.

"You're not really considering staying in hicktown, are you?" Meredith whines.

"I'm not sure."

"I think you should move here regardless of the fellowship."

"I know you do. But what would I do?"

"Whatever you want! Anything! Nothing!"

"Meredith, I've done the calculations. Even with the money I get from my dad. I couldn't make this work long-term."

"So? You get a job waitressing! It can't be that hard!"

I smile apologetically at the waitress who bends down deeply to put small plates of vegetables—some identifiable, some not—on our table. Meredith didn't mean to be rude; it was just bad timing.

"Meredith, waitressing isn't going to get me into grad school. I need experience. Applicable experience."

"Philippe…" she coos.

He puts down the piece of … aloe? cactus? zucchini? … he has been examining and looks up. "Yes, Meredith?"

"Tell her about your magazine."

"Oh, that's not a thing yet. It won't be for several years."

"You don't have to wait that long, if you have Alice, and a big scoop—like why Hot Chris Thompson is leaving his band just as it's about to take off. Your dad would give you the money now, if you asked."

I register Chris' flinch in my peripheral vision.

"What are you even talking about?" I ask.

"Philippe is into journalism. And music. And his plan has always been to get a magazine off the ground."

"After I'm done having fun, Meredith. When I'm ready to be in charge of something. Not now."

"What about in the fall?" she asks.

"Meredith, you are not going to bully someone into changing their five-year plan just so I have something to put on my resume!"

"Why not?! It's like a win-win-win—" she points to me and Philippe and herself and then looks at Chris—"win-ish?"

"Meredith, I love your enthusiasm, I really do. But that's not how it works. And I'm not going to tell Chris' story if he doesn't want it told. I don't even write music pieces."

"I'd let you tell it, if it would help you," Chris says, putting his hand back on my knee.

"See?" Meredith is beaming. "We all want what's best for you."

"I am over this conversation," I tell the table. "And I'm over this 'food.'" I use air quotes.

"Me too!" Philippe says.

"Agreed," Chris says.

"Fine," Meredith says with a pronounced pout. "Next stop. Burgers and fries."

"Thank gawd," I say.

Meredith pays the bill for everyone. The waitress asks if we want any of the food to go, but we pass.

"Hey, did your mom tell you who we saw last week?" she asks me, as we step out into the night.

"No, I haven't talked to her."

"That girl Tracie who was a couple years behind us at Frazer, remember her? We were just walking back to my place after dinner, and she was right there on the street."

"Weird," I say.

"Not really. You never know who you're going to run into in Manhattan. It really is the best place to be."

CHAPTER 20*

If there's a small benefit to not drinking, or not drinking too much, it's waking up without a hangover the next morning. We get up early, and Chris lets me walk him all over Manhattan. He's never been to the city, and he's happy to have me take the lead. In each neighborhood, I point to places where Meredith has taken me for dinner, and places we've seen bands, and I tell him about the historical facts I know, but mostly we just drink iced coffee and wander, holding hands, like a real couple.

We end up on the Brooklyn Bridge, surveying the skyline and watching runners and other tourists. What would it mean to not be a tourist here?

"So, this is your home now?" It's like he reads my mind.

"I hope so."

He kisses me.

I sense people watching us, so I don't let it go on too long. "That's your answer to everything, isn't it? You think I'm helpless to fight you when you kiss me?"

His head is on my shoulder, his face in my hair. "Why do you want to fight me?"

"I don't mean that. I just mean I'm feeling pulled in a lot of directions, and obviously none of those other directions can make my knees weak with a kiss."

"What do you want to do?"

He knows it's a loaded question, and what surprises me is that I have an answer, but I'm afraid to say it out loud. Not to him. Not here.

"What time do you have to be at the club?" I ask.

"That's not a response."

"I know."

"Soundcheck's at 5. Then we're all grabbing dinner together down the street. The label's paying tonight."

"Okay. Should I make plans with Meredith?"

"You can come to soundcheck. You can come to dinner."

"And have Tau glare at me?"

"You don't have to come if you don't want to. But you and Meredith are on the list. Philippe, too. You can just come for the show."

"No, I want to come. I just don't want to butt in."

"Alice, I want you around. I don't care what anyone else says. I can handle Tau. You're the only one who's being weird about us."

Us? Us.

"Okay," I say, running my fingers through his hair. "If I'm being honest, this caught me off guard. It's like you had all the time in the world to know you'd be playing State College, and I found out the day before. Then you break up with me, or whatever, and in the next breath, you invite me to meet you here."

"You think I knew it was going to work out like this? That you'd be single? That you wouldn't hate me? You think I planned this?"

"No, I'm just saying, it's a lot. Everything's a lot. Ten days ago, I thought I was going to spend the summer getting shitfaced with my friends in State College and then start my real life with a fellowship in New York City. Now, I'm standing on the Brooklyn Bridge with the first person I ever loved, and I have no idea what I'm doing next. It's all just a little much."

"Whoa."

"Yeah. You don't have to say anything. I know I never said anything. But it's true. And I've spent the last five years chasing that feeling and running from it at the same time."

"I love you, too."

What?

"What? Don't say that. I was talking about five years ago. I was talking about when you disappeared and broke my heart, and it took me forever to admit it to myself. Don't say that now. Here."

"Alice, I love you. I may never forgive myself for leaving like I did, but I can make up for it now."

I sit on the wooden slats of the pedestrian walkway, my back up against the barrier. Chris sits next to me. Our knees to our chests, we hold hands between us.

"You don't have to say anything," he tells me. "I just thought you should know."

Tears are coming down my face, and I cover my eyes with my free hand.

"I love you, too. Of course, I do. But that doesn't make any of this easier. It makes it harder. You know that, right?"

"I do," he says.

We tip our heads together as people step around us. He runs his hand through my hair and kisses my face. We can't get back to Meredith's apartment quickly enough. She's been kind enough to crash at Philippe's this weekend.

*　*　*　*　*

I fall asleep when we're done and wake up to a note on the pillow next to me that says, "Come by The Merc whenever you feel like it. We go on at 8." I'm trying to determine what time it is when Meredith lets herself into her room.

"No pretend knock?" I ask with a laugh.

"I ran into Chris in the lobby on his way out a while ago. It's not like you're doing anything private in here without him."

"Safe bet, I guess. What time is it?"

"Six. What's your plan for tonight?"

"I don't know. I was going to go to soundcheck and dinner with Chris, but I guess he let me sleep."

"Maybe he didn't want you to come."

"Meredith. He wanted me to come, but he knew I was exhausted. He put us all on the list. You, me, and Philippe. He's not trying to get rid of me. He's not going to bail on me."

"Are you seriously moving back to Pittsburgh?"

"I seriously don't know what I'm going to do, okay? But…"

"But, what?"

"He told me he loves me. And I told him I love him."

I don't know why I tell her, except for the fact that she's my best friend, and you're supposed to tell your best friend these things, even when they hate the person you're in love with.

"Oh, Chicken," she says with a sigh—a warm one, thankfully, not an exasperated one—as she sits down at the foot of the bed. "So, this is going to be a thing?"

"I think it already is."

"You'd really rather move to Pittsburgh than come live with me?"

I let out a pretend primal scream and throw a pillow at her. "Can we please talk about anything else?!"

"Why won't you let me help you?"

"You can't help me. I need a job in journalism to make J-school work, and despite your best efforts to force Philippe to create a magazine for me to work at, you can't make a job materialize."

"We could figure something out," she says, and she means it.

"I think it's just easier for you because what you do doesn't really matter."

"Excuse me?"

"No, I just mean if something doesn't work out, you just pick something else."

"What are you talking about?"

"I don't know. What about the time you changed your major from International Relations to Art History because you didn't get into the MUN club?"

"That was bullshit. They should have taken me."

"You were completely hung over for the final selection round."

"But I had already proven myself."

"That's my point. You don't follow the rules. And when someone actually calls you on it, you just move on to something else."

"They just didn't want to accept a freshman."

"Regardless, it didn't really matter, because you didn't need that degree. You just did something else. Because ultimately whatever you do, you'll be fine."

"This again?"

"What?"

"This is about money?"

"A little, yeah."

"Why is it always about money with you, Alice? Why can't you just be happy I'm willing to share?"

"This isn't you paying for the movies in high school, Meredith. Or giving me the clothes you cast off after one wear. This is rent. This is life, my real life, and I need to make it work myself."

"How is living with your dad and interning for him any different than living rent-free with me?"

"Well, it isn't. Which is why I want to get the fellowship and housing from Klein, so I can do things for myself. I don't want someone handing me something. I don't want an unfair advantage."

"You already have an unfair advantage. So what? That's life. You can't walk away from something just because someone else doesn't have it."

"What do you mean?"

"You don't think the fact that the Klein fellowship is only open to Jewish applicants isn't an unfair advantage?"

"Well, no … there are lots of programs that are only for certain groups of people, right?"

"Yeah, because Jews are so underrepresented in the media, right?"

"Meredith!"

"I'm not wrong."

"You're being a bitch."

"Okay, well forget that. You don't have student loan debt, right?"

"You know I don't." It was money her dad got from Karl Bell that paid my tuition.

"So, some people have student loan debt, and you don't. You don't feel guilty about that, do you?"

"Sometimes, I actually do… "

"Fine. Bad example. You're going to have a response for anything I bring up. I'm just saying, having a rich friend is not the worst thing in the world, and I'm not going to beg you, but I think we could figure out how to make this work."

"I don't know. Do you even really want me around?"

"What does that mean? Because I brought up the fact that you're Jewish? Please. I don't give a shit about that and you know it. I never have."

"Right, but—"

"But nothing! I'm not a bigot!"

"I know. But what if we fight?"

"We've fought in the past. It's never been a deal breaker. There are no deal breakers with me and you."

"Even Chris?"

"Even Chris."

"Wow. Okay. Listen, I'm not saying *no*. I'm just saying, *I don't know*."

"Fine. That's good enough for me. For now." She throws the pillow back at me.

"Can I ask you a question, though?"

"Anything." Meredith is standing in front of her full-length mirror checking herself out.

"You're really not worried about ruining our friendship by living together?"

"No." She turns back to face me and looks a little stunned, maybe even hurt by the question. "Are you?"

"A little."

"Why?"

"Living with Nate is one thing. Obviously we love each other, but we've never really liked each other, so the fact that we annoy the crap out of one another is, you know, expected. But thinking about the roommates I had before him…"

"The ones from the lacrosse team? They were horrible."

"Right, but people who didn't live with them didn't think they were horrible. What if I'm horrible to live with?"

"You're not horrible to live with and you know it. You're worried I'm horrible to live with."

"I just don't want to lose you."

"Oh!" She gets a devious smile on her face. "So, if I made you pick between him and me?"

"You wouldn't."

"Of course I wouldn't." Her smile is sweet now, which is unlike her. "But it's good to know where I stand."

"Very funny." At least I hope she's being funny. "Where do I stand?"

"What do you mean? What would I give up for you?"

"No, not that, but why is it so important to you that I move here? I mean, do you think we're always going to live in the same town? Do you think our friendship can't survive being apart? We just did four years apart."

"Except for every break and at least one weekend a month."

"Right, but still."

"Are you asking why I want you around?"

"I guess. I'm sorry, it's dumb. I'm just feeling pulled in a lot of directions right now. It's hard to know what's real or why anything is happening."

"I want you around because everyone here likes me for my money, and you like me in spite of it."

CHAPTER 21*

The Mercury Lounge is packed for ACE's set. I think the piece in *Time Out* must have made a difference. Nightswimming doesn't seem bothered by the extra attention ACE is getting, and the bands go out to Katz's together after the show. Philippe, Meredith, and I go, too.

Meredith won't eat anything at the deli. It's all too greasy for her palate.

"I prefer Lois Burton's Jewish cooking to this," she says, gesturing to the fatty corned beef a man behind a counter is cutting for me. I make an apologetic grimace towards the man, but he's not paying attention to us, only to the knife he's wielding and the slab of meat he's cutting. "This lighting is also a problem."

"You know what my mom makes isn't really 'Jewish cooking,' right?"

"I don't know why you say that. She's Jewish, and she cooks it." Meredith cackles. It's a cosmo-laced cackle. I've had a few pink drinks myself, but not as many as she has.

"I like that you eat what you want when he's around." She says it as an afterthought, but it makes me smile. I like it, too.

ACE, Nightswimming, and a few other hangers-on take up several booths in the corner of the restaurant. Chris makes room for me, Meredith and Philippe at his booth, but Meredith chooses to sit a booth over, next to the drummer from Nightswimming, who is hot, but married. Philippe sits with me and Chris.

"You know not to say anything about me leaving the band, right?" Chris asks Philippe quietly.

Philippe mimes zipping his lips and throwing away the key.

"And Meredith?" Chris tips his chin towards her.

Philippe shrugs.

"She wouldn't," I say.

"She's drunk," Chris says.

"She's drunk a lot. She's never told my secrets before."

His shoulders relax, and he smiles at me. "You have a lot of secrets?"

"Doesn't everyone?"

"You two are adorable together!" Philippe tells us.

I instinctively look at Tau at the next table, but it doesn't appear he's heard anything.

"We're not together," I say, in case Tau has heard anything but isn't letting on.

"Really?" Philippe asks.

"No labels," I say.

Chris slings his arm over my shoulder and kisses my temple.

"Really," Philippe says. "Adorable."

Chris and I eat off each other's plates. Eating with him is nourishing in a way I haven't experienced in a long time. Everything here is so salty, but we wash it down with Dr. Brown's sodas, and I'm reminded of all the times I had deli with my grandparents before they died, and before my mom became a health food guru who had very strong ideas about what I put into my body.

"You okay?" Chris asks, noticing I've drifted.

"I'm great," I tell him.

It's like no one else is in the restaurant, no matter how loud and bright and crowded it is. Everything else just falls away. When thoughts of him leaving tomorrow creep in, I push them away by looking at his face, his hair, his body. He lets me stare; he likes it.

"You want to get out of here?" he asks.

I nod.

"I guess that's my cue!" Philippe air kisses both of us and slides over to the booth where Meredith is squished next to the guy from

Nightswimming. Philippe whispers something to her, and she nods and smiles at me. She won't be home tonight.

On the street, Chris wraps his pinky around mine, and before I can even enjoy the tingling in my core, there are tears falling on my shirt. I wipe my face, but they keep coming.

"Oh no," he says, and stops walking to hug me. "Please don't."

"I'm sorry," I say between gasps. It's getting worse not better.

"Don't be sorry. I just hate seeing you sad."

"I'm trying not to be sad. I don't want to be sad. But we just have a few hours left. And then, who knows…"

"I know. But, you're right. Who knows? Anything could happen."

"Anything?"

"Sure."

"*Anything* can't happen," I tell him. "One of a very few things is going to happen."

"My point is, if we don't know what's coming next, let's not assume the worst. Let's pretend this is real life."

"Why can't this be real life?" I don't mean to float this idea on a street corner in front of Katz's, but it just comes out.

"What do you mean?"

"Move here. With me. If I come alone, I could really only afford to sleep on Meredith's couch. But if we come together, we could split the rent, and then maybe I could get an unpaid gig in a newsroom or volunteer at a couple of places for experience or something."

"Oh, I don't think so Alice."

"Why not?"

"What would I do in New York? I don't want to live in New York."

"Why not? It's so great here. There would be tons of opportunities to play shows. Don't leave the band. Get them to relocate here. To New York."

"They have families in Australia, Alice."

"But all signs point to the band really making it big, if you don't leave. So, don't leave? Get big. Move here. We could be together."

"So, you get everything you want? You get away from your family, and we're together, and we don't have to sneak around, and the only concession is, I don't want to be in a band anymore or live in this city."

I take a step back from him. "It's not a competition to see who can get more of what they want. It just sort of came to me."

"I'm sorry. I know. But I'm not moving to New York. I need to be in Pittsburgh."

"Why? What's there for you?"

"When we were there last week, I went down to Pitt and registered for classes. I'm going to finish my degree."

"What? That's great! Why didn't you tell me?"

"I guess I was worried about what you would say."

"Why?"

"I think you like the fact that I'm in a band and going back to school is the opposite of that."

I do like the fact that he's in a band. I like being backstage and in clubs before they open. I like the way people look at him and the way they look at me when I'm with him. He's not wrong, but I don't want to be that person.

"I'm glad you're going back to school, if that's what you want to do."

"Thanks. I think telling you makes it real. And now I really have to do it."

"Well, I'm proud of you." And I really am. I can't help but be bummed that he's looking to settle down right when I'm ready to take off, but timing has never been our thing.

"Proud of me, huh?" he asks with a sweet smile. "I guess that's something."

He swings his arm around my shoulder, and we turn to walk uptown, when a group of large men pass, nearly knocking us off the sidewalk. They are loud and not paying attention to anyone but themselves. Some of them are wearing athletic gear and others are wearing suits and gold jewelry. Most of them have sunglasses on, despite it being one in the morning. They burst into Katz's, and we can see through the windows that everyone stops what they're doing to gawk at them. I'm intrigued by who this group of men might be, when I see him.

My body goes rigid under Chris' arm. He looks at me and then back through the window.

"What's up?" he asks.

"It's him," I say. "We should go."

"It's who?"

I try to walk, but my feet won't cooperate.

"It's Karl… I don't get it. Was he traded? Or maybe his team is in town? Is it baseball season? Are those baseball players?"

"Oh shit, that is him," Chris says, as his body stiffens as well. "Weird. You okay?"

"I don't know. Let's just get out of here," I say, but I still can't make my feet move. I'm trying to put one foot in front of the other when Karl turns his head, and though I can't be sure, it certainly seems like he's staring right at us. "Fuck."

"Okay, let's go," Chris says, trying to nudge me forward.

"But. Meredith."

"What about her? Do we need to go get her? You can stay here. I'll get her."

"No, don't leave me." I wrap my arms around Chris' waist and bury my face in his chest. I'm having trouble taking deep breaths, but I can at least inhale his scent in short, violent bursts. "I'm not worried about what he'll do to her. I'm worried about what she'll do to him."

"Too late," Chris says.

"What?"

I turn my face to the windows, and sure enough, even though I can't hear it, I can tell Meredith is definitely yelling at Karl Bell, and everyone he's with, while they're trying to order smoked meat.

"I can't look," I say burying my head back into Chris' chest.

"Uh, she is really scary," he says. "She has a whole baseball team cowering."

"Really?" I allow myself to peek, and he's right. The men who took over the whole sidewalk just a moment ago look like little boys in the face of Meredith's pointing and scolding.

"Looks like she has everything under control."

"It certainly does." I'm able to laugh a bit.

"Do you want to go in?" he asks me.

"Not at all. She'll tell me all about it in the morning."

CHAPTER 22

Chris has to leave before it's light out. He wakes me to say goodbye, but I mostly hide my face in my pillow.

"You're pretending to be asleep," he says.

"You don't know that," I mumble.

He sits down next to me, and I curl my naked body around him. The soft vulnerability of my skin is pressed up against his jeans and t-shirt. He gently runs the pads of his fingers up and down my leg.

"I gotta go," he tells me.

"I know."

"I'm only on the West Coast for a week."

"I know."

"I'll come see you when I get back. We'll figure this out."

"Will we?"

"We don't have a choice. I'm not letting you go this time."

"So, if I get the fellowship, you'll move here with me?"

"No. I didn't say that. But we could do long distance."

I flop over and bury my head again.

"I know," he says, "long distance never works. But New York to Pittsburgh isn't that far."

"Not like Australia-far," I tease.

He pokes my side, and I shriek.

"Come here." He guides me to a sitting position and holds me in his arms. "I'm not letting go this time. Not until you tell me to."

"You know you broke up with me, like, a week ago, right?"

"I'm sorry. I thought you wanted something I couldn't give you."

"I just want you. In my life. Somehow."

"I know that now. And you've got me."

He holds me for a long time, so long I slip back to sleep in his arms and wake only slightly when he lays me back down in the empty bed. I know he's gone when the door clicks shut, but I pretend he'll be right back.

Hours later, Meredith, Philippe, and I are in SoHo, brunching at yet another healthy find my mom introduced her to. I want to sit outside, but Meredith says it's too hot for her hangover.

"I'm just trying to understand what went down last night," Philippe says, between sips of organic Bloody Mary. "One moment, Meredith is hitting on a hot, married drummer and another, I'm pulling her off a hot, Major League Baseball player. Or at least, that's what the guy working the register told me."

"He's not hot," I say.

"He's scum," Meredith says.

"Did you really attack him?" I ask her.

"Gawd, I don't remember."

"She did, but like in a really sloppy, ineffective way," Philippe says with a cackle. "Who is he?"

Meredith and I look at each other.

"That was Karl Bell," I tell Philippe. "He used to be friends with my dad. And when I was sixteen, he … did stuff to me … and then, he and my dad had a fight or something, and then my dad ended up in a coma and Karl Bell took off with my car."

"Whoa. I'm so sorry. What kind of place is Pittsburgh? Did you grow up in a made-for-TV movie?"

"Philippe!" Meredith swats at him.

"No, it's fine," I say. "You know, when I say it out loud like that, it does seem … surreal."

"Did he get in trouble back then?" Philippe asks.

"Not really. I mean, thanks to Meredith's dad, I got some money from him."

"He paid her college tuition."

"But, like, he's still just walking around like a regular guy?" Philippe asks. "America is so weird."

"Do you know if he saw me?" I ask them.

"Last night?"

"Yeah, through the window? I thought he looked right at me."

"Honestly, I don't remember what he said or what I said. I just remember wanting to kill him."

"Gawd, I hope you're never that mad at me," Philippe tells her.

"Don't fuck with my friends, and you'll be safe," she tells him, and then looks at me. "You okay?"

"I guess. I don't love that he's here. I didn't realize he had been traded. But, it's a big city, right?" This isn't exactly how I'm feeling. I'm actually thinking about how small the city is. How weird it is that we ran into him. How it could happen again at any time.

"Oh, I wasn't asking about him. I was asking about Chris. You look … sad." And she sounds a little bit sad for me.

"Oh. That. Right. Yeah, you could say I'm sad."

"Did you, like, break up for real?"

"No, actually we didn't."

"Oh." Now Meredith seems slightly concerned, but uncharacteristically, she's trying to hide it.

"That doesn't mean I'm moving to Pittsburgh," I assure her.

"So, long distance?"

"I don't know. We're going to see each other when he gets back from recording and try to figure it all out."

"I've never seen someone so sad to be dating a hot rock star," Philippe says.

"Listen, I'm in love with Chris Thompson. I don't know if that's the same thing as dating a rock star."

"Well, for another week it is," he says.

"So why the sad face, Chicken?"

"I didn't expect this summer to be so complicated."

"I got news for you," she says, drinking from her mimosa. "This isn't just a summer anymore. This is your life."

"I don't know what's scarier," I say with a genuine laugh. "Being your enemy or being your friend."

"Doesn't matter," she says, proud of herself. "I always tell it like it is."

CHAPTER 23

The bus back to State College on Tuesday is sticky and smelly, but I don't even mind. The scenery out the bus window is, as always, amazing once we cross into Pennsylvania. The sky is a clear deep blue. It's not like a robin's egg, which is a thing people say in books. Robin's egg blue actually has a lot of green in it, and the sky rarely looks like that unless there's a tornado coming. I'm not a fan of robin's egg skies. No, this sky is cobalt, the color of racquet balls, no tinge of green, no threat of rain. The trees are in full bloom. Every possible shade of green is present, but not in the sky, in the leaves and the grass and around the streams. It's like it's all there, just for me. I always feel this way coming back from Meredith's. Like I've just had an adventure, but the scenery reminds me I don't belong in the city, like that's her place and this is my place. Except I want that to be my place, but now I know Karl Bell is there, too.

When I get off the bus, I go right to work. The minute I open the door, Cassie is in my face.

"Oh! My! Gawd! You're back! Alice! Alice! Alice! Tell me everything! Everything! Everything!"

I look to the register where Brian is standing. He looks like he's had a long, hard, boring shift. "She's had a lot of iced coffee today."

"I can tell," I say.

"Zach said I could leave when you got here." He's already halfway out the back door.

"No problem."

"Good luck," he says with a nod to Cassie.

"Tell me everything!" Cassie is bouncing up and down on her toes. "Did you get to meet Nightswimming? How did the Mercury Lounge show go? Are you dating Chris Thompson? Is the sex good?"

"Slow down," I tell her, though I do find her enthusiasm a nice switch from her typical bitter disinterest. I also like the way she's looking at me, like I'm someone just because of my connection to Chris. I don't like that I like it, but I can't deny that I do. "Where's Zach?"

"I don't know."

I walk over to look at the schedule behind the counter. He's put me on opening with Cassie the rest of the week. That's when he's least likely to be here. Closing together used to be our thing.

"Is he avoiding me?"

"I don't know, is he?" she asks.

Oy. I should have not said that out loud.

"Uhh … no, I'm kidding."

"No, you're not! He loves you and you love Chris and now you're worried he hates you."

"It's not that simple, Cassie."

"If you say so. Tell me about New York, now!"

I recap the trip, leaving out the parts I would prefer didn't get back to Zach, but making sure to give her just enough insider knowledge— like the squalid condition of what passes for a green room in the Mercury Lounge's basement—that her eyes get wide and she squeals a few times.

"When I grow up, I want to be just like you!" she says.

"That's the nicest thing you've ever said to me."

"You're like a real groupie."

"Uh, that is actually the worst thing you've ever said to me. Is that how you see me?"

"Well, I mean, you hook up with musicians, and you went away for the weekend with a band, so…"

"Cassie, I went to see Meredith in New York and ACE happened to be there. I'm not a groupie. You should want to grow up to be like me because I graduated with a 4.0, and I'm going to do great things…

eventually, I think. Not because I know someone in a band from when I was a kid."

"Whatever," she says and wanders away, and I'm left with her version of me and my version of me and no idea which is true.

I don't want Chris to drop out of the band, and I don't want to move to Pittsburgh to be with him. Because then I'm just some dumb girl who works at her dad's radio station and moved home to be with the first person she ever loved. That can't be my story, even though when I was Cassie's age that's the exact story I wanted for my life.

I want Chris to stay in the band, and I want him to move to New York to be with me. That's a much better story.

I can hear Zach upstairs. He's avoiding me, and I've made a mess of everything. Not that I was really planning to stay here, but I hadn't written it off just yet. The longer I go without an acceptance to Klein, the more willing I'm going to be to consider just about anything.

The store is quiet, so I go up to the office to get the reports I'm working on. I consider knocking on Zach's door just to say hi, but I'm not sure he wants to see me and I'm not sure I could handle being right about that. It's better not knowing exactly where his head is right now. I take the papers and markers down to the store and work on them while Cassie dances around the store and helps the few customers who come in: a guy looking for the new Ben Harper release—she's not impressed and informs him it's not out until later this month—and a group of high school girls Cassie knows but clearly does not like.

After we do the closing checklist, I send Cassie home and take a minute of quiet for myself behind the counter. Zach is usually in the store when I'm working whether he's on the schedule or not. It's rare for me to be here longer than a few hours and not see him. And I can still hear him upstairs. He's definitely avoiding me, and I don't like how it feels. I get why he's doing it—that part isn't a mystery—but I don't get why I'm so bothered by it. He has every right to be pissed at me, I totally deserve it. I'm literally the worst. Which is why I go upstairs and knock on his door.

"Hey." He doesn't open the door all the way. He doesn't step back to usher me in. He just stands there.

"Hey, what's going on?" I ask.

"Nothing."

"I thought you might want to see the progress I made on the reports today. I think I'll have something for you to send to corporate soon."

"Oh, thanks." His tone softens a little. Like maybe he's glad we have something work-related to talk about. "You can leave everything in the office. I can look at it tomorrow."

"Anything going on tonight?" I ask.

"No."

Awkward silence. I almost wish he would just call me out on my shitty behavior instead of pretending I haven't been shitty. Maybe I should call myself out?

"Listen, Zach—"

"Alice, can we talk later? I'm trying to finish cleaning up the apartment and everything."

"Right. Sorry. Yeah. I figured you must be busy when you weren't downstairs today."

"Yeah, I hate cleaning. I just want to get it over with."

"Sure. Sorry to bother you."

In four years of knowing Zach I don't think I've ever said, *sorry to bother you*, to him. This is a nightmare.

CHAPTER 24

I lug my duffle bag out of the store and stop to get cash at the MAC machine, but my balance is low. Like, really low. Which is weird, because it's June 3rd and even though the 1st hit over the weekend, my monthly allowance should be here by now. It's never been late. Unless. Unless I've been cut off because of graduation. Which, whatever, it makes sense, but like, my dad could have told me that was going to happen. I was counting on that money to make New York work. This is so like Burton. I wonder if he'd reinstate it if I went back to Pittsburgh, or even if I just told him when I was "planning" to be back.

By the time I get to Nate's, I'm furious. I know I'm lucky to get anything from my parents, and so many people have it so much worse, but it's not like I have a trust fund. I call my dad at the station, and they tell me he's just coming out of the booth.

"What's going on, Alice?" He sounds tired, his typical post-show slump. When he was younger, the shows invigorated him, but not so much since the accident.

"Um, you tell me, Dad. Is there anything you forgot to mention when you were up here last week?" *Gawd, how could that have only been a week ago?*

"Alice, you're going to have to be a little more clear than that."

"The money, dad. There's no money in my account."

"And?"

"And, is there a reason for that?"

"I don't know what you're talking about, Alice. Did someone steal something from you?"

"Really, Dad? For the last four years $400 has showed up in my checking account on the first of every month."

"Oh, that."

"Yes, that."

He takes a long, long pause and slow deep breath. "You should probably call Art."

"What?"

"Arthur May. Talk to Arthur May about this. I can't help you; but let me know what he says."

"Dad, is that money from you, or not? We've talked about this before. I know mom doesn't have anything to do with it. It's not from you?"

"Alice, call Art. That's all I can tell you."

I click the phone off and plop down on the couch. It's after 8pm. I consider calling Meredith to ask her how to best reach her dad—is he even in town in June? how late does he work?—but I'd rather not involve her in this just yet, so I try her parents' house, and her dad answers.

"Hi Mr. May. It's Alice Burton. How are you?"

"Alice, I'm fine. Is everything okay? Is Meredith okay? Where are you?"

"I'm in State College. I got back today. I was with Meredith for the weekend. She's fine, this isn't about her."

"Oh. Okay. What can I do for you?"

"Uh, well, this is weird, I guess, but my dad told me to call you about something in my bank account."

"Something in your bank account?"

"Well, something *not* in my bank account, actually. See, ever since I started Penn State, $400 has been deposited into my checking account on the first of every month. And it's not there for June. I assumed it was from my dad. I mean, he always led me to believe that it was, but tonight he said it wasn't him. Do you know anything about it? He told me to call you."

"Yes, Alice, give me a moment." I hear him tell Meredith's mom that everything's okay, and it sounds like he's moving to another room. "Okay, I'm back."

"I'm sorry to call you at home. I guess I thought that'd be okay."

"Oh, it is. I'm glad you did. I wouldn't want to talk about this at work. Let me ask you this, are you okay without the money?"

"What do you mean, 'am I okay?'"

"Well, if it stopped, if you got the last of it already, would you be okay?"

"I mean, I wouldn't starve. I have a job."

"Well, let's set the bar a little higher. What are your plans for the fall?"

"They're still up in the air. And I had counted on that money, but, like, I'm not committed to anything, so if it's gone, it's gone. I'll figure it out."

"Good, that's good to hear. You know, we can always help you out if you need it. But I think both your mom and dad are doing well for themselves these days, aren't they?"

"Oh, yeah, sure. We're fine, thanks. But Mr. May, can you tell me what's going on?"

"Alice, a while back, after … that night... I made some arrangements for you at the request of your dad. I think you know about your tuition payments, right?"

"About Karl Bell? Yeah. I know a little."

"Well, it's not how I would deal with things now, but you know your dad is pretty persuasive, and you know our family cares about you a lot, so I did what was best for you. On top of your tuition, I arranged for money to go directly into your account. But there was no end date discussed. I don't think it has anything to do with graduation. I haven't had communication with … him… in a while. Unless he's been keeping tabs on you. Do you want me to look into it?"

"Um, wait, so this was essentially blackmail money? Buying my silence? You knew what happened?"

"I don't think you should look at it like that. Blackmail is a crime and not a term I would use lightly."

"Right, sorry, but, that's what you're describing, right? Like, the idea was, what? We'd stay quiet about his shit behavior—sorry—if he put money into my account every month?"

"Basically," Mr. May confirms.

"Hmm. Well, at least it makes more sense now."

"What does?"

"I saw him this weekend. In New York City."

"You did? On purpose?"

"No, just on the street."

"Well, he was just traded. He's playing there now."

"I had no idea."

"Did you talk to him, Alice?"

"No, but Meredith did."

"She what?"

"Um, she made a little bit of a scene at Katz's Saturday night. Well, Sunday morning, I guess."

"But she's okay?"

"Yeah, I mean, I was outside when it happened. I saw her through the window, but I didn't go in. I couldn't. And she was with friends, so she was fine. But, I guess there are always consequences, huh?"

So, Meredith gets to mouth off, and it costs me $400 a month, and it costs her nothing. But it's actually cost me something all along. When Karl Bell was making my life hell, I couldn't think of anything except keeping myself safe, but I'm not that kid now. I should have spoken up then. I should be speaking up now.

"Alice, I'm sorry. It wouldn't be right for me to approach anyone about this. I think we should let it go."

"What if I want to tell someone? What he did?"

"Well, I'm not a criminal attorney, but you'd have to look into the statute of limitations, and the fact that there has been money involved won't help."

"But he's probably hurt other people."

Mr. May doesn't say anything, but I know I'm right. I didn't speak up five years ago, and because he arranged for money on my behalf, I can't really speak up now.

"Maybe talk to your mom?" Mr. May says cautiously. "This really isn't my area."

"Right, yeah, sorry," I say. "Thanks for … everything … I guess."

"You'll be okay, Alice. We're here if you need us."

He means for money. But I don't need money, his, or anyone else's.

I'm ready to drown my sorrows and shame in whatever beer I can find in the fridge when I see the letter on the table. It's a small envelope with the Klein Fellowship logo on the upper left corner. A small envelope. Shit.

I wait for the tears to come, but they don't. It's a stunned feeling more than anything else. An empty void, like I'm frozen in space and time.

I open the envelope, just to make sure.

I've been waitlisted and encouraged to make other plans. I'm informed it's rare to be accepted from the waitlist.

There are two beers in the fridge, a Rolling Rock and a Honey Brown. I grab them both and head up to my room. I'm still not crying. I'm still not collapsing. I'm moving like a phantom, floating on autopilot. When I drop the letter on my desk, I see it. The picture of "us." Suddenly, I'm not a phantom anymore. I'm not on autopilot. I'm awake. I run down the stairs to call Meredith. I tell her I'm moving home.

CHAPTER 25

The news still doesn't feel real, even though it's not new anymore. It's been four days since I found out I was waitlisted from Klein, and Meredith is still the only person I've told. I think part of me hopes it was a mistake. Or that I'll be pulled off the waitlist and won't have to tell anyone, but each day that goes by makes that seem less likely.

"Why don't you ask Burton to make a call?" Meredith asks.

I'm surprised it's taken her this long to make the suggestion. "No."

I'm on Nate's front porch in a rocking chair with the cordless, a sweating mason jar of vodka spiked lemonade on my knee.

"Alice, he could probably help."

"He probably could," I say. "But the whole point was to do something on my own. And now we know I'm just not good enough. I'm *almost* good enough. I'm *waitlist* good enough. But that's as far as my natural ability and work ethic will take me."

"Aaaalice! Don't say that."

"No, it's fine. It's good I found out now. I mean, this is helpful." I take a long swig of my drink. It's four in the afternoon and hot.

"You realize it's just one program," she says, kindly for her.

"The best program."

"Right, but still. Lots of people pull strings. I don't think I'm dumber than anyone else just because my dad could pay full tuition at NYU and make a sizable donation. It's just how the world works."

"It's how *your* world works."

"It's how the *whole* world works."

"It's not how *my* world works."

I want my merit to matter.

"How is asking your dad to make a call for you any different than you taking a job at his station?" she asks.

It's not like I haven't thought about this. I know I have more advantages than some. But somehow nepotism seems less nefarious than my dad bullying other people into helping me. But it is one of the reasons I wanted the program so badly. Because it would mean not falling back on a job my dad hands me.

"I know. Fuck. But still. I don't want to involve him in this. And even if I did, it would mean I had been keeping this from him the whole time, and that would be a whole other thing. And anyway, you know he doesn't want me in New York, so I don't know that he'd be that eager to help out."

"I'm sorry, Chicken. But you can still move here, right?"

"No, I don't think so."

"But we've talked about this."

"Well, it turns out I was counting on some money I don't have anymore."

"What does that mean?"

"It's a bit complicated." I don't know if it's the shame that my dad made her dad do something illegal, or the fact that it's her fault I don't have it anymore, or the fact that I just want all of it behind me, but I don't tell her about the $400 a month.

"Are you sure? My couch is still here for you if you want to come up and just figure things out here."

"I know. Thanks. You're the best."

"But I get it if you think that's taking advantage of the system and my family's resources." Her tone is mildly snotty.

"Meredith!"

"I'm just saying, it's all connected. You can't ignore how the world works just because you don't like it."

"I get that. And I'm not not moving in with you because of nepotism or whatever. I just can't right now. But hopefully I'll end up there for grad school, and you know, real life."

"Real life, ha! What's that?"

"Seriously."

"How are things with Zach?"

"Done. There's nothing with Zach."

"Was that hard?"

"It wasn't… anything. We're mostly just working opposite shifts."

Zach isn't completely avoiding me, but I do see him less than I normally would. And we don't get together after work anymore. It wasn't a discussion, it just stopped. He stayed in a few nights the rest of us went out, and I got the message.

"You told him you're leaving?"

"No, I still haven't told anyone but you."

"Not even Chris?"

"No."

"Things okay there?"

"Do you care?"

"Only in a totally voyeuristic way."

I want to tell Chris, but his calls from California have been sporadic and tense. He doesn't seem upset with me, just tired and stressed. He claims the recording sessions are going well, but his tone doesn't match his words. I know telling him about my move back to Pittsburgh might cheer him up, but I would hate to tell him and then have to tell him otherwise if I get pulled from the waitlist.

"Well, at least you're honest," I tell her.

"Always." She cackles.

"I think we're fine. He's been a little cranky when we talk, but I don't think that's about me."

"Of course it isn't. You can do no wrong."

"What does that mean?"

"He sort of … dotes on you. It's weird."

"Uh, thanks."

"I don't know. I have concerns."

"Oh my gawd, I get it! You don't like him."

"It's not that. I'm over that. I'm trying to look at this whole thing objectively, and I just don't like it."

There's something in her tone that makes me want to hear more. "Go on."

"I just, you know, it's one thing for you to move back to Pittsburgh and work for your dad and apply to Columbia, but after two or three years there with Chris, would you even go to Columbia? Would you leave him for that?"

"No, but I'd try to get him to come with me."

"But, like, he could come to New York now if he wanted to, you both could. He doesn't want New York. He's done with ... you know ... all this." I imagine her waving the glass of whatever she's drinking at her window in the direction of Washington Square Park.

It gives me pause.

"I don't even know if we would stay together that long, Meredith. But if I get into Columbia, I'm going. You don't have to worry about that."

"Okay." She sounds much less than convinced.

"Meredith, what are you getting at?"

"I don't think you can say no to him."

"Excuse me? Are you kidding? Since when am I someone who lets a guy tell me what to do?"

"He's not a guy. He's 'the' guy. You've never cared about guys, because they weren't him. He's going to get you knocked up, and you're not going to go to grad school. You're going to marry him and live in Pittsburgh and run your dad's station and Chris'll probably work for you."

"Meredith!"

"And you know what, Chicken? That's fine. It really is. If it will make you happy. There's nothing wrong with living back there. Or running a radio station. You'll be good at it. But you'd be good at a lot of things. So, just be careful, because if you go back there, you might never leave."

I finish my drink. Gawd, I hate it when she's right.

"I won't get stuck there. I promise. I already told him I don't want to be with him if it means sneaking around, so given that neither of us have the desire to tell my dad, I think this is going to crash and burn pretty quickly."

"You'll cave," she says.

"What?"

"You'll cave. You'll sneak around with him."

"What? Why would you say that?"

"Think about it. You've snuck around with him before. You snuck around with Zach before he asked you out. It's not a big deal. But you're not going to let something with Chris Thompson crash and burn, even if it's a flaming wreck."

"Whatever."

"When's he back from LA?"

"Tomorrow."

"And when are you back?"

"Nate wants me out by August 1st, so I still have almost two months to figure this all out."

"I foresee sneaking around in your future."

"Well, that may be the case, but here's hoping I'll be at Columbia in a few years. Maybe I'll even live on your couch while I'm in school. If you're nice to me."

"Sounds good, Chicken. Looking forward to it. I'm going to get ready to go out. What are you up to tonight?"

"Hmmm... Saturday night? I'll be on whatever porch has a keg on it."

"Good girl, Chicken. Love ya."

"Love ya."

CHAPTER 26

"Your boyfriend's on the phone." Nate is standing in my doorway holding out the cordless.

"He's not my boyfriend," I say reflexively, though I'm groggy and not sure what's going on.

When I get out of bed to reach for the phone, I realize I probably didn't put myself to bed last night. My Liminal Space t-shirt is for going out, and I never sleep in boxer shorts in the summer. But at least they're mine.

The next thing I realize is how dizzy I am. Shit.

"Hello?" I say into the phone when I take it from Nate's hand, the tell-tale deep-throated gravel of a hangover in my voice.

"Morning, Princess," Chris says.

"Hi."

Nate rolls his eyes at me, and I slam the door shut. The sound reverberates through my head, and I crawl back into my bed.

"You don't sound so hot. Are you hungover?"

Such a loaded question.

"I'm fine," I try to say brightly. "Are you back? Are you in Pittsburgh?"

"Yup. Yesterday, I was in a band in LA. Tonight, I'm having dinner with my parents."

"That's nice," I say.

"Is it?" he asks.

"Isn't it? For you? For them? This is what you want, right? Are you okay?"

"I am. It is what I want. Are you okay?"

"I said, 'I'm fine.'"

"I hate talking to you on the phone," he says.

"Excuse me?"

"You would never lie to my face, but right now you're full of shit."

"Fine, I'm hungover. Does it really matter that much?"

"I don't know. Does it? What'd you do last night?"

I scan my memory, but it's foggy. "Just a party. You know, a keg on a porch."

"With Zach?"

"No. Is that what you're worried about? There's nothing to worry about. Especially not Zach."

"I just want you back here. Okay?"

"Well, you're going to get your wish. I didn't get the Klein fellowship, so Pittsburgh it is."

"Really?"

"Yeah."

"Are you serious? When did you find out? Why didn't you tell me?"

"You sounded really stressed in LA. And I actually got waitlisted, so it's not a done deal, but at this point, I don't think I'm going to New York."

"That's fantastic!"

"Is it?"

I take a deep breath and notice a glass of water on my nightstand with two Tylenol next to it. Whoever put me to bed knew what they were doing. I take the Tylenol.

"Listen, Alice, I know you wanted to get into the program, and I know you don't want to come back here, but I really want to be with you. I want us to be together."

When he says it like that, it doesn't sound so bad. I imagine how much worse it would feel if I were headed to Pittsburgh and he wasn't going to be there.

"Sorry, I guess I'm in a weird mood right now. How did it go with the guys?"

"Not horrible. Derek was cool about it. Tau was pissed at first, but then he calmed down. I think they both knew something was up."

"Good. And your parents? Happy to have you home?"

"It's all going to take some getting used to. But the term starts tomorrow, so I'm just going to jump in and make it work."

"Oh wow. That was cutting it close. Are you ready to be back in school?"

"I mean, it's not my favorite part of this whole plan, but I just have to knock out a couple credits, so I'll survive."

"I'm really proud of you."

"Are you?"

"Of course."

"I thought you wanted me to stay with the band."

"Well, I didn't want you to go back to Australia, so if this is what keeps you stateside, then so be it. I can get on board."

"Big of you," he says with a laugh.

I laugh, too and then feel nauseated. "Hey, can we talk later?"

"You're going to puke, aren't you?"

"I'll call you later." I switch the phone off and throw it on the bed while simultaneously making a run for the bathroom.

*   *   *   *   *

Downstairs Nate and Angela are at the kitchen table, a pitcher of lemonade between them. I pour myself a glass.

"It must have been you who put me to bed," I say to Angela.

"I helped," she says.

"Who did you help? Nate?" I can't imagine Nate being that kind, even with Angela in the room.

"I had nothing to do with your drunk ass last night," he says.

"Zach brought you home," Angela tells me.

"Oh."

"You don't remember anything, do you?" Nate asks.

I shake my head and then have to steady myself.

"Wow," he says.

"I've been dealing with a lot. You can lay off," I tell him.

"Oh, poor baby, dating a pseudo rock star and freeloading off your brother, rough life."

"I pay rent, Nate. Jeez. I'll be gone soon enough."

"Johnny said you still won't tell them when you're starting at the station, but you know you have to be out of here before August 1st."

"Yes, I know. I'll be gone, don't worry."

"How do you feel?" Angela inserts herself into our stink eye contest.

"Like shit. Did Zach say anything when he brought me home?"

"Yeah, he said something about Tequila."

"Wonderful. I'll get the details from him."

"You're a mess," Nate says.

"I think you'll be just fine," Angela says to me with a loving smile that's only slightly tinged with pity.

We kiss cheeks, and I head back upstairs to throw up one more time before I get back into bed.

CHAPTER 27

I'm propping the store's sandwich board sign out on the sidewalk when Zach walks up with a carry-out tray of iced coffees. "Happy Monday!" he says.

"Thanks," I say, carefully taking one out from the corner and trying not to disrupt the tray. There are four of them, but Cassie and I are the only ones working.

Zach reads my mind. "Two for Cassie."

"Of course," I say.

He holds the door for me despite carrying the tray of coffees and a bag of bagels. He stands close to me and smiles when I pass him. When we're inside Cassie immediately appears to grab her two coffees and a bagel.

"Feeling better this morning?" Zach asks.

"Better than yesterday? Yes. Thanks. Angela said you got me home. I appreciate it."

His smile falters.

"You don't remember?"

Oh. Shit. Did I have sex with Zach Saturday night? No. That's not right. He wouldn't have brought me home. I would have crashed upstairs if we hooked up.

"Saturday night? No, not much." I twist my face into a cringe.

"I guess that's not really a surprise." He sips his coffee.

"Hey, since when do you drink iced coffee?" I'm not really trying to change the subject; I've honestly never seen him drink iced coffee.

"I thought today was a good day to try something new," he says with a shrug.

Zach assumes his position behind the register.

"Come on," I nudge him. "I'm on the schedule, you're not. I'll take register."

He moves to the next stool. I find it strange he's here at all, when he could be upstairs, or wherever he's been hiding from me the last week, but he just sits there picking at his bagel and sipping iced coffee.

After an awkward moment we speak at the exact same time.

"Zach—"

"Alice—"

And then we laugh.

"Go ahead," I say.

"No, you."

"I was just going to ask you if you could fill me in on Saturday night."

"Sure. We had a good talk. Before you got completely wrecked. I thought you might remember that part."

"Sorry." More cringing. "Mind giving me a little bit more?"

"Yeah. You're in love with Chris Thompson, which was pretty clear from the beginning—"

"Zach, I'm really sorry. The timing and everything…"

"Don't worry about it. We're good."

"Are you sure?"

"I am. And you told me you're moving back to Pittsburgh at the end of July. And I told you I'm leaving, too."

"Really? Leaving State College? The store?"

"Yeah, I'm going to grad school. Berkeley."

"What? Really? When?"

"End of July. Like you. We'll do one last Arts Fest, and then we're out. Makes sense, right?"

"But what about the store?"

"My mom has agreed to be the 'manager,' but mostly Brian can handle anything that comes up. And Cassie will still be bossing everyone around. I sent your reports in to corporate and they get it."

"Wait, what? I'm not done with them. I was going to—"

"They're fine. They worked."

"But I wasn't ready. They weren't perfect! Zach, I was working so hard on those!"

"Alice, sometimes things don't have to be perfect. Actually, things rarely have to be perfect. I'm not sure anything is ever perfect. But what you did was good. Sometimes good is enough. They get we're not like a regular store. You did it."

"What did I do?"

"You got me out of here. You got me to Berkeley. You got me to grad school. You don't remember any of this?"

"Is that why we were doing tequila shots?"

"Yes. You remember the shots?"

Salt. Lick. Shot.

"Not really. Angela said you told her that's why I was so messed up."

"Do you think maybe you need to … ease up on drinking?"

"What are you saying, Zach? You think I have a problem?"

"I think you think you have a problem."

"What does that mean?"

"You said some stuff between shots."

I smirk at him. "I've always considered myself a binge drinker, not an alcoholic."

"I know. I read that article you wrote on that study for the paper last year."

"Right. So, what are you saying?"

"I'm saying maybe ease up on the 'binge drinking?' Maybe it's not so cute anymore?"

"Oh, come on, Zach. I've never been cute. Cute is not my thing."

"You know what I mean, Alice. You told me all about it. Chris doesn't drink and you're worried you're going to mess it up if you keep getting black-out drunk. You told me it's one of the reasons you wanted to go to New York instead of Pittsburgh."

"I did not say that!"

"You did."

"Really?"

"You said Meredith doesn't give you shit about your drinking, and Chris 'monitors' you. If you're worried about being with the person you want to be with … the person you love? … because you think he's going to impede your drinking, don't you think that's reason enough to stop?"

I make a low grumbling noise.

"You love it when I'm right, don't you?"

I stick my tongue out at him.

"Get a room!" Cassie yells from the stacks.

"Listen," Zach says. "I know you have all kinds of willpower. Obviously you have no problem watching what you eat."

"That's because she has an eating disorder," Cassie practically yells.

"I do not have an eating disorder. We've talked about this. Me sticking to my mom's plan is far healthier and more balanced than what a typical college student eats. Pizza? Fries? Bagels? There's hardly any nutritional value there at all."

"I know, Alice. I'm not saying you need to eat anything different. I'm saying maybe it's time to bring that discipline to drinking."

"He's saying you can use your freak powers for good instead of evil," Cassie says with a cackle, and then she drains her first iced coffee and launches the empty cup towards the trash can.

"Cassie, please, you have horrible aim," Zach tells her.

CHAPTER 28

Chris pulls up in front of Nate's in his old truck. He taught me to drive stick shift on it when I was in high school, even though he normally drove a motorcycle. All of the energy that's been rattling around in my body and ricocheting off my organs for the past three hours bursts out of me in the short sprint I do to meet him on the street.

"It took you forever!" I tell him before I wrap my arms around him and squeeze him tighter than I've ever squeezed anything in my life. His muscular frame can take it. "I thought you'd have your bike!"

"It's getting tuned up in the shop. No one rode it the whole time I was gone. That was a mistake." He holds me tightly. "It's so good to hold you. How has it only been two weeks?"

"Well, before that it was like five years, so…"

"Is Nate around?" Chris asks as we walk towards the house.

"No. Angela and I conspired to get him to change his schedule around, so he has to stay on campus with the soccer camp kids this weekend."

"Perfect."

I'm naked before I hit the top stair. He talks more during sex than I'm used to, telling me how much he loves my body, how much he loves me. It's intoxicating and unnerving. I've never slept with someone I've been in love with before. Because I've always been in love with him. And that has allowed for some distance with those guys. Sex may have been good with some of them, but my feelings were never involved. I never said, "I love you," during sex and now it comes out of my mouth in a guttural whisper with my lips pressed against Chris' ear. Damn. Meredith's right. I'm going to let myself get swallowed whole by him. And I'm going to enjoy it.

"Tell me about classes," I say after I wake up from a short nap next to his naked body.

"Not much to say. It's only been a week, but because it's a short term, it's been a long week."

"Is it hard being back?"

"In Pittsburgh? No, not really."

"No, in school."

"No, I was ready."

"Do you still see Johnny?"

"Yeah, of course. You know he moved into my apartment? The one above his studio."

I roll over and prop myself up on my elbow. "No. He never mentioned that."

"It's a little weird being back there. Sleeping on the couch."

"Gawd, that dusty couch! But you're getting your own place, right?"

"Not right away. I'm mostly staying out at my parents, but I crash at Johnny's sometimes."

I crinkle my nose.

"You really hated that place, didn't you, Princess?"

"This is not about me being a snob." I say in mock protest, as if he actually injured me.

He kisses my forehead.

"But seriously," I continue, playfully pushing him away. "If you're living at home or on Johnny's couch and I'm living at home..."

"Yeah?"

"How is this going to work?"

"You mean, where are we going to have sex?"

"Well, yeah ..."

"Where do you want to have sex?" he asks with a glint in his eye.

"I'm being serious," I tell him.

"I want to hear you say it. Where do you want to have sex with me?" He slips his hand between my legs.

"Stop!" I giggle, but I don't mean it.

He pulls his hand away from me. "No problem." He laughs.

"Hey! Don't stop!" I climb on top of him.

"Then tell me where you want to have sex with me."

"Everywhere!" I say straddling him. "Anywhere! Preferably somewhere bigger than this bed!"

I lean down to kiss him, our bare chests pressed together.

"I'll have it figured it out by August, okay?" he says.

I bite his ear, and he yelps.

*   *   *   *   *

After we're done a second time, we shower and get dressed. I've stocked the fridge with root beer, sparkling lemonade, and seltzer in several different flavors. I make a plate of cut veggies for us to take to the porch as a sort of fake cocktail hour.

"This is nice," he says, rocking slowly in the rocker, holding my pinky with his between us.

"It is," I say. "But how can it compare to being on tour, or living on a beach?"

"It's better."

I huff out a laugh because it sounds so cheesy, but he's serious.

"Well, first of all, you're here."

I bat my eyelashes at him playfully.

"And secondly, I was just done. I was done trying to be something I never wanted to be. You know that. I don't like being looked at. I don't like being on stage. I don't like living out of a suitcase. I didn't even really like being in Australia. Not after it wasn't new anymore. Not after it was clear Talia and I weren't going to last. Being in the band felt uncomfortable. Like I was wearing someone else's clothes. You know I was only in Wasted Pretty because Tess made me. It was always her band. Her thing."

"I know … but you're so good at it."

"At what?"

"What do you mean?"

"At being a rock star? I suck at being a rock star. I hate giving interviews. I hate being recognized."

"But what about guitar?"

"I'll always play guitar. I don't have to make my living doing it to do it."

"Yeah, but it's not the same."

"You're good at sex," he tells me with a smirk. "I certainly hope no one's paying you for it."

"Very funny," I say.

"I'm not kidding. Promise you'll only have sex with me, and I'll promise I'll only play guitar for you."

"Nice try," I tell him.

"What?"

"I'll promise to only have sex with you, if you promise only to have sex with me."

"Oh, well, that goes without saying, doesn't it?"

"Does it?"

"Alice, I don't want to have sex with anyone but you. And I don't want to play guitar for anyone but you."

"Well, I'm much more concerned about who you have sex with, but the guitar thing is sort of hot, too."

He leans over and kisses me. "Do we have plans tonight?"

I look at my watch. "I thought we'd have dinner in town, and we can stop at the store on the way. I'm sure Cassie would love to hit on you for a bit."

"And Zach?"

"No, I don't think Zach would want to hit on you."

"Ha ha," he fake laughs. "What about you?"

"I always want to hit on you. It's amazing I'm not constantly making a fool of myself."

"That's not what I mean." Chris raises his eyebrows at me.

"Zach and I are fine. We had a good talk. When I leave for Pittsburgh, he's leaving for California. We're happy for each other. Because we're friends, and friends get to be happy for each other."

"A friend you've had sex with…"

"Yes, I've had sex with Zach. And the night you played The Hook, he had asked me out. But I have not been with him since you've been back. Promise."

"Fair, now come have sex with me." He stands up, takes my hand, and we're back upstairs before I even have a chance to put my seltzer down.

CHAPTER 29*

It's Sunday morning before I know it. We didn't make it out of the house last night. No dinner in town or wandering the quiet streets at dusk, no stopping at the store to watch Cassie throw herself at Chris and laughing at his artful misdirection—an equal mix of distant chill and ingratiating humility. Just us, in this tiny bed. We ate Butterfly Bars and shakes for dinner in the middle of the night by the light cast from the warm sulphur glow of the streetlights.

Chris rolls over, sees I'm awake, and nuzzles into my shoulder. "Morning," he sighs.

"Morning."

"What time is it?"

"Just after 10. When do you have to go?"

"Not too late. I don't want to drive the truck that far in the dark."

"I get it. I'm surprised the truck made it this far to begin with." I interlace my fingers with his. "Do you want to go for a run?"

"Sure, if you want."

"Well, I know you're not a fan of swimming laps."

"No, I'm not. A run'll be good."

I'm too lost in conversation to hear Nate before he's knocking on the bedroom door. "Alice, you decent?"

I pull the sheet up over our chests. "No!"

"Can you get dressed? I want to show Scott the room."

"What are you talking about?" I yell.

"Just get dressed and come downstairs."

I wait until I hear his steps on the stairs before I say anything. "Shit!"

"He doesn't know I'm here?"

"I don't know what Angela told him. She just made sure he was sleeping at the dorms with the camp kids."

"He doesn't scare me, and he shouldn't scare you." Chris gets out of bed and pulls on a pair of Umbro shorts.

"I'm not scared of him. He's just such a pain in my ass."

I get dressed, and Chris and I go downstairs together. I can see the bitter look of disgust on Nate's face, but before he says anything, Chris greets the guy standing next to him.

"Hey, Scotty, long time."

"No shit! C.J. Thompson?!" Scott/Scotty/the guy next to Nate reaches out to shake Chris' hand. "I thought you moved to Hawaii to be a rock star."

"Is that what people are saying?" Chris asks with a knowing smirk.

"I think that's what I heard. What are you doing here?"

We all turn to look at Chris. As usual, he's not rattled.

"I'm finishing up my degree back at Pitt, and I'm here seeing Alice. Do you know Alice?"

"No. Hi." He puts his hand out to me. "I'm Scott Nash. I played with C.J. at Indiana his freshman year. Huge talent," he tells me, as if Chris isn't standing right there. "Also sort of a mess, but I always liked him."

I can tell Scott means well, but Chris flinches.

"Nice to meet you. I'm Alice, Nate's sister. What are you guys doing here?"

Nate hasn't acknowledged Chris at all even though Chris had initially extended his hand.

"Scott's moving in. I wanted to show him the room."

"Really, what happened to Dan-o?"

"Dan got a new job at Lafayette, so I got bumped up to head assistant and Scott's taking my place. He needs the room July 1st, Alice, so please tell me you've figured out where you're going next."

Now Chris and I both flinch, which is weird, but I have no time to worry about him.

"What? You said I could have the room until August 1st. I can't just … move. That's like two weeks from now!"

"Chill out, Alice. Don't make a scene. Aren't you just moving back to dad's? Does it really matter when you go?"

"It does to me!"

"Listen," Scott says, "I don't want to screw anything up for anyone—"

"It's fine, really," Nate says, steely and cold. "Right Alice?"

"Yeah, whatever. Nothing like missing my last Arts Fest."

"Seriously, I don't mean to mess you up," Scott says.

I turn my attention to him. "Really, it's fine. This is absolutely not about you."

We stand at the bottom of the steps awkwardly until Chris puts one hand on the small of my back and reaches out his other to shake Scott's. "Really good to see you, man. We were just headed out for a run."

"Yeah, I'll get your number from Nate. I'd like to be back in touch. You are some kind of rock star aren't you? Or was that all rumor shit?"

"I played music for a while," he says with a nod.

"And whatever happened with you and...was it Stacy?"

"Stephanie." Chris says quietly.

It feels like a punch to my gut. I don't want to think about Chris' college girlfriend right now and the possibility that she had his kid.

"Right, Stephanie. She was wild!" Scott says, and then he turns to me. "Sorry."

"Whatever," I say.

"We're not in touch," Chris tells Scotty. "Nate, always a pleasure."

This time Nate shakes Chris' hand, probably reveling in the fact that Chris' past is being thrown in his face.

I let the screen door slam behind me and kick my leg up on the porch railing to stretch.

"You okay?" Chris asks.

"I don't know, are you?"

"Yeah, I guess," he says.

I keep stretching.

"I was in touch with Stephanie. A few years ago," he tells me.

"Okay," I say.

I don't really want to know more. I don't want to know if she kept the baby and if it was his. I do quick math. The kid would be around eight now. I used to babysit an eight-year-old. Eight-year-olds know things. They're like little, fully formed people who need their dads. Oh gawd, is he a dad?

"She wasn't pregnant."

"What?" I whip around.

"She wasn't pregnant. It was a false alarm."

"I—But—You—"

"I know."

"That's a lot to take in."

Stephanie "being pregnant" was why Chris left Indiana, why he stopped drinking, and at least one of the reasons we didn't have sex when we were "together" or whatever we were when I was in high school.

"That 'pregnancy' changed the course of your life," I say with air-quotes.

"Probably for the better," he says.

"I guess."

"Seriously, are you okay? We can talk about this if you want."

"I mean, what's there to talk about? I guess it's better than you having a kid, right?"

"Definitely."

"But like, are you sure?"

"What do you mean?"

"Are you sure she doesn't have a kid? Doesn't have your kid? Are you sure she's not lying?"

"Well," he pauses, as if this option never occurred to him. He's very good at taking things as they come. He doesn't seem to assume people are lying to him the way I always do. I don't know if that makes him trusting or just lazy. "I mean she doesn't have a kid, so…"

"Okay," I say with a shrug, even though I'm not sure that's true. But if he doesn't want to think about it, neither do I. "To be honest, I think the more pressing issue is I'm getting kicked out of my room in two weeks."

"You really don't want to come back to Pittsburgh, do you?"

"That's not it. It's just … I thought I had time. I thought …"

"You thought you might figure something else out?"

"No. That's not it. I'm coming back. I just … Zach and I had plans for the store during Arts Fest, and I thought I had more time to get used to the idea."

"Yeah, I get it. I thought I had time, too."

"What does that mean?" I put my other leg up on the railing and look over at him. His foot is also on the railing and his nose is to his knee. I can't see his eyes.

"You know, to figure out where I'm going to live. I know you don't want to sneak around, but, if I got myself a place, maybe you could just practice omission and it would be less like sneaking around."

I put both feet on the ground and turn towards him. He twists his body so his cheek is on his thigh. "You know I'm going to practice omission. I'm not going to tell my parents we're together, so as long as neither of them sees us together, they can't use our relationship to get at each other. But I am going to be living with my dad, and if you're living at your parents …"

"I know. It's not ideal."

"Not ideal? It's worse than when I was in high school. At least you had your own place then. Where are we even going to hang out?"

"I'll figure something out."

I put my face in my hands and make a noise that sounds something like a growl. I expect Chris to comfort me, but he just keeps stretching. I sit in a rocker and wait for him to finish.

"You still up for a run?" he asks.

"Sure. Whatever."

He doesn't ask if I'm okay, he just steps off the porch. And I follow him.

*   *   *   *   *

I thought I would feel sluggish on the run, but without my ever-present low-grade morning hangover, and fueled by rage at Nate, I am able to easily keep up with Chris, who is in amazing shape. I even pass him when I sprint at the end. We're both panting and dripping with sweat when we get back to the house.

"I'm starving," Chris says while he stretches on the little patch of grass out front.

I grunt something in response. I'm edgy and jittery.

"Should we go somewhere to eat?" he asks. "Or do you just want to do shakes?"

It's then I realize I haven't had real food in over twenty-four hours.

"Yeah, I could do breakfast. You should experience The Waffle Shop while you're up here." And then I think, I should experience it one last time. I can't believe my tour of lasts is starting today.

"Cool," he says, but I can almost hear the constriction in his chest. Something's not right.

"I'm going to do another loop around the block to cool down," I say.

"I'll come with you," he says standing up.

"No, I'm gonna go alone. You grab a shower. I'll be back in a few."

"Princess?"

I turn back to face him but don't say anything.

"What's wrong?"

"You tell me."

"Alice."

"What? Something's off."

"You're the one who's upset about moving back."

"No, it's something more. Are you embarrassed by me?"

"No! What are you talking about?"

"That Scott guy. Are you embarrassed that you got caught with me? Here? When he thought you were a rock star… in Hawaii?"

"I don't care about that shit. You do."

"Are you sure? Are you sure you're ready to fade into oblivion? An undergrad at Pitt? No soccer team? No band? Just a regular guy?"

"Yes! How many times do I have to tell you? I don't need any of that. I'm tired. Touring and playing shows all over Australia? That's exhausting enough. But maintaining my sobriety through all of it is a whole other thing. I want to fade into oblivion. I'm ready to fade into oblivion. I think it's you who doesn't want me to. You don't want to be with just some guy. You want to date a rock star and move to New York City. You want to walk into a bar and turn heads. And honestly, you turn heads with or without me, so if that's what you want, you should go. If you're going to be this miserable in Pittsburgh, figure something else out. I love you, but I won't force you into a life you don't want."

I purse my lips and take a deep breath through my nose. My nostrils flare so wide I can actually see them myself.

"I'll be back in five," I finally say, and jog away without waiting for an answer.

I take longer than five. I loop the block twice, walking not jogging, looking at this place I'm about to no longer live. When I get back to my room, Chris has showered and dressed. He's made my bed and is sitting on the edge of it, like he's trying not to mess it up, his hair damp and plastered to his forehead. His bag's packed at his feet. There's a sense of finality to the tidiness of it all. I don't know what to say when my lower lip starts to tremble and a cry escapes from my mouth. I think it startles him as much as it startles me. He's off the bed and hugging me before I can push him away.

"No, I'm all sweaty," I say. "And snotty!"

"I don't care," he says with a laugh.

"But you're all clean!"

"I don't care. You're crying. Why are you crying?"

"Something's off," I manage to say. "Something's not right."

"What do you mean?"

"Are you sure there's nothing you're not telling me?"

"Is this about Stephanie?"

"No. I don't think so."

"There's nothing. Remember, I'm the one who doesn't lie to you."

I do remember. Something inside me settles.

"Except about being able to see me from the stage," I say with a little laugh. The panic in me seems to have left just as swiftly as it came on.

"Except for that," he says with a laugh of his own. "So, waffles for breakfast?"

"Sure. Let me shower first."

"I could do with another shower," he says, taking off his shirt. He follows me to the bathroom.

CHAPTER 30

The sun is warm, but the light is soft this late in the day. Still, the rays sparkle when they hit the emerald water of The Quarry like little diamonds floating on the surface. Chris is jumping with Cassie, and Zach and I are lying on our towels. I've just done laps the long way across the water to work off my Waffle Shop breakfast, and I'm spent.

"I can't believe this is it. This might be my last time at The Quarry," I say, my cheek flat on my towel, Zach's cheek flat on a his a few feet away.

"Don't think like that. You still have a few weeks."

"I guess," I say.

On the edge of my vision, I see a fat, green caterpillar, the kind that looks like an alien, inching along. I prop my chin up on my hands to watch it. "Did you know I used to think caterpillars just grew wings when they were in their cocoons?"

"You mean in their chrysalises?"

"Yeah, when I was a kid, I thought the cocoon–sorry, the chrysalis– was like a sleeping bag, and the caterpillar crawled in and just slept while the wings grew, like the way girls slowly get boobs over time."

"That's such a … gentle read of the situation."

"Tell me about it. The caterpillars turn to actual mush. Goop. Soup. It's so gross and violent, but in, like, a slow burn way, you know? I think I'm goop right now. I think this summer is my goop phase. I thought I was already a butterfly when I got to college, 'cause you know, boobs, but I think right now I'm as much of a mess as I've ever been."

"You're not that much of a mess. Just because you didn't get a fellowship doesn't mean it's all over for you. Trust me."

"If you say so, Zach. And I'm really sorry about missing Arts Fest."

"Don't worry about it," he tells me. "And anyway, maybe you could come back for the weekend?"

"I guess. But people say shit like that, like 'I'll be back all the time!' and then life happens, and you never see them again."

"You'll be two hours away. You can come back if you want."

"But then you'll be 2500 miles away, and I'll never see you again either."

"Alice…"

"No, Zach, you've been really good to me. Even when I was shitty to you. I can be such a bitch."

"You're not a bitch, Alice."

"Alice? Alice is definitely a bitch!" Cassie says with a laugh. She and Chris are dripping wet, and their feet and ankles are covered in dirt and pebbles from climbing up the side of the quarry.

"Shut up, Cassie." I sit up and throw a pebble at her knee.

"No really," she turns to Chris, "I don't see what you see in her. She's so perfect and pretty and smart and she actually swims laps when she's supposed to be having fun. Really, you could do soooo much better!" She wraps a towel around her waist and flips her hair like she's a supermodel.

"I can assure you, Cassie, I could do no better than Alice," Chris says, sitting next to me on his own towel. "There is no better."

"Okay, this is a little much," I tell them. "I'm not dead, just leaving town."

"Yeah, well, with you and Zach both leaving town, this should be my funeral."

"Oh, come here, Cassie!" I pull her onto my lap. "I'll come back and see you. And I'm sure Zach will come back during breaks."

"Blah, blah, blah," she says, but she puts her head on my shoulder, and I make a promise to myself to follow through on the things people say in moments like this. The things they say to make everything okay, even when things are actually very messy.

I have to admit, I feel warm inside. Happy. With Chris and Zach getting along and Cassie on my lap, if this is my last time at The Quarry, it will be a good way to remember it.

"So, you started classes already?" Zach asks Chris.

"Yeah, just knocking some stuff out during the summer."

"What are you taking?" Zach asks.

Chris shifts on his towel. "Just some communications stuff. Quickest way to finish my degree."

"Cool. Cool," Zach says. "Then what?"

"Excuse me?" Chris asks. More shifting.

So much for everyone getting along. "I think he means what are you going to do after you get your degree?"

"Well, I'm not running off to grad school, if that's what you mean. I'm never going to be a philosophy professor."

No one says anything until Cassie pipes up. "This got awkward fast."

"I'm sorry," Zach says. "I didn't mean to pry."

"No, sorry, my bad," Chris says. "Of course you didn't."

I let out a breath too loudly, mostly because Zach seems to be really trying, and Chris seems to really be on edge.

"I'm hungry!" Cassie announces.

She gets up to fish a sub out of the bag she brought up from the sub shop. She hands one to Chris and one to Zach. I take a bar out of my bag. We eat silently and watch as the high school boys in their cutoffs jump off the ledge, whooping and jeering each other on.

It didn't occur to me how much I needed Zach to forgive me until he did. It didn't occur to me how much I needed him and Chris to get along until we went by the store after breakfast and they concocted this plan for today. I guess I thought if they could get along, there'd be hope anyone could. Maybe I could tell my parents about Chris, and maybe they wouldn't totally make it all about them. Maybe everything would work out. But now I can't tell whether Zach and Chris are getting along or not. I guess it's good they even bothered to try.

"I need to get going," Chris says, as he wraps up the paper his sub came in and wipes his mouth with a napkin.

"Don't gooooo," Cassie croons. "You can't leave me here with these two losers."

"I think you'll be fine," he says. He points to the high school kids. "I think the guy with the mullet has been checking you out."

Cassie sticks her finger in her mouth and pretends to vomit at the suggestion.

Chris and Zach stand up and shake hands. It warms my heart, which is also breaking.

I stand up, too. "I'll walk you down to the truck."

We don't say anything on the walk, but he wraps his pinkie around mine and my lip starts to tremble again.

"Two weeks," he says quietly.

"I know," I say.

He gets into the driver's seat and rolls down the window. "I gotta ask…"

"What?"

"Are you sure you shouldn't be with someone like Zach?"

"I repeat: 'What?'!"

"You know, someone book smart, Jewish, with a five-year plan? Probably a ten-year plan?"

"Chris. Is that what this is about?"

"What 'what' is about?"

"You've been acting a little weird."

"Have I?"

"Yeah. I'm not choosing between you and him. You know that, right?"

"What are you choosing between?"

The question stops me cold. It's like a cloud has just passed between me and the sun. I actually look up, but there's not a cloud in the sky. What I'm choosing between is Chris' dream and mine. I could say the choice was made for me. But if Chris weren't going to be in Pittsburgh, would I really be going back there? Or would I find a way to make something else work?

"Princess?"

I snap out of it. "Nothing, I'm not choosing *between* anything. I'm coming home. And I love you." At least that part is not a lie.

"I love you, too. See you in two weeks."

"Two weeks," I say.

CHAPTER 31

For our last Friday lunch in State College, Burton takes us to The Tavern. It's me, Nate and Angela, and Zach. Cassie wanted to come, but Zach left her and Brian in charge of the store and told her she could play whatever she wanted to on the sound system. It's dark and cool in The Tavern, a stark contrast to the sticky late June day outside. I've always felt like the restaurant, with its dark wood and low ceilings, was underground, even though it isn't.

"I don't understand why you don't come home with me today," Burton says after we order. "You've had four years here. You really need two more days?"

Before I can answer, Nate steps in. "I have Monday off, so I'm bringing her home Sunday night," he says. "I'm coming home to have dinner with mom anyway."

That stops the conversation cold. While I'm happy to let Burton and Nate bicker—because it takes the heat off of me—it does make it awkward for everyone else. Angela puts her hand on mine under the table and gives it a little squeeze. I look across the table to Zach.

"And we have big plans for the weekend, anyway," Zach says, answering the plea in my eyes.

It works. The conversation goes back to its normal flow. Zach tells Burton about the festivities the store has planned, and Angela chimes in saying how much she's going to miss me and how she wants every last minute possible to hang out with me. I know they're doing it mostly to get Burton off my back, but they say some really nice things about me which I guess I really need to hear. Because this is it; I'm really moving back there. Burton came up for lunch last Friday and took a bunch of my boxes with him. He'll take the rest of my boxes today, leaving me with just a duffle full of stuff for the weekend. It's hard not to feel like a failure. Like I was made for school, but I'm just going to flounder in the real world. I focus on the fact that I don't have to be nervous. No first-day jitters for the radio station, because even though I haven't been back in a while, I basically grew up there. And Chris. I focus on Chris. We still haven't figured out the logistics, but we'll be in the same city. That's something to look forward to, even if I've had to make peace with the fact that we'll be sneaking around like kids.

"You're going to have your hands full," Burton says, catching me off guard.

"What? Me? With what?"

"The summer interns, they're even bigger idiots than normal this year."

"You say that every year," I tell him.

"Well, they're all yours as of Monday morning, so get ready."

"Great," I say.

After lunch, Zach heads back to the store, and my father drives Nate, Angela, and me up to the house. Nate and I bring my boxes to the porch, and my dad loads them into the Caprice.

"When should I expect you?" Burton asks me.

I look to Nate.

"Not 'til after dinner with mom on Sunday," he says.

My dad grimaces. He grimaces at any mention of my mom. This is just another complication I'm walking into. I give my dad a hug and then take a seat next to Angela on the porch. Nate joins us after Burton pulls away.

"Good luck with that," Nate says.

"With what?" I ask.

"With him. With mom. The station. Your life."

"Uh, thanks," I say.

"Be nice," Angela gently chides him.

"I am being nice," he says.

"Nate, why haven't you mentioned Chris to Dad?"

"Two reasons," he says.

"And they are?"

"You have enough on your plate as it is."

"And?"

"And, you and Chris are going to fuck everything up on your own without Dad needing to be involved."

"Nate!" Angela chides more strongly.

"Nice." I say.

"I'm serious," Nate says, with no edge in his voice at all. "If I thought you and C.J. Thompson were going to survive being in the same city, I might say something to Dad. But it's not worth you dealing with Burton's B.S. when you're going to figure it out on your own."

"Figure what out?"

"He's just not right for you." Again, I expect Nate to sound mean or cruel or bitter, but he doesn't. He sounds matter-of-fact. Almost caring.

"How can you say that? You barely know him. You barely know me."

"Alice, I've known you your whole life. I've lived with you for the last nine months. As for C.J.—"

"Stop calling him that."

"Fine, as for Chris, I know what I need to know. You're both retreating to Pittsburgh to figure stuff out, but you will figure that stuff out. He won't."

I work hard not to sound hurt or defensive. Or worse, convinced. "I don't know how you can say that."

"Because I know guys like Chris, I've known them all my life. And I've known Chris since high school, too. All talent, no follow-through. That only carries you so far. He never worked hard. He never learned how because he didn't need to. But soccer talent doesn't get you anything in the real world. I'm not coaching because of my talent; I'm coaching because I learned what I needed to learn to make a career out of it."

"I don't think he wants a career in soccer." There's a slight whine in my voice, and I wish there weren't.

"It's the same with his music. All talent, no craft."

"Well, I think he's done with music, too."

"Okay, so what exactly is next for him?"

"I actually don't know. But I don't see how that matters."

"It matters. You'll see. It matters."

I look at Angela for some clarity, but she knows when to stay out of things between me and Nate.

"If you say so," I say. "I'm going to take a nap."

CHAPTER·32·

We start Saturday night at The Hook. It's me, Cassie, Zach, Brian, Angela, and a few other people from the store. Nate's not with us because he's doing an overnight in the dorms with the soccer camp kids so he can have Monday off. After the two guys with guitars are done with their set, I get control of the jukebox. I let people buy me drinks, but I pick all the music myself. Zach stays close, but not too close, like he's keeping tabs on me to make sure I'm not breaking down. But part of me is breaking down. Nate's words have been bouncing around in my head since yesterday. I hate how he ignores me most of the time, is mean to me the rest of the time, and then every once in a while drops this really insightful wisdom on me, like he's been paying attention the whole time. Like he can see things so clearly that I should have been able to see all along. Or that I have seen, but had hoped weren't true, or at the very least were invisible to others.

"Time to move on," Zach says, handing me a red plastic cup of water.

"What does that mean?"

"You didn't think we were going to spend the whole night at The Hook, did you?"

"Uhh, I guess I did…"

"Let's go, Alice."

"Where to?"

"You'll see."

I go over to the bar and give Uncle Stu a big hug goodbye. He looks so much like Rod. I must be drunker than I realize, because I actually think I'm hugging Rod, like he's still here and he's telling me everything will be okay. Zach belongs in California; I belong in Pittsburgh; Cassie will be okay without us and will get out of here as soon as she graduates. When Stu finally releases me, there are tears in my eyes.

"It's going to be fine," he says. "You're going to be fine."

"Thanks, Rod, I mean, Stu. Sorry. I'm so sorry."

"It's okay. You're going to be fine."

"Thanks, I needed to hear that."

"No problem, kid. We'll miss you, but you can always come home."

Home. I let out an ugly cry.

"Oh, sorry, kid," Stu says.

"That's okay," Zach says, slinging his arm around my shoulder. "We got her, Uncle Stu."

"Zach, where are we going?" I ask.

"Just come with me," he says, leading me outside to the street where everyone else has already started walking up College Ave. "Do you trust me?"

I wipe the leftover Rod/Stu tears out of the corner of my eyes and straighten my back.

"Yes," I say, squeezing my eyes shut, willing the drunk tears to stop. "Always. I've always trusted you. I will always trust you. You've been so good to me, Zach. I'm so sorry—"

"Nope," Zach says, holding up his hands to stop me. "No sorries tonight, Alice. You've always been good to me, too. And good for me."

"Have I?"

We're not walking. We're standing close, and I'm holding his right hand in mine. I've lost sight of everyone else.

"You really have. You never promised me anything you couldn't deliver. You didn't lead me on. I fell for you, that was my mistake."

"But Zach, it wasn't a mistake. It was just bad timing. You know that, right? You're great."

"Don't Alice. Not tonight. We had years to figure it out, it wasn't timing. I should have said something earlier. I think too much about everything. So, no sorries tonight and no lies. We're good."

"You're the best, Zach. I'm going to miss you."

"I'll miss you, too."

Zach and I hug and when I look over his shoulder, I see Cassie standing there, hip cocked, arms folded across her chest.

"Ew. Gross. Get a room!"

"Ha ha, Cassie. I'm sure you're going to miss saying that," I say.

"Well, you're going to miss Grilled Stickies, if you don't get a move on it!"

"Grilled Stickies?! No way! Wait! I can't eat Grilled Stickies! I'm definitely not drunk enough!"

"No farewell tour is complete without Grilled Stickies," Zach says.

"Here," Cassie holds out her red Solo cup, and I take a drink.

"Cassie! This is straight vodka."

"Actually," she says with a laugh, "it's on the rocks."

Zach and Cassie flank me—he with an arm around my shoulder, she, with an arm around my waist—and I know I'm going to miss them even more than I am capable of comprehending in my current state.

When we get to the diner our friends are spread across two tables in the back. We sit down just as the waitress brings the Grilled Stickies, an order for each of us, all à la mode.

"I can't eat a whole order!" I say. "A la mode!"

"Drink more," Brian says, nodding to Cassie's red plastic cup in my hand. "You'll end up puking them all up anyway."

"For the last fucking time, I'm not bulimic!"

"I didn't say you were," Brian says. "I don't think you are. I think you're an alcoholic."

The whole table laughs except Zach.

"Shut it, Brian," he says.

Zach pays the bill with the store card because he says this is my official goodbye. He makes a sweet but sappy toast with a milkshake he ordered, as if a cross between a cinnamon roll and a sticky bun covered in ice cream isn't enough for one night. Everyone claps and says nice things about me. We all go back to Zach's place, just like we always do, as if this is any other night. And it's nice, because with all the toasts and sappy stuff out of the way, it does feel like a regular night, and I can enjoy myself. Until I throw up in the kitchen sink, and Zach puts me to bed on the green Power Couch.

CHAPTER 33

Cassie wakes me up by pretending to be a mother cat grooming me. She does that sometimes. I might even miss it, eventually, but I shove her away.

"Meeeooow," she says, drawing the word out like a whine.

"Morning Cassie," I say with a fuzzy tongue and cottonmouth. She is noticeably showered and not in the same clothes she wore out last night. I wonder who walked her home. I hope she didn't go alone. I don't know who's going to walk her home, now that I won't be here.

"Meeeeoooooowwww," she whines again.

"Uh. Not today, Cassie. Today—oh shit! What time is it?!"

She doesn't answer, just shrugs and pantomimes being a cat.

"What's going on out here?" Zach is standing in his bedroom doorway. His hair is a tousled mess. I also notice Angela curled up in the orange wingback chair. She shifts and pulls a multi-colored blanket that Zach's mom crocheted over her head.

"Cassie thinks she's a cat," I tell Zach.

"Great," he says.

"Meow," Cassie says and then points to the door.

"I think she's trying to tell us something," I say.

"Come on, idiots." Cassie hops up onto her two human legs and is back to her bitter self. "We gotta get to The Waffle Shop, if we're going to eat before we have to open."

"Right," Zach says, sleep in his groggy voice.

"What?" I ask.

"Waffle Shop, final stop on your farewell tour," Cassie informs me.

"Is this something I agreed to?" I ask.

They both nod.

"Was I sober when I agreed to it?"

They both shake their heads.

"I can't, I'm sorry. I'm having dinner at my mom's tonight. I can't start the day at The Waffle Shop. She'll smell the sugar on me."

"But Alice, it's your last day here," Zach says. "You're not going to just eat bars and shakes are you?"

"Oh, I am. On the heels of Grilled Stickies, which I can sort of still taste? Yes, I'll stick to Butterfly Food today."

"Gross!" says Cassie.

"Alice, eventually you're going to have to eat more than one meal a day."

"Please, Zach, not this. Not this morning. Not today."

"There's not going to be another day," he reminds me. "And if no one else is going to express concern for you, I will."

"Come on, Zach." I get up from the couch and move to the kitchen area where I scavenge for my stash of bars.

"No, you come on, Alice. This isn't about health or nutrition or weight, this is about control."

"You're not making sense," I say, not turning around.

"You know there are calories in beer, right? And carbs. And sugars. And whatever else you count, right?"

"Don't remind me," I say.

"So, you'll break your diet for—"

"It's not a diet, it's a meal plan," I correct him, parroting my mother's words.

"Right. A meal plan. Whatever. Do you think she knows about all the alcohol you consume?"

"No," I turn around. "She doesn't."

"Exactly. You break your 'plan' for shitloads of alcohol, but you won't come to The Waffle Shop with us?"

"What's your point, Zach?" I turn back to the cupboard. I don't want to sound as annoyed as I do. Not because I'm not annoyed, just because I don't want him to know I'm annoyed.

"You drink so you have an excuse to break the rules that you've set up for yourself."

"I don't know what you're talking about," I say over my shoulder. "Are you stoned?"

"It's about control," he says. "Everything for you is about control. Even our relationship was about control. You knew I wouldn't tell anyone, so you kept coming around."

I whip around to face him. "Zach!"

He doesn't say anything.

Angela pushes the blanket off her head. "I knew."

"I suspected," Cassie chimes in. "But, still, gross."

"Seriously? Zach?"

"Seriously. Alice."

"One day you're going to come up against something, or someone, you can't control. Then what? It's why you don't want to move home. Because you can't control Burton."

"Zach! You're a philosopher not a psychologist. No need to analyze me. I'm not going to The Waffle Shop. Nothing you say is going to make me change my mind, and anything else you do say is going to piss me off more."

"Alice, I'm not trying to piss you off. I'm only saying this because I care about you."

"Right, I get that. But I don't have to justify myself to you. From what I remember, last night was lovely. Let's leave it like that. I gotta get home anyway."

"No one else has anything to say about this?" Zach asks Cassie and Angela.

"I don't," Cassie says quickly.

We all look at Angela.

"I mean…" she says cautiously and trails off.

"What?!" I snap at her.

"I'd say all Burtons have an issue with control, so it's possible you wouldn't realize if you had a problem. Like, it would seem normal to you. So, like, it wouldn't be your fault."

"Seriously, Angela?" I unwrap a bar, gather what's left of my stash, and throw it in my bag. "I gotta get out of here. Love you all bunches. It's been real."

Zach moves between me and the door.

"Really Zach? You're going to hold me hostage?"

"Of course not. I just want you to understand how much I care about you. If something happened to you, and I hadn't tried my hardest, I couldn't forgive myself."

There's something about the sincerity in his tone that shakes me out of my hangover and defensiveness.

"What do you think is going to happen to me?"

"Well, I don't think you eat enough."

"I assure you, and have assured you in the past, what I eat is far more healthy than what most college students eat. My mom has designed the products really well. The whole time she was testing the products I went to more check-ups than anyone I know."

"But that was years ago."

"And I'm still fine."

"But also…" Zach looks like he's in pain. Is it pain on my behalf? Or does he think I'm going to hit him?

"Yes?"

"But also, you're not going to be able to control Chris Thompson. And I'm worried you're following him home, and it's going to end badly."

My instinct is to slap Zach. Or at least throw my bag at him. Lash out in some physical way. I've never had an impulse like this before. At least not towards Zach, the kindest, most laid-back person I've ever known who has only ever been accommodating to me. I realize he is both worried I might hit him and is possibly in pain on my behalf. It's this realization that breaks me.

"You're right," I say, quietly, so only he can hear me. "It might. But I still have to try."

He gives me a hug and lets me pass.

CHAPTER 34

After what I know will be my last swim at the campus pool, I squeeze out my suit and put it in a sandwich bag. It's so humid today, there won't be enough time for it to dry before Nate and I take off for Pittsburgh. Except I don't actually know when we're taking off, because Nate just said to be ready so we can leave whenever he's able to get away, and I don't really know what that means. All I can do is wait around the house and be ready. I call Meredith, and miraculously, she picks up.

"So, this is really it?" she asks. "No last-minute change of plans?"

"I wouldn't call this a plan," I say. "I'd call this a last resort. But no, no change of destination."

"Are you sad? You sound sad."

"No. Maybe. I don't know. It doesn't feel real. I haven't been back there in so long; I don't know what to expect. And now I just want to go, but I have no idea when we're leaving."

"Dinner at Lois' right?"

"Yeah, that's our first stop. And then my dad's."

"You might as well start calling his place home."

"I guess."

"And you start at the station tomorrow?"

"Yeah, he's giving me the summer interns again. Like, the exact same thing I did five years ago. Like, I don't even know how this is going to be beneficial at all to my J-School applications. But he says it's just for the summer, and then I can do some reporting. Or the traffic.

Or the weather. Who knows? He'll change his mind six times before then."

"Oh, you'd be a great weather girl!" Meredith says with a heavy laugh. "You're even pretty enough to do it on TV."

"Thanks … I think."

"Have you said all your goodbyes?"

"Yeah, I went out with Zach and Cassie and Angela last night and then, this morning…Zach said some stuff."

"Oh gawd, he's in love with you, isn't he?"

"No... I mean, he cares about me, but no, not love, not like that."

"So, what did he say?"

"He thinks the thing with Chris is going to explode. And Nate does, too. Basically, everyone is against this working out."

"I mean… you're not wrong."

"Thanks, Meredith."

"Well, I agree with them. I'm sorry."

"No, you're not."

"You're right, I'm not. Just feels good to know I'm not alone. Are you going to listen to Zach? Or Nate?"

"You mean, break up with Chris? No."

"Right, so now what?"

"I don't know. I guess I'm just sad."

"Well, at least when your relationship implodes, I'll have 'I told you so' buddies."

"Thanks, Meredith, you're a peach."

"I'm always here for you."

We get off the phone and I try Chris at his parents' house. His mom tells me he's out and asks for my number.

"He has it," I say. "But I'm not sure I'll be around. Maybe I'll try him later."

"Well, not too late," she says.

"Right, I know." I'm not allowed to call his house after nine at night. And it's just plain weird talking to his mom. Who seems perfectly nice, but like, it's just weird.

I wander around the house, stopping in each room to take a picture in my mind of what it looks like, feels like, smells like. The hardwood is slick but forgiving under my bare feet. I've already changed the sheets on my bed so they're fresh for Scott/Scotty, but I sit on the edge as delicately as someone who is 5'10" can, and memorize the space around me, how far it is to the window, the desk, the door. I'm zoning out, looking at myself in the mirror when I hear the cordless ring downstairs. I rush to get it, noting how large I feel on these steps made for people who were—what? smaller in the 1800s?—and grab the phone.

It's Chris.

"Hey," he says.

"Hey," I say. And all the melancholy and all the confusion and everything else just leaves my body.

"When are you outta there?"

"I don't know. I'm on Nate's very fuzzy timetable."

"Are you ready?"

"I am." Hearing his voice makes me ready. "I'm just bored."

"How was last night?"

"It was fun. They got me to eat Grilled Stickies."

"Did they really?"

"Yeah. They are really good."

"Glad you had a good night."

"What are you up to?"

"I was out playing pick-up with Johnny earlier, and I'm just staying in tonight. Are you sure I can't see you?"

"I can't make any plans. I don't know when we're getting in. And we're having dinner at my mom's. Tomorrow night?"

"Yeah. Okay."

"What time are you done with class?" I ask. "I won't have a car, so we'll have to figure out where to meet and everything. It's not like you can pick me up at the station. Maybe we can meet at Johnny's? I can catch a ride with him."

"Uhhh ... that could work."

"You okay?"

"Yeah. Fine. Let's plan on that. Listen, my mom needs the phone. Do you still have your own line at home?"

"No, my mom was using it for her business, so my dad stopped paying for it when she moved out. I'm going to try to get it put back in once I'm settled. Or maybe I should just get a cell phone?"

"Maybe," he says. And then his voice quivers a little when he asks, "Listen, will you call me when you get in tonight?"

"Yeah, sure. You okay?"

"Uh-huh. But before nine, right?"

"I know. Before nine."

"Alright, I'll talk to you tonight. Love you."

"Love you, too."

CHAPTER 35

Nate and I pull into the parking lot at my mom's building on Walnut Street just after seven, but because it's the tail end of July, it's still light out. Nate knows the code to the entryway, so we don't have to ring or knock to be let in. The door to her condo is cracked open slightly. I feel like I'm breaking and entering because I've never been here before, but Nate, of course, seems right at home. The large white peninsula that separates the very white kitchen from the equally white living room is set in her trademark polished-but-casual style: small salads are on glass salad plates, bumpy clear glass goblets hold sparkling water with lime wedges, there's no bread. She greets us with hugs. I pull away quickly and awkwardly. Nate's lasts longer.

"I'm so glad to have you here. I can't believe I had to wait years to have both my kids in my home."

It feels like a dig, and I respond with a pained smile.

"Alice, did Meredith tell you I saw her last month?"

"She did. She took me to the raw vegan place you took her."

"Wasn't it amazing?" my mom coos.

"It was … um …" I consider lying just to avoid the conversation, but I decide on honesty. "… not my thing."

"Oh really? Honey, you should definitely try to make peace with raw food. It's so good for you. And cleansing."

"I guess."

"Well, you look good, that's for sure."

I know 'You look good' is the nicest thing she can say to someone, so my smile is less pained this time.

"Let's sit!"

It's clear she and Nate have their regular seats, back to the living room, so I take the stool on the end. Unlike the two they sit in, this one doesn't have a back.

"How is Angela?" My mom asks. "I'm sorry she couldn't come."

"She's fine," Nate says, "just busy teaching. Our schedules are hard to line up in the summer."

"And you, Alice, are you seeing anyone?"

Nate turns towards me, his back to our mom, and raises his eyebrows.

"Mom, you just saw me last month. It's not like it's been years."

"Well, eventually you'll meet someone, won't you? It could have happened last week!"

"It didn't," I tell her, which is vaguely true.

"I'm so glad you're back here for a while," she says. "I'm just sorry you can't stay here with me."

"Well, you should have thought of that before you bought a one-bedroom condo," I say.

"Alice!" Nate and my mother chide me in unison.

"Sorry, that was rude."

"It really was," Nate says.

"I said, 'I'm sorry.'"

"I never expected you to move back," my mom says. "I really thought you were done with Pittsburgh. And with how much time I spend on the road, it didn't make sense to get a bigger place."

"I know. That was shitty of me. It makes sense for me to live with dad anyway, if I'm going to be commuting with him."

"Well, this place is walkable to the station, if you ever want to spend the night on the couch. Or use the place while I'm away."

This seems like a genuinely nice—and potentially very helpful offer. "Thanks, Mom."

The rest of the meal is uneventful, though not necessarily enjoyable. Thankfully, Lois doesn't force raw food on us. She grills the salmon to perfection, but I'm distracted by the fact that this is home now, if not this apartment, this city. Nate and my mom banter about food and the upcoming soccer season and Scott/Scotty, the new roommate, and a bunch of house-related stuff, and I just chew slowly and occasionally nod my head.

Lois serves us fruit salad for dessert, and then laments that we have to leave so quickly. It hasn't felt quick at all to me.

"I just want to get settled in at home," I say.

She flinches when I use the word 'home,' but hugs me anyway.

"Let's see each other soon," she says. "For dinner this week?"

"Maybe," I say. "I have to figure out my hours and everything. I'll call you."

"And Nate, come back again soon? Before the season starts? Bring Angela?"

"I'll see, Mom."

She watches us until the elevator door closes.

"So, you're just not going to tell anyone you have a boyfriend?" Nate asks as soon as the door closes.

"Um, no."

"That hardly seems reasonable given that you'll be living with dad and working at the station."

"Well, reasonable or not, we haven't figured things out yet, so, no, I'm not going to tell anyone. And mom and dad would just use the info against each other anyway. I'm sure Dad still hates the idea of Chris, that is, if he even remembers him. And mom would probably be ultra-supportive, just to be 'cooler' than dad."

"I don't understand you. I know how smart you are, but sometimes you make the worst decisions. You know it can't go anywhere if it's a big secret."

"I get your point. It's not a perfect situation. We'll see what it feels like once I get settled in."

Nate is still shaking his head when we get in the car. The clock on the dash says 8:48.

"Shit," I say.

"What?"

"I was supposed to call Chris tonight, but I can't call his place after nine."

"Oh, this just keeps getting better. Is he living at home, too?"

I don't say anything, but I nod.

"I give you guys two weeks."

"Thanks, Nate."

CHAPTER 36

My father tries to get me out of bed to go to the station with him, but I pretend to sleep through his efforts and catch a ride with Nate before he leaves town.

"Are you going to come up?" I ask, while he idles outside the station.

"Nah, I need to get back." He has no desire to see my dad; he's so my mother's son. Which I guess makes me my father's daughter. I thought I had outgrown that role, but once I enter the building, I'm nothing more than the boss' kid again.

"Okay, well, thanks for schlepping me around."

He mumbles some kind of affirmative.

"And thanks for letting me live with you."

Another mumble.

"Okay, so, I guess this is it."

"Just go upstairs," he says. "It's not the end of the world."

I lean over the console to give him a hug and he lets me, though I wouldn't say he reciprocates.

"Bye Nate," I say before I slam the car door shut.

He offers a chin tip in response and pulls out of the parking lot.

Upstairs the air is on full blast, just like my dad likes it. I greet the receptionist, and she hands me a name badge on a lanyard.

"What's this?" I ask.

"You know Doug in HR, right?" she asks, snapping her gum.

"Yeah."

"Well, he's rolled out this whole new program with more accounting," she says.

"Accountability." Johnny comes around the corner and corrects her. "And that includes no gum at reception, right Cindi?"

"Right," she says with a sigh and spits the gum into the trash can without even leaning over.

"At least she has good aim," Johnny says as he walks me towards my dad's office. "He's not in a great mood."

"When is he ever in a great mood?" I ask.

"Well, I think he expected you to come in with him this morning, so he had a meeting planned for the interns. You know, to like, turn them over from my control to yours?"

"Thrilling," I say.

"Well, that meeting was supposed to start an hour ago."

"Well, then, he should have told me that."

"He said he did. And you pretended to be asleep."

"Yeah, that might have happened."

"Just be extra … sweet with him? Are you capable of that?" he asks me.

"I don't know. It certainly doesn't come naturally."

"I'm aware of that," Johnny says as he deposits me in my father's office.

My dad looks up, not at me, but at him. "Oh? She's here? Get the interns together," he tells Johnny.

Johnny nods and then raises his eyebrows at me, a warning to be on my best behavior.

"Hi Dad."

"Alice," he says.

"Johnny says I'm late. Sorry."

"I know you were pretending to be asleep this morning. This isn't going to work unless you take it seriously."

"I know. You're right. I don't think this is going to work."

"What?" he finally looks up from his desk.

"Dad, this is not the right fit. I need to be out on my own."

"Then you should have gone out on your own," he says.

"You didn't really give me much of a choice: come home and live with me and work for me or you're on your own."

"That actually is a choice, Alice. And you made it. So, shape up."

I have nothing to say in response. He wasn't the one who cut off the $400 a month. And I wouldn't want that money anyway, now that I know where it was coming from.

"Johnny has the interns gathered in the conference room. Let's go," he says.

I trail behind my dad as we walk through the cubicles. Doug intercepts us right before we turn the corner to the conference room.

"Alice, congratulations on graduating!"

"Thanks, Doug. Nice to see you."

"Glad to have you back. I do need you to fill out some paperwork. Johnny was supposed to bring you by my office first thing."

"Doug, leave her alone," my dad says. "She'll get to your paperwork when she gets to it."

"The thing is," Doug says to me, "we're doing things a little differently now."

"I'll talk her through it," my dad insists.

"We had a lawsuit recently," Doug continues. "We need to do things a little bit more 'by the book.'" He actually uses air quotes. And looks really dorky doing it.

"What happened?" I ask.

They look at each other but neither of them speaks.

"Come see me after you meet with the interns," Doug tells me.

"I'd like to know what's going on now," I say.

"I fired someone and they're saying it's because I didn't like them," my dad says.

"So?" I asked. "That doesn't sound new."

"Well, it's unwise and opens us up to lawsuits," Doug says. "So, we're making sure we do things a little more carefully these days, instituting some training and regulations. Discouraging fraternizing, that sort of thing. Come by my office?"

"Ew! Dad?! Did you fraternize with someone?" *Gross.*

"No, I did not fraternize. I did fire someone because they wore ugly clothes, though. And a lot of Baltimore Ravens gear."

"He was from Baltimore, Burton, and you knew that when you hired him."

"You're trying to turn us into a stupid, bland corporation," my dad says to Doug, and then he walks into the conference room without me.

"I'm trying to protect the station on behalf of all of us who love it," Doug says to me. "Alice, just come see me after the meeting."

"So I can sign a pledge not to fraternize?" I say with a laugh. "My pleasure."

"Really glad to have you back, Alice. We all are."

"You think I'm going to help you control him."

"A guy can hope, can't he?"

*   *   *   *   *

My dad has left a seat between himself and Johnny at the "head" of the oval conference table. It's not easy to maneuver my way in, and I wish they would just have left an empty seat by the door. I hate the feeling of taking up too much space, especially because everyone is watching me.

After my dad does a grand introduction, mentioning my recent graduation, all my undergrad journalism chops, and my history of growing up at the station, which I wish he would have left out, he has the interns—most of whom are white, and ninety-percent of whom are guys, which frankly is progress from when I worked here five years ago—go around the room and introduce themselves. I'm smiling and nodding when one of the interns in the back of the room, who I haven't been able to see previously, leans forward.

It's Chris Thompson.

"I'm Chris," he says. "I'm finishing up a degree at Pitt. I've been working mostly in the studio booth."

And then he leans back. He's obscured once again by all the other faces.

I know how important it is for me to keep a straight face. To not betray whatever it is I'm feeling, which, honestly, is easier to do than to actually figure out what it is I'm feeling. It's maybe thirty percent confusion and seventy percent rage. I make sure to look straight ahead at each intern as they introduce themselves. I continue to smile and nod. I don't look to my sides, to Johnny to ask what the hell is going on or to my dad, to see if there's a sly, knowing grin on his face.

When the introductions are over, my dad turns the meeting over to me. I don't even know what words are coming out of my face. Something about being happy to be back and looking forward to getting to know everyone. But I just want out of the room. Or more appropriately, I want my dad out of the room. I dismiss everyone as soon as I sense Burton is bored, but I put my hand on Johnny's forearm, so he stays seated with me while everyone files out. My dad is long gone, and Chris is the only intern left in the room by the time he makes his way up to the front.

I remain seated and glare at him.

"Can we talk?" he asks, checking the door.

"Not here," I say.

"Okay, where?"

I look at Johnny and then my watch. When I speak, it's to him, not to Chris. "Meet me at eleven forty. Both of you."

They seem frozen as I get up to leave.

"Where?" Chris asks as I pass him.

"Johnny knows," I say. "I have to get to Doug's office now to sign a no-fraternizing pledge."

CHAPTER 37

Sitting at my desk just outside my dad's office, I watch Chris slip out of the studio and meet up with Johnny by the stairs. I count slowly and silently to ten before I get up from my desk, grab my red water bottle, and take the same staircase, the one by the break room. Part of me actually wondered if Johnny would remember where we used to meet when we were waiting out my dad's bad moods, but he does, because when I get to the landing between the seventh and eighth floors the two of them are sitting on the concrete steps.

"I really want to explain," Chris blurts out.

I hold up my hand. "In a million years, I can't imagine anything you have to say that will explain this."

"I should go," Johnny says.

"No," I say firmly. "You're a part of this, and the last thing I need is to be seen alone with him."

"Will you talk to me and not him?" Chris asks.

"Yes, please," Johnny says.

I turn towards Chris. "Okay, I'll talk to you. Are you out of your mind? What is the one thing I made very clear?"

He looks at me but doesn't say anything.

"I said I would be willing to try to make this work if it meant not lying outright. By which I meant, I was willing to try this if I never had to be in the same building as you and my father, let alone the same room! Was that not clear?"

"I can explain."

"I should really leave," Johnny says.

"No," I snap and turn to Chris. I have no idea what I want him to say, what he could possibly say to make this any better, but I'm listening.

"You're not supposed to be here," Chris says.

"Excuse me?"

"I told him not to say that," Johnny interjects.

"You weren't supposed to come back until after my internship was over. So, we wouldn't have been here at the same time."

"That's your explanation?"

"That's the truth."

I notice my eyes are blinking fast. I force myself to take a deep breath. "So, this is my fault?"

"No," Chris stammers. "I don't mean that. It's no one's fault. It just wasn't supposed to happen."

"Oh, it's your fault, Chris," I tell him.

"Well, right, I mean, I know this looks bad—"

"No, it *is* bad. There's a difference. This is not okay."

"I didn't mean to catch you off guard. But you didn't call last night."

"Wow," I say.

"I also told him not to say that," Johnny says.

"Okay, you can go now," I say with a fake smile.

"Thank gawd." Johnny takes the steps down two at a time.

"I was going to tell you last night, but you didn't call. And you know I can't call your house."

"Two weeks, Chris. You had two weeks to tell me. You found out I was coming home the same day I did. The same minute. Two weeks. We've talked a million times since then."

"I know."

"'I know!' That's all you have to say? 'I'm taking some Comm courses,' you said. 'I don't lie to you,' you said!"

"I'm sorry."

I look at the floor, shake my head and exhale through clenched teeth.

"Alice, I am sorry. I know I screwed up. Again."

"Yeah," I say. "You did." And I don't know what else to say.

"I needed this internship. It was the only one available by the time I registered. If I didn't take it, I wouldn't be able to graduate in December. It would mean a whole extra term."

I look at my watch again. "I should get back."

"I get it. But I'll see you at Johnny's later?"

"Uh, no. We're through, Chris. We can't be together like this. Maybe after your internship is over, but not while we're both here."

"Alice, don't do that. Please. Let's just meet up at Johnny's later. He told me he was going to bring you by and then head to his parents' for dinner. We can have the old place to ourselves. We can have some time."

"Why would I do that?"

"Because I'm asking you to."

There's a look on his face that I never imagined even considering saying no to, but I'm considering it now. He reads my mind.

"Don't answer me now," he says. "I'll be there tonight. If you come by, that would be great. If you don't, I'll understand."

I feel myself relax a little bit, but I still don't know what to say.

"I'm going to go back down," Chris says, pointing to the stairs. "Unless you want to go first."

"Go ahead," I say.

He takes my hand and squeezes it gently when he walks past me and the tingling sensation of being touched by him is just as strong as it was the first time. I wish it weren't.

CHAPTER 38

It's a quick drive from the station to Johnny's place. My dad was not thrilled that I wasn't coming home for dinner, but I reminded him we could have dinner anytime we wanted now that we lived together. Luckily, he didn't make too much of a scene when Johnny and I headed out after the drive-time show.

"No parking as usual," I say, while Johnny idles outside his place.

"Oh, I'm not coming up. I want nothing to do with the two of you," he says.

"You know, you could have told me about his internship."

"Alice, I love you like a sister, but seriously, leave me out of your shit."

"Fine." I should get out of the car, but I don't. "It's really weird."

"What is?"

"Seeing his bike here." It's parked between two cars, perpendicular to the curb, just like it used to be. I feel my long hair and sort of pat myself down, as if the physical presence of my body could somehow confirm it was 1997 and not a time warp back to 1992.

"You okay?" Johnny asks.

"I don't know."

"You're going to break up with him, aren't you?"

"I kinda have to."

"Why? Because you signed some paper in Doug's office? Doug is a doofus."

"No, Johnny, because my dad will fail Chris. Or kill him. I can't believe he hasn't already."

"I'm not sure he realizes it's him. Your dad doesn't miss much, but I know he has some holes around … that night."

"Regardless, Johnny, this can never be real. Don't you get that? Like, I don't know, maybe other people can be in relationships with people their parents hate, but I can't. Can you imagine Lois and Burton using my relationship as a bargaining chip?"

"But you are with him. You have been all summer."

"Right, but that was before I was here. Summer? In State College? It doesn't really exist. It's like, I don't know, Brigadoon, do you know that show?"

"Uh, a TV show? Called, what?"

"No, it's a musical. It's about a town that only appears once every hundred years. And then it's gone again. It has nothing to do with the real world. The earthly world. It's magic. That's what this summer was. Or was supposed to be. I was fooling myself. I can't have a serious relationship with Chris Thompson. Or if I do, I have to be sure it'll be worth it. Like, I can't complicate my relationship with my parents for something that's going to flame out, you know?"

"Not really, no. Are you high?"

"No, I'm not high. I just … I can't take any chances here. Even if there weren't the whole no-fraternizing thing, I would have to know it was going to work."

"You can never know that."

"Right, I know, which is why this is too much of a mess."

"Well, Wonderland, it's your mess now. And you have to go upstairs, because I'm already late for dinner." He flicks my forehead like he did when I was a kid.

I swat his hand away.

"Fine. Thanks for the ride. You'll take me home later?"

"Really Wonderland? I'm not here for you. I have my own life to live." But he laughs, and I know he has my back. "The same trick still works to open the door."

Walking up the narrow, low-lit stairs to the attic where Chris Thompson is waiting for me in what once was his apartment, I feel like

I'm watching myself from above. I do the pat down thing again, making sure I'm real, making sure I'm here. I'm not quite convinced I'm not imagining all of it when I reach the landing. The apartment door is cracked open. I stop for a moment outside and take a deep breath, but before I can release it, in what I hope will clear the lump in my throat, Chris opens the door all the way.

"I was hoping that was you."

I'm a little taken aback. "All the same steps still creak, don't they?"

Chris reaches for my hand. I hesitate before I take it. He leads me inside, past the same dusty couches—they've always been here and always will be—to the Formica table in the kitchen. We sit across from each other, nothing between us. If he thinks I'm going to talk first, he's going to be waiting a long time.

"I've already said I'm sorry, right?"

"Yeah."

"And I explained how it happened. How originally I was going to be done before you got home, and then your schedule changed."

"Doesn't make it my fault. You should have told me you were working for my dad. Actually, no. You shouldn't even have been working for him in the first place. Does he even realize who you are?"

"I don't think so. He hasn't called me C.J. once, so probably not. I do my best not to interact with him, but every once in a while, I get the feeling that he's looking at me weird."

"Awesome," I say, deadpan. "Sounds like you have this whole thing figured out."

"Honestly, if Nate hadn't kicked you out this wouldn't be a thing."

"Yes. It would. You took an internship with my dad and didn't tell me."

"I didn't want you to get messed up in it."

"And if he did recognize you?"

"Then I would hope to get to you before he did."

"Great plan."

"Alice, it's just one more week. Four more days."

"You let me walk in there this morning with no warning!"

"Yes, I did. And I'm really sorry about that. I thought we were going to have a chance to talk last night."

"Right, so because I didn't get home until after nine, it's my fault?"

"It's not your fault."

"I know it isn't!"

"I mean, I'm not saying it's your fault. Shit. Alice, please. We knew this would be complicated. I'm doing the best I can."

He's pleading for me to let him off the hook, but I can't, because the real issue is this whole thing can't work.

"I don't know if I believe that."

"Please believe me. I really am trying."

"Yeah, I mean I get that you're trying. And maybe you're doing your best. Maybe we both are. But this can't be happening right now. Let's just take a break for a week. We can figure this stuff out once you're not at the station anymore."

"You don't mean that," he says.

"What don't I mean?"

"You're done with me."

"I'm not 'done with you.' I just need some time to get settled. And to not date someone at the station. Especially you."

"Don't lie to me, Alice."

"You mean like you lied to me? For the last month? Every time I asked you about class?"

"You're right. I'm sorry. But I want to work it out. I want *us* to work out."

"Maybe it will. But not this week."

"So, we can talk about it next week? You're not just putting me off."

"Yes," I lie. "Just try to avoid me at the station. And my dad. Stay in the booth. Keep your head down and give me space."

"Understood." He lets out a little sigh like he's glad this is all behind us.

It's not.

"Are you hungry?" he asks.

I scan my body and check my watch. "Not really."

"Do you want to …?"

"What? Sit around this apartment and pretend it's 1992?"

"Johnny has a TV," he says, part statement, part question.

I shake my head and shrug.

"Well, he won't be back for a while. Do you want me to take you home?"

"On your motorcycle? Nah, that's not very discreet."

"Right. Sorry. Listen, I know you're mad. And I get that. And I know you need time. Do you want me to leave you here? I could head home if you'd rather be alone."

I should want him to leave, but the mere fact that he's offering—that he's trying so hard to give me what I need—makes me want to cut him some slack.

"You don't have to leave."

"Do you want to take a ride?"

The thought of being on Chris Thompson's motorcycle, arms wrapped around his waist, my chest pressed up against his back and a helmet shielding me from the outside world and the need to talk to him and to stay mad at him, is enticing. But part of me holds back, not wanting to give him anything he wants because if I do, I might give him everything he wants, and I need to save something for me.

"What about the roof?" I say.

"You want to go up? Sure." His whole body responds with eagerness. I hate how much I love how much he wants me to forgive him. Like I'm the only thing he needs in his life to be content. Like I'm his world. And as much as I love it, I hate it, too. Because I need to be my world. And it's not that I don't want him to be a part of it. But I'm realizing I need it to be on my own terms. I'm not trying to make it more complicated than it needs to be, but I don't think he realizes how complicated it is.

He grabs a blanket, and we climb the ladder from the landing to the roof. It's not dark yet, not even dusk, just a hazy grey. Everything to one side of us is lush and green—Schenley Park, Panther Hollow—and to the other side, up the hill, above all the row houses and student apartments, is the hospital my dad was in the night Chris left for Australia. In the distance, directly in front of us, I can even see the station tower. It's like a map of my life, my past, and unfortunately, my future.

"You okay?" he asks, spreading out the blanket, but not sitting. He's staying close to me, but not too close.

I give him a look like, *are you kidding?* He reads me easily.

"Aside from being mad at me, are you okay?"

I smile. "It's hard to stay mad at you."

"Thank gawd." He smiles back.

"But I am still mad." I can't stifle my laugh quickly enough.

"Of course you are." He can't contain his smile.

"I am!" I insist.

He smiles, genuinely, one of the many smiles that clearly conceals a laugh, and nods slowly like he's saying, *sure you are.*

And then he tilts his head and bats his eye lashes like a puppy dog.

"Chris! Stop it! I'm mad at you!"

He stays silent and keeps doing what he's doing. Looking adorable. And inching closer to me.

I purse my lips, a failed attempt to hide my own smile and conceal a laugh.

He gets close enough to put his head on my shoulder. I don't move away or stop him. Instead, I reach up and stroke his hair.

"Dammit," I say.

"You love me, you really love me," he teases.

"Don't be so sure," I say. "I tolerate you."

"Ah, but will you kiss me?"

I don't answer, I just kiss him. I press my body up against his and feel the relief and exhilaration passing back and forth between us.

"Do you want to sit?" he asks, pointing to the blanket when he pulls away.

I shake my head. I realize it will be my last chance to be with him for a while. I'm not sure I'm going to break up with him anymore, but even if I do, nothing will be final until after we get through this week apart. "Let's go downstairs."

He grabs the blanket and leads the way back to the ladder. I take one more look at the city sprawled out around us before my head goes into the building. If I can make peace with us, maybe I can make peace with this city.

In the apartment he lays the blanket out over the brown couch and kisses me, but he notices my hesitancy.

"Oh, sorry, I thought we were on the same page," he says, looking sheepish.

"No. Yeah. It's just… the couch … I've always hated this couch."

"Uh, Johnny's bed?"

"No, that's worse. That's definitely worse."

With a laugh, he pulls me down on the couch and takes off his own shirt before he removes mine. With him lying on top of me, I can tell he's already hard, but he takes time to pay attention to me, like he's using his mouth to map my body. He's interested in all of me, not just the normal places guys typically focus, if they focus on me at all. Everything else falls away, the dusty couch, the dingy apartment that isn't even his anymore, my resolve to be mad at him—to break up with him—because he lied to me, even if it was a lie of omission. We come at the same time and as our breaths move from panting to long deep sighs, Chris holds me tight against his chest like he may never let go.

*　　*　　*　　*　　*

Chris makes fun of me for making a post-sex shake, but then he asks me to make him one. We sit at the Formica table drinking my mom's patented concoction.

He checks his watch. "I think Johnny'll be back soon."

"Yeah."

"Will you call me when you get home? I'm gonna stay here tonight."

"Chris, I don't mean to be a bitch, but we can't talk this week."

"Are you serious? We just had sex, and you won't even call me here?"

"No." I shake my head. "Effectively, we're not together this week."

"Really? As of… now?"

"Yeah, as of now." He's kidding, but I'm not. "I have to take this stuff seriously."

"Because of some paper Doug made you sign?"

"Well, that, and because my dad would fuck you up."

"Your dad's not going to touch me."

"He'll fail you."

A look of understanding takes over Chris' face.

"He will make sure you fail."

He puts his elbow on the table, and his head in his hand. He doesn't say anything for a long time. When he finally looks up at me, he says, "Sorry."

CHAPTER 39

Monday is my first day at the station without Chris, and I can feel the difference in my body. I'm relaxed, no longer dreading every task my dad requests of me with the fear I'll have to interact with Chris in front of everyone. I'm convinced my attraction to him is too strong to hide. Whereas five years ago, the illicit nature of our interactions added to the excitement, and possibly even fueled our connection, last week just took too much out of me. We successfully avoided each other in the building, but all the interns went to The O on Friday after work to say goodbye to the ones who were finishing their four-week term, and that was a little more complicated. In his mind, we were in the clear, but grades haven't been turned in yet and Chris still seems to underestimate my dad's pettiness.

I did meet up with him at Johnny's Saturday night, but just for a few hours and Johnny was with us the whole time. I could tell Chris was getting impatient with me, expecting things to be the way they were in State College, the way they were five years ago, but they're just not. I'm not at ease with him here in Pittsburgh, not now. It still sort of freaks me out that he kept the internship from me that whole time.

"Alice!" my dad bellows from his office. I jump from my desk and stand in his doorway. "What are you working on?"

"Just getting ready to do the orientation with Doug for the new interns."

"Okay. Let me know when you need me. But I have meetings the rest of the afternoon."

"I know, Dad. I have a trusty computer that tells me your schedule."

"Computers are not 'trusty,' Alice."

"I know, Dad."

"I can hear you roll your eyes," he says.

"Very funny."

"Do you want to have dinner tonight? Can you wait until after the show?"

"Sure," I say on my way back to my desk.

The drive-time show is from four to seven, so it's usually eight o'clock before my dad makes it out of the office. When I know dinner is going to be that late, it's doable, I just have to portion out my bars and shakes and celery differently. It's always easier to enjoy spending time with my dad in a restaurant. Once we get home, we watch TV in silence or retreat to our own rooms. There's no animosity these days, but it's not like we sit around talking and doing jigsaw puzzles. There's something about being out where he knows he's being watched that encourages Burton to play the good dad and something about being home, where there used to be four of us and now there are only two, that makes him close up.

When I first got back, I was struck by how empty all the cabinets looked. There were generic products where there used to be name-brands—except for the Caffeine Free Diet Coke, can't skimp on that. But then I remembered the house was meant for a family of four, and for as long as I'd lived there, my mom had been doing the shopping. I tried to accept that the house should look different with just my dad living there, but it just doesn't feel like home. And with all his salary increases over the years, why would he be buying generics? The thought that he is gambling again—or still, who knows, it's this thing that no one acknowledges but probably hasn't cured itself—crosses my mind, but I'm happy to ignore it if it means not having a fight with him.

"Alice? Hello?" Doug is standing at my desk, waving his hand in front of my face.

"Sorry, yeah, I'm with you."

I follow Doug to the conference room and sit next to him as he goes through the new orientation checklist with this crop of interns. They actually look young to me, which means I feel old. At the appropriate time, I get up to get my dad. He comes in to do his "Burton thing," in which he attempts to instill the fear of God in these kids and imbue me with his authority. I understand how it's supposed to work, and I probably needed it when I was sixteen, but now it makes me feel weak. I wish he would let me develop a professional relationship with them on my own. I can tell Doug is equally uncomfortable as he monitors my dad for things people might be able to sue the station over. Burton leaves the room when he's done, and Doug and I split the interns up into their departmental assignments.

"How busy are you today?" Doug asks me, once the interns leave for their various projects.

"Typical Monday," I say. "What do you need?"

"Can you input the grades for the last crop of interns? It's just pass-fail. Everyone passed. Technically, your dad is the supervisor, but because he refuses to use the computer …"

"Yeah. I think I have the log-in info."

When I get back to my desk, my dad and Johnny are in a meeting with marketing, so I log into the Pitt system to submit the grades. It's a three-step process. You have to enter them, then approve them, then submit them. I get a warning when I hit "submit" that lets me know once I've hit the button again, the grades can't be changed. Hitting the button feels good. It removes any power my dad has over Chris. I wish there were a button to push to remove any power he has over me.

I see my dad, trailed by Johnny, come in and out of meetings all day, until 3:50 p.m. when he stops by my desk to check his phone messages before heading into the studio.

"We're still on for dinner?" he asks.

"I'll be here," I tell him.

They've just shut the door to the studio when Burton's line rings.

"Dennis Burton's line," I say.

"I'd like to talk to Dennis, please," a man's voice says.

"I'm sorry. He's in the studio and can't be disturbed."

"Oh, right. I'm in Chicago today, different time zone."

"I can take a message."

"Voicemail would be better."

"I'm sorry, Dennis Burton doesn't trust machines. That makes me his voicemail."

"Why does that not surprise me?" the man asks with a small laugh. His voice is warm and kind. A smooth radio voice without snark or edge.

"Dennis Burton, world famous luddite," I say. "But I'm happy to have him call you back tomorrow. Or after the show."

"Well," the man pauses. "I usually deal with Johnny. Is he around?"

"He's been promoted and is in the studio now. I can help you."

"Okay. This is about his daughter. And it's urgent. Can you pass him a note?"

I stop myself from telling the man that I am his daughter. Something tells me it's best to take this conversation slowly. "Okay. Sure. Go ahead."

"This is Steve Berger. I run the Klein Fellowship. Alice—that's his daughter—had applied to our New York program, and he had asked me to waitlist her. I think he didn't want her in New York City. But we have a spot in the newly formed Chicago cohort, and we'd like to offer her that spot. It starts next week, and if she can't take it, we have to move on to another applicant. So, the sooner I hear back from him the better."

I don't know how long the silence lasts, but I am unable to move or breathe. I get a head rush, the kind that feels like my skull is either going to collapse or explode.

"Hello?" The nice voice says. "Did you get all that?"

"Sure, sure. Got it. Let me take down your number in case he doesn't have it handy."

Steve Berger gives me the number where Burton can reach him, and I read it back to him to make sure I took it down properly. When we hang up, I let out a sigh-growl and attract some attention from those around me. I don't bother putting them at ease. I dial Meredith's number, but she doesn't pick up. I don't leave a message, mostly because I can't even put into words what I'm feeling, almost as if there are no words to make sense of my rage. If I put words to it, it would have the effect of minimizing the seething, white-hot energy surging through me. Propelled by my fury, I get up from my desk.

"I'm going out. Can you cover Burton's phone?" I ask the receptionist with the jet-black hair.

"Sure," she says.

"Want anything?" I ask her.

"Where you headed?"

"To get a slice. Or six."

"I'd take a pepperoni," she says.

"Great."

"And a fountain Coke?"

"No problem," I call over my shoulder, unable to stop moving.

Walking, ordering, paying is all a blur. I stand at the counter next to the register, slice in hand. The cheese is not hot enough to burn my mouth but just hot enough to change my body temperature. The tang of the red sauce and the fat of the cheese feel like home and freedom and power. Everything is different now.

CHAPTER 40

I'm sitting in my dad's office, at his chair, eating another slice of pizza, when his show ends, and he and Johnny come in.

"I thought we were having dinner tonight," my dad says. "And get your feet off my desk and out of my chair."

"Since when do you eat pizza?" Johnny asks.

I don't move while I finish chewing. Then I say, "You both can sit down."

"Alice. Up. Now," my dad says.

"Sit," I say.

Johnny makes a move for the door.

"Johnny," I say. "Sit down."

"Alice, I don't know what kind of strange pseudo sibling rivalry is going on with you and Johnny, but this is not how you talk to me. And when the two of you are here, I expect you to keep it professional."

I still don't move.

Johnny plops down, exasperated, and grabs a slice from the box I've left open on my dad's table.

"Alice, if you have something to say, say it." My dad has never been patient.

I pass the pink "While You Were Out" message pad where I've written Steve Berger's info across the desk, like I'm negotiating a big business deal, and this is my final offer.

My father picks it up, reads it, and drops it on the desk again. His face doesn't change. Although he's spent the last decade in radio, he's always maintained an ability to control his countenance. He likes it when people don't know what he's thinking, but I think I know. I've had years of practice.

Neither of us speaks.

Johnny picks up the pad. He's chewing and his mouth is full, but I see the exact moment he realizes what's going on. He looks at me and back at Burton, and the minute he swallows, he stands up to leave.

"I'm going to head out now."

"You're part of this, Johnny," I say.

He looks to Burton, but Burton doesn't give him anything. He just stands in the middle of his office, stone-faced.

Burton's a master of the silent treatment, but I out-silent him. Finally, he says, "So you want to move to Chicago?"

"I want to know why you had me wait-listed. I want to know why I'm here. I should be in New York. I'm good enough to be in New York!"

"This isn't about being good enough," Burton says. "This is about being where you need to be. You'll get to New York, when the time is right, for grad school, if you want."

"You really think that managing a staff of interns, which I did when I was *sixteen,* is going to get me into an Ivy League journalism program?"

"I think working for me will."

"So would Klein. Dad! Why didn't you tell me about this?"

"Why didn't *you* tell *me*?"

"Because I wanted to do something on my own! I wanted to get in on my own merit."

"You think I don't know people there?" My dad bellows from somewhere deep in his gut.

"I'm sure you do. Obviously you do! But I didn't think you'd get in my way!"

Johnny stands up. My dad and I yell his name simultaneously.

"I'm just closing the door," he says, gingerly stepping backwards. Once the door is shut he returns to his seat, lips pursed tightly together while my dad carries on.

"How do you think it made me look when Steve called to ask me if you were my daughter, and I had no idea about your application?"

"So, you had him waitlist me because you were embarrassed?!"

"I had him waitlist you because you need to be here."

"Why? Why do I need to be here?"

My dad doesn't respond, so I turn to Johnny.

"And you? You knew about this!"

"This isn't his fault, Alice."

"No, nothing is ever Johnny's fault, 'cause all he ever does is exactly what you tell him to."

"Johnny's smart enough to take my advice when I give it. Unlike you and your brother who think you know better."

"Call Steve Berger. I'm going to Chicago," I say.

"You know no one in Chicago."

"Exactly."

"You're not going to Chicago. The program starts next week. That's not enough time to relocate even if they're giving you a place to live."

"I'll be fine. I'll handle the logistics. Just make the call."

"I thought you wanted to go to Klein to be with Meredith in New York. Apply next year. I'm sure you'll get in. Maybe you'll be ready to go then."

"You think I just wanted the program so I could move to New York? I could have moved to New York if I just wanted to move to New York. I could move to New York tomorrow! I wanted the program because it would set me up with the best chance for grad school! This wasn't yours to decide. This was mine. I worked for this! Make the call!"

"You won't get anywhere yelling at me, Alice. You think I'll 'behave' because Johnny's here?"

"You never behave. You always do whatever you want. Johnny's here because he could make the call. Steve said he was used to dealing with Johnny. If Johnny called and said Steve Berger could accept me, he would."

"Come on, Alice," Johnny pleads.

"He wouldn't do that. He knows I'd fire him."

"And then he could sue you."

"He wouldn't sue me."

"You signed all the same paperwork I did. You're not allowed to fire him without Doug weighing in, and Doug won't let you fire him for a non-work-related incident."

"You're overplaying your hand, Alice. You're not going to Chicago."

"Why?"

"Because I said so. If Johnny makes that call, I'll just make my own call. You're here for a year, maybe two. The sooner you accept that, the sooner everything goes back to normal."

"What do you think I'm safe from here? Were you worried Mom would visit me in New York and win me over?"

"Leave your mother out of this," my father commands. "And leave Johnny out of this. This conversation is over."

I knew it would come to this. I didn't want it to. But I knew it would.

"Dad, I'm seeing Chris Thompson. We're in a relationship, and if I stay in Pittsburgh, we'll probably move in together."

"Chris Thompson? C.J. Thompson?"

"Yes."

Johnny puts his face in his hands.

"Did you know about this?" my dad screams at Johnny.

"Let's leave Johnny out of this," I say more calmly than I thought possible. I hold up the message pad.

"Wait a minute. He's interning here, isn't he? I knew that little shit looked familiar, but I couldn't place him."

"He's done," I say, very satisfied with myself.

"I can still make sure he fails."

"No, you can't. Doug had me submit grades today. They're locked. He doesn't work here anymore and neither do I."

My dad is boiling over, but he's out of moves.

"Make the call, Dad."

I'm shocked, when he actually picks up the pad and starts dialing the phone. My body is vibrating, and I realize I didn't expect any of this to work. But, I won. I don't know what I would have done if I didn't—probably crash on my mom's couch for the foreseeable future—but it doesn't matter, because I'm moving to Chicago.

CHAPTER 41*

The fallout from my power play is a little more serious than I had expected. Johnny leaves the station before I can catch up with him, so I call Chris from my desk hoping to get to him before Johnny does.

"He's not home from class yet," his mom tells me. "His schedule changed this week."

"Right! Thanks Mrs. Thompson," I say.

"Should I have him call you?" she asks.

"I'll try back." I wonder if she's caught on yet to the fact that he can't call me.

My dad drives me home from the station, but we don't talk at all. Once we get in the house, my dad goes to the kitchen, and I head up to my room. I try Johnny's place and thankfully, Johnny's home and picks up.

"Hi, it's me," I say.

"He's not here," he says.

"Okay, thanks. How are you?"

"Alice, you could have seriously fucked up my life tonight."

"I know. I'm sorry."

"Somehow that just doesn't seem to cut it."

"You knew about the waitlist, didn't you?"

"I don't have to answer your questions, Alice."

"You don't have to, no. But you could."

"Are you seriously messing with me right now? Do you know what he'll do to me if he thinks I knew about you and Chris? Do you even care?"

"For what it's worth, I think he's far too pissed at me to be pissed at you, too."

"He doesn't work like that, and you know it. He has enough anger to go around, and it can last for days. Weeks, even! And now that you've quit, I'm back to managing the fucking interns."

It's possible I didn't think through the consequences of my actions too clearly.

"Johnny, I'm really sorry. I did what I had to do, but I'm sorry you got caught up in it."

"I told you when you were in high school that you and your fucking hormones were going to get someone fired. I'm the only one left to fire."

"He's not going to fire you, Johnny."

"I don't think you get it. You're protected because you're his kid. You're reckless. Throwing the rest of us under the bus."

"I didn't mean to put you in any danger of losing your job."

"You just didn't think. I'm so pissed at you right now."

"Okay. I guess I should let you go then."

"Yeah, probably."

"Can I just ask you one thing first?"

"What?"

"Are you going to tell him?"

"Tell who what?"

"Are you going to tell Chris I'm leaving?"

"Oh, no. That's on you. I'm not carrying any messages and you cannot meet here. Do you understand me? Not anymore. That shit is over."

"Okay. I got it. I'll talk to you later."

"Yeah, whatever."

He hangs up, and I worry how long he's going to stay mad. I get it, I really do, but he screwed up, too. Keeping secrets for my dad was never part of the deal before. We kept secrets from him, not for him.

The clock in my room reads 8:52 in red numbers. I dial Chris' parents' house, and he picks up.

"Hey, it's me," I say.

"Hey. How was today?"

"Eventful."

"When can I see you?"

"Actually, I was thinking I could head out towards your parents' place. Can you meet at The Venus on Route 8?"

"The one you can't go into with me because the owners know your dad?"

"It'll be okay tonight."

"Are you sure?"

"Yeah, I know it's getting late."

"No, it's fine. I'm an adult. They just don't like the phone ringing after nine, but I can leave the house." He laughs quietly.

"Okay. I think I can get there by ten."

"I can't wait to see you."

"Yeah," I stammer, allowing myself to feel for the first time what it might be like to tell him I'm leaving. "Me too."

My dad is still at the kitchen table when I come downstairs.

"I need to take the car for a bit," I tell him, picking up his keys from the counter by the radio.

"You need to go see him?"

"I need to go break up with him."

I don't wait for my dad to say anything else. I don't wait for permission. I just leave.

CHAPTER 42

When I pull into the parking lot of the Venus Diner, Chris is sitting on his bike, helmet off. He doesn't recognize me in my dad's Caprice Classic, and I watch him for a bit before I get out. Aside from his hair being shorter, he looks just like he did when I first saw him in the weight room on Pitt's campus five years ago. I'm transformed into that girl who couldn't breathe at the sight of him. The girl who thought someone that beautiful would never talk to someone like her. I'm transformed into the girl who first spoke to him at the movie night on Flagstaff Hill, tripping over my words and jealous of Tess, who turned out to be his cousin, not his girlfriend and who turned into one of my closest friends, even if only for a few months. I pat down my body, confirming I'm here, that this is real, that Alice Burton is going to get out of this car and break up with Chris Thompson, The Hottest Guy Ever. As if that's something the sixteen-year-old part of me—a part I imagine will always live somewhere in me—can even comprehend.

"Hey," he says when I get out of the car. The pink and green neon of the sign bounce off his bike.

"Hey," I say as I walk towards him. The air is humid, thick with the promise of rain.

When I reach the bike, he wraps me in a hug and kisses me, burying his face in my neck. I hate myself for letting him—for not blurting out that we're through—but I want to be devoured by him. I kiss him back, but he must sense something because he pulls away quickly.

"I should have known something was up when you said you wanted to meet in public."

"Let's go inside," I say.

He holds his helmet on one side of his body and wraps his other arm around my waist, letting his hand rest on my hip.

We sit across from each other in a booth next to the window. I try to look outside, but I can only see our reflection.

I order decaf, and he orders iced tea. I expect the waitress, whose name tag says Dottie, to be annoyed that we're not ordering food, but she smiles at me warmly. It feels like the kindest gesture I've ever received, and I certainly don't deserve it. As soon as she turns away, tears well up in my eyes.

Chris watches me like he's not sure if he should say anything.

"I'm sorry I'm crying," I tell him.

"You don't have to apologize to me," he says. "But can you tell me what's going on? I'm worried."

"Yeah." I wipe away the tears and nod. "I'm … leaving town."

He looks momentarily relieved. "For how long?"

"A year … maybe two … maybe forever? I'm moving."

"Oh." He doesn't look upset, but he does look confused.

"Yeah, so, I'm moving to Chicago on Sunday."

"Chicago?"

I explain the whole thing to him about the program and the waitlist and my dad. I tell him how I'm going to have to ask my mom for a loan for the plane ticket. I don't get to the part about how I got my dad to make the call before he interrupts me, but I do tell him Johnny's pissed at me, and I'm not so happy with him.

"So … this isn't about me?"

"What do you mean? I don't understand the question."

"Are you breaking up with me or are you moving or both?

I take a long sip of hot decaf. "Both?"

I can see the sting he's feeling.

"Why?"

"Because part of the reason I'm moving to Chicago is to start over. On my own. And long distance never works."

"How do you know?"

Is he serious? Would he really want to try? "There's something else I need to tell you."

"Okay."

"You're not going to like me once I tell you."

"I wouldn't be so sure about that. You're still talking to me after everything I put you through." He reaches his hand out on the table, and I take it.

"Um, my dad didn't want me to go to Chicago. I made him make the call."

"What does that have to do with me?"

"I told him about me and you."

His hand flinches in mine. "What do you mean?"

"I told him we were together. I knew it was the only way he would send me away."

"To keep you away from me?"

"Yes."

Chris Thompson laughs with his full body. I'm not sure I've ever seen him laugh like this before.

"What's so funny?"

"You thought I'd be mad about that?"

"Well, yeah, I guess."

"Alice, it's sort of brilliant."

I'm laughing now, too, but only because he is. I don't know what we're laughing about. "What do you mean?"

"I was always worried I'd hold you back, but I was actually your ticket out of here? It's ... well ... it's brilliant."

"You're not mad?"

"No. I'm thrilled for you. It's what you want, and I helped you get it."

"But I'm breaking up with you."

"Eh, for now. We've always had shitty timing."

"I don't know what to say, I really thought you were going to be pissed."

"Am I going to get credit for my internship at the station?"

"Yes. I made sure to submit and lock the grades before I said anything to him."

"Great. So, I'll be done by December. Maybe I'll leave then, too?"

"I thought you wanted to be here."

"I thought I did, too. And it's good to be spending time with my parents, but maybe it's not really what I'm looking for."

"Oh my gawd. You came home for me, didn't you?"

He's quiet for a minute, but I can tell he's carefully working out what he's going to say next. "Can I come around and sit next to you?"

"Of course!"

He slides into the booth and pulls my face in to his to kiss me. I breathe him in. There are so many emotions running through my body, but I choose to focus on his scent, his touch, his belief in me and my belief in him.

"I didn't come back here for you, and I certainly didn't come home to hold you back. I thought if we were both here, we might be able to figure something out, but that's not going to happen right now, and that's okay. I won't love you any less because you're in Chicago."

I weep openly. "This hurts so badly."

"I know."

"I was so mad at you for lying to me."

"I know."

"But it became apparent very quickly, I can't stay mad at you."

"I know."

"Which made me more mad at you."

"I know."

"Gawd, I love you."

"I love you, too."

I put my head on his shoulder.

"What did Meredith say about all this?"

"Eh, she's 50/50 on the whole thing. She's glad I'm breaking up with you—"

"Of course she is."

"But she's not thrilled about Chicago. She thinks this means I'm going to end up at Northwestern instead of Columbia."

"Sounds like her," he says with a knowing smile.

"Wait, if you leave in December, where would you go?"

"You know, I've been thinking about Chicago…"

"No, you haven't," I say with a playful slap to his shoulder.

"No. I haven't. Actually, Tess has been bugging me about touring with her. They're coming to the US in January."

"What? That's amazing! I mean, if you want to. That's not what you want to do, is it?"

He looks down at the table. "I didn't think it was. But maybe it wouldn't be so bad. I like being with Tess. And I wouldn't play with them; I'd guitar tech. I like that stuff."

And it's like my heart explodes and deflates in the same moment. "Oh my gawd, I'm a horrible person."

"What do you mean?"

"This is about me. If I were here, you wouldn't go on tour."

He doesn't meet my eyes. "I wasn't considering it before, but I am now."

"That's a hedge," I say. "You were going to give up touring with Liminal Space to be in Pittsburgh with me, and I'm not even willing to give up a fellowship."

"You're not a horrible person. You're young."

"What does that mean?"

"It means you have stuff to figure out. I do, too, but I've had time you haven't. You need to do this. Our bad timing is just that. Bad timing."

"I'm so sorry. I feel selfish and … stupid."

"No one could ever confuse you for stupid."

"This hurts so much I can actually feel it in my stomach."

"You're probably hungry," he says.

"Very funny," I say, even though it doesn't sound like a joke.

"I'm actually serious. You need to eat more. Your mom's bars are a snack, they're not real food. And you need to drink less."

"Whoa." I sit up straight and scoot over to get some distance from him. "That took a sharp turn."

"Sorry, I thought I'd have longer to ease into this discussion, but if all we have is tonight, we have a lot of ground to cover."

"I'm not an alcoholic," I say. "I know you are, and I applaud your sobriety, but I'm not you."

"I don't need you to applaud me. I need you to take care of yourself. Especially if you're moving somewhere where you don't have close friends. Your friends look out for you. I saw it in State College, even Meredith watches what you eat and drink, and Johnny and Nate, they keep tabs on you. I know you're excited to be on your own, and I'm sure you feel ready. But what if there's always been a safety net and you didn't know it."

"I need to take a minute," I say. "I'm going to go to the bathroom."

He stands up to let me out of the booth but doesn't let me pass. "Don't leave me here."

"I won't. I wouldn't. I promise."

CHAPTER 43

The bathroom is bright, even brighter than the diner, which I didn't think was possible. My eyes are puffy and red. When I pee, it smells like burnt coffee. I can see why I'd rather be drunk right now, why anyone would rather be drunk right now. Everything feels too real. But it's not like I have a flask on me. I don't carry a flask; I've never carried a flask. But I wonder if Chris is right. I went from being Burton's kid to Nate's little sister. I've never been anonymous anywhere. There have always been people looking over my shoulder. That was one of the things I liked about being with Chris when I was in high school. Only a few people knew where I was and none of them were privy to what was going on unless I wanted them to be. He, and his dingy apartment, were my chance to be anonymous then.

Chicago is a fresh start. I'm desperate for that, but I may need to change some stuff up as well, and not rely on just being somewhere else.

When I come out of the bathroom, Chris is once again on his side of the booth, and he's talking to the waitress.

I smile at her as I slide back into my seat.

"I'm thinking of getting an omelet," Chris tells me. "Do you want one?"

I've already had pizza today. "Can I get it made with egg whites?"

"Are you asking me or Dottie?" he asks.

"Dottie, I'll have a spinach and tomato omelet made with egg whites, please. No toast."

"Fries, home fries, or hash browns, Honey?"

I bite my lip. Chris smiles across the table at me, half support, half challenge.

"Home fries, please."

"Sure thing," Dottie says as she glides towards the counter.

"So, you're not mad at me?" Chris asks.

"No." I move around to his side of the booth and snuggle in next to him. "I'm not sure I agree with you. But I know you mean well. And Zach also made sort of a big deal about the whole eating thing last week, before I left. I get it. I think you're all wrong, but it's probably unlikely. So yeah, I'll look into that."

"I'm sure I speak for everyone who loves you when I say, 'thank you.'"

"It's really not a big deal," I say, uncomfortable with the idea that all of these people may have been talking about me behind my back. "I'm perfectly healthy."

"Well, you're perfect, I know that." He kisses my forehead.

When our food comes out, it's not Dottie, but Nick, one of the owners, who brings it.

"Is this little Ally Burton?" he asks. His face looks the same as it always has—he's had deep wrinkles as long as I've known him—but his hair is all grey, not the salt-and-mostly-pepper I remember.

"Hi Nick," I get up to hug him and tower over him.

"Isn't it late for a school night, young lady?" Nick asks.

I don't even know what time it is.

"I graduated from college last month, Nick."

"No! You do look all grown up, but has it been that long since I've seen you?"

"Yeah, I haven't been back to the 'burgh in a while. And no one's called me Ally in even longer."

"Oh, I'm sorry!" He looks mortified. "Did I embarrass you in front of your boyfriend?"

"No, it's fine, Nick. This is—" I take a gulp of air to try to pass the lump in my throat "—my *friend* Chris Thompson, and I go by Alice now. Chris, this is Nick. He owns The Venus with his brother. They're friends of my dad."

"Nice to meet you," Chris says.

"My pleasure," Nick says with a head nod that is almost a bow. "Any friend of the Burton's…"

Chris and I both laugh.

"I'll be right back," Nick says and scampers away.

"What was that about an invisible safety net?" I ask while putting ketchup on my omelet. I'm back on my own side of the booth now.

"Exactly," Chris says.

He smiles as he watches me eat, like he takes pleasure in it. It's weird. But then Nick returns with two Strawberry milkshakes.

"I remember you always liked these," he says, putting the sweating glasses and metal overflow tumblers down on the table between us. "On the house. Just make sure to tip Dottie well. Happy Graduation!"

"Thanks, Nick."

I think Chris is watching me to see if I'm going to drink the shake, but he's actually looking over my shoulder. I turn around to see Johnny coming in from the vestibule.

"What's going on?" I ask. "This better not be an intervention. I'm seriously fine."

"It's not an intervention."

Johnny is as surprised to see me as I am to see him.

"This is what you made me come out for at one a.m.?" he says to Chris.

"Just sit down," Chris replies.

Johnny stands over me. "Move. I'm not sitting with either of you."

I once again move to Chris' side of the booth.

Johnny takes the milkshake that was in front of me and takes a long sip.

I raise my eyebrows at him.

"It's not like you'd ever drink this," he says to me. "What am I doing here?"

"Yeah, what is he doing here?" I ask Chris.

"I called him when you were in the bathroom."

"He didn't tell me you were here," Johnny adds.

"Well, he didn't tell me he called you. This isn't my fault."

"Shut up both of you," Chris says. "Johnny, obviously you know Alice is leaving for Chicago. I just wanted to get you two together so you could hash out whatever beef you have before she goes."

"You know she tried to get me fired."

"No, I didn't! Do you know he knew my dad blocked my application to Klein? And he didn't tell me!"

"Guys, it doesn't matter. Johnny, were you fired?"

"Not yet."

"Alice, are you going to Chicago?"

"Yes."

"Fine. Then everyone's fine. Put it behind you."

Johnny and I stare at each other across the table. He narrows his eyes, and then I narrow mine. Then he sticks his tongue out at me, and I smile.

"Thank Gawd," Chris says.

"Why do you care so much about me and Johnny not wanting to kill each other?" I ask.

"I still want to kill you, I'm just pretending I don't," Johnny says, but he's not serious.

"Because you'd both eventually blame me for ruining your bizarre-o friendship, and I'd rather not have that hanging over me."

"Fair," I say.

"Did you bring cards?" Chris asks Johnny.

Johnny produces a deck of cards. "You realize it's the middle of the night?"

"Okay, old man," I say.

Johnny orders a burger, and we play poker with pennies just like we used to in Chris' apartment after Wasted Pretty gigs. Nick even joins us for a few hands, but eventually Johnny needs to leave.

"I can't stay here all night," he says. "Some of us have to deal with Burton in the morning. I'm sure he'll be in a great mood."

"Sorry," I say.

"Not to mention I'll be doing your job again. I can't believe you didn't last a week."

"I lasted just over a week," I say. "And we wouldn't have had to go through any of this if you had told me what was going on."

"Don't," Chris says, putting his hand on my forearm.

"Where does Burton think you are, anyway?" Johnny asks me.

"Breaking up with C.J. Thompson."

"That's one sure way to get the car," Johnny says. "Did you break up?"

Chris and I look at each other and shrug.

"Yeah," I say. "We're just friends."

"If you say so." Johnny gets out of the booth and I get up to give him a hug. "Will I see you before you go?"

"I don't know. I have to find a flight and figure out a way to get my mom to loan me the money. It's going to be a weird week. And I won't be coming to the station."

"Let's grab dinner before you go?"

"I'll call you," I say.

He hugs me and then flicks my forehead. I walk him to the door, and when he leaves I can see it's finally raining.

"Looks like you're stuck here with me for a while," I tell Chris when I slide into the booth with him.

"No complaints," he says.

*   *   *   *   *

Hours later, Chris and I are half-heartedly playing cards when I realize I need to get the car home, if my dad's going to be on time to work.

"I should go," I say.

"Do you have to?"

"Yeah. Don't you have class today?"

"Yeah, but I can get by on very little sleep. Professional hazard."

"Fair enough."

"So, this is it?"

"I think so. Like I told Johnny, I don't know what this week is going to be like. I can't promise anything."

"I get it."

"But I do love you," I tell him.

"I love you, too. Get me your number when you get one?"

"For sure. Thanks for being so understanding."

"Alice, five years ago I left for a different continent—"

"The farthest continent."

"Yes, the farthest continent. Without saying goodbye. I'm lucky you still talk to me."

"You're lucky you're so hot."

"Stop objectifying me!" he teases.

"You're right, you're also kind and caring and amazing."

"That's better," he says.

"But I really need to go."

"I know you do."

We hug in the vestibule for a long time. It's not raining anymore, and the sky is morphing from slate grey to light blue with shocks of pink and purple. When I get home, my dad will leave for work. I'll pull the blinds shut in my room and go to bed in an empty house. By then, the ache in my core—the one that has already started to form—will be so intense it will probably keep me awake, staring at my ceiling. But that's ok, because sometimes that's what doing the right thing feels like.

ACKNOWLEDGEMENTS

Thanks to Black Rose Writing for the continued support.

Thanks to my writing community near and far, especially Michele Lombardo, Emily Popek, Dena Ogden, Daniel Southwell, Lauren Tanabe, Michele Bacon, Evan Wasserstrom, Chris Blackwell and Chelsea Moore, Meghan Kenny, Monica Prince, Hannah Grieco, Lauren Tanabe, Emily Maloney, Molly Pascal, Write Now Lancaster, Fear No Lit, the Binders, and all of the Lancaster creatives who inspire and embrace me. Thanks to the editors who have continued to select and publish my work, especially those of you who say nice things about it and help me make it better!

Thanks to the State College Summer of Rusted and Bitter Love, especially Scotty Nick, Dan-O, Schwinger, and–as always, for everything–KMay. Thank you to Pittsburgh and NYC and Bitter Delores and Searay.

Thanks to Dave Hall, my go-to English fact-checker, any mistakes in British-isms are all his fault. Just kidding! And thanks to Mel May, my go-to Australian.

Thanks to Rachel Smith, Chris Anderson/Ms. Grimes, Curt Gettman, Peter Sanderson, Jamie Argento, Reenie Kuhlman, and Liz Fulmer, all for different reasons.

Thanks to Melissa Colasanti and Jenny Block.

Thanks to Genevieve Miller Holt, Susan P, Melissa Ressler, Jessamyn Violet, and Ed Granger, for their eagle eyes.

Thanks to The Fridge, Mean Cup, The Candy Factory, Prince Street Café, The Highlights Foundation, Lancaster Theological Seminary, and my bedroom, where I retreated to write once COVID-19 hit. My weighted blanket was my true hero in 2020.

Thanks to my family of origin, my found family, and my friends near and far, especially and always, Erica C, Lindsay T, Rachel T, Naomi O, Melissa S, Eva T, and Mr. Fish.

And always and forever, thanks to Sam and the Hopweisers. What I do isn't easy, for any of us. Thanks for loving me anyway.

ABOUT THE AUTHOR

Photo credit: Michelle Johnsen

Jamie Beth Cohen writes about difficult things, but her friends think she's funny. Her writing has appeared in TeenVogue.com, The Washington Post/On Parenting, HuffPost, and several other outlets. She lives with her family in Lancaster County, PA where she co-founded and co-hosts the Write Now Lancaster writing group. And she hosts the spreadsheet podcast, "There's a Column for That!" where she talks to writers and others about how they use spreadsheets to organize their work and their lives.

Connect with Jamie at www.JamieBethCohen.com
or on Twitter at Jamie_Beth_S.

NOTE FROM THE AUTHOR

Word-of-mouth is crucial for stories like this to succeed. If you enjoyed *LIMINAL SUMMER*, please leave a review online—anywhere you'd like. I'm also available for book groups and school visits. Please be in touch.

Thanks!
Jamie

We hope you enjoyed reading this title from:

www.blackrosewriting.com

Subscribe to our mailing list – *The Rosevine* – and receive **FREE** books, daily deals, and stay current with news about upcoming releases and our hottest authors.
Scan the QR code below to sign up.

Already a subscriber? Please accept a sincere thank you for being a fan of Black Rose Writing authors.

View other Black Rose Writing titles at
www.blackrosewriting.com/books and use promo code
PRINT to receive a **20% discount** when purchasing.

CPSIA information can be obtained
at www.ICGtesting.com
Printed in the USA
BVHW070404091021
618518BV00002B/6